I0578890

Published by: Cinnabar Moth Publishing LLC
Santa Fe, New Mexico

Cover Design by: Ivan @ BookCoversArt

ISBN-13: 978-1-953971-16-6
Library of Congress Control Number: 2021941946

Pixies in the Mist

RASTA MUSICK

Content Notes

If you would be triggered by, find disasteful, or be negatively impacted by any of the following subject matter, please refrain from reading the contents of this collection. The following is a list of the types of subject matter contained in the story or stories you are about to read.

Forced body modification
Emotional manipulation and gaslighting
Abandonment
Abduction
Imprisonment
Arachnids
Wasp
Maiming
Death
Non-graphic reference to sex

CHAPTER ONE

Jake stood up and walked into his shower room to get ready for a night of dancing. It was only recently that the separation of his toilet and shower didn't make him uncomfortable. To someone else, it might have been strange that he felt pride from having gotten used to such a minor aspect of his life in Japan, but it was part of his life that he had to deal with daily. Every small comfort mattered when adjusting to a new country, as Jake had quickly found out. Things were different than visiting on vacation. It had already been a few months since he had moved to Japan on a student visa. The five-day-a-week Japanese course he was taking filled up his mornings and some of his afternoons. Jake once again wondered why he had signed up for morning classes when he hated waking up early. Thankfully, he had studied Japanese before coming. He couldn't imagine being as lost as some of the people he met during class. The thought made him shudder as he started the water.

Running a hand through the brown curls of his hair to slick it back, Jake began cleaning his body. Living in Japan had started off fun, and he had just built a rhythm for himself. The rhythm wasn't exactly what he had imagined when he first decided to try it out. The Japanese course was more time-consuming than he expected, even knowing a lot of the material. The first flare of excitement had gradually worn off over the admittedly brief time he had been in the country. He liked to imagine that it meant he had grown used to living in Japan, but he had a feeling it was actually the opposite. Life was meant to be exciting. Novelty wasn't the only source of that.

Jake felt like his life still had as little direction and purpose as it had when he chose to leave home in the United States. His instincts had said Japan was the right place to be. When he followed his gut, things tended to work out for him. Thankfully, his parents were supportive of his choices as well. But things weren't going how he had hoped. Japanese class was a grind that left him unsatisfied. When was he going to figure out what his future was meant to be? Where was he supposed to go? He felt lost and alone. Shaking his head, he tried to turn his mind to happier thoughts.

Focusing on his dancing plans for the evening, Jake wondered if he should write a story about his experiences dancing Salsa in Japan for his blog. It wasn't what his audience, almost nonexistent as it was, would expect, but that abnormality might be the key point of interest. It broke away from the normal, tourist-destination oriented approach he had been taking. He wasn't sure if blogging was the path for him, but it wasn't going to go anywhere if he didn't find a way to build his audience faster. He needed to start making a name for himself somehow. To that end, he would have to pay special attention to his experience that night. Remembering details was key for good writing, after all. As his mind turned toward dancing, Jake felt a tingle of excitement. His salsa plans were one of the brighter points of his week. They felt right.

Once he was finished bathing, he dried himself off, stood in front of his sink, and looked into the mirror. He stared at the reflection of his brown eyes as he started to run his fingers through his hair to style it. Every time he did this, he was reminded of home. His mother hadn't washed his hair for a long time, but she had taught him everything he knew about taking care of it.

A smile lit up his face as he remembered the feeling of her hands when she showed him how he could move his fingers to adjust the weight of his hair or change the shape. While he reminisced, his hands automatically started to follow the same motions of his mother's fingers in his memory. The process soothed him and reminded him of what his mother had told him before he left. Jake could feel the tension in his body go away as he continued in his bathing routine.

"You're a citizen of the world. Home is anywhere you can feel happy, comfortable, and be yourself."

He hadn't understood her at the time, but in moments like these, he felt like he got it. At that moment, he was home. Jake once again resolved to do his best to make Japan his home. He knew he had to change things up somehow. Going through the motions was fine when he had first arrived, but it was about time for him to find a lifestyle that truly fit him. One that felt right. He needed real connections. His life so far was full of superficial friendships based around the activities he chose to do. Still, forging a proper home for himself in Japan was a concern for another time. For now, he had a party to go to. Grabbing his bag, he locked the door behind him as he walked to the subway. Another Wednesday night. Another night of dance. He wondered what moves the teacher would go over this week, and he couldn't help but dance a few steps from last week's lesson while he walked. He imagined the regulars and other people who only came in once in a while, and the anticipation brought extra spring to his step as he made his way down the street.

Jake walked through the wicket, pulling out his wallet, taking out his commuter card, and swiping it over the machine in one smooth motion as the train he was supposed to catch slowed to a stop at the platform. Perfectly timed. He appreciated how lucky he was to be in a less popular part of town as he once again had no problems finding a seat on the train. He hummed to himself. Life was working out nicely for him. He saw no reason for tonight to be any different.

Kenneth smoothed out the short, red spikes of his hair with one hand as he stood in front of the train's mirror. He could feel the glances of the other passengers, though he pretended not to notice. He finally had a night to himself. While it had only been three months, it felt like a century had passed. He would know, having lived long enough. The constant grind of finding magical humans, or marks, and handling them rarely left him with any opportunities to enjoy himself. He tried to loosen the stiffness in his shoulders as he thought back over his responsibilities. Over the next few days, he would have to work to increase trust with two marks. And he would need to squeeze in time to reach out to his connections to several others that he had already gotten processed. The life of a pixie was never dull.

For the evening, he had the opportunity to put those concerns to the side. He resisted the urge to smile as he thought about it. A night of dancing was exactly what he needed to feel relaxed and settled. Despite the years of experience, adopting different personas to deal with people still took its toll. A single night of free expression was the perfect fix. It also allowed him to meet people in a community that was mostly consistent. There was very little chance of him meeting someone that could be magical. He thought back to remember the names of the people he had met, trying to make sure he would recognize anybody new.

Instinctively, he did a quick scan of the people sitting around him, using the mirror to do it without being obvious. They all appeared to be harmless and human. Though that didn't guarantee they were. He kept a careful eye out for anybody that seemed out of place or too interested in him. While he was on the way to somewhere he could relax, he wasn't there yet. Kenneth turned away from the mirror and leaned back against the wall. While he kept a watchful eye out, his focus moved to the future.

It would be nice to cut loose and have fun. Last time he went salsa dancing, some year or two ago, he had stayed out until morning without any problems. He hoped there weren't many new people. The less he had to be worried about coming across a mark or a magical threat, the better. Still, he wouldn't know until he went. The only thing that he knew for certain was that he was going to dance. He was going to dance, and he was going to milk it for all it was worth.

Jake strode into the salsa club, waving at some of the other regulars as he passed them by. He had arrived with only a few minutes to spare before the lesson started. The teacher beckoned for everyone to move onto the dance floor and make space behind him as he started everyone off with stretches. The place was small enough that even the dozen people who attended the lessons took up most of the space. Jake groaned softly as he felt his body pop as he stretched. Despite coming every week, his body reminded him of the fact he never stretched on other days.

After they finished warming up, the instructor paired people off for the next part of the lesson. Each pair watched as the teacher and his assistant showed them the steps they would be learning and practicing for the day. Jake watched intently. Every step and hand motion the teacher made, he attempted to imitate when it was his turn to try the pattern. He felt bad for his partners since many of them struggled to learn these new routines, but it only took a couple of tries for him to start picking things up. When he had first started dancing in Japan, the number of older people had surprised him, as well as the fact that nobody seemed to be below 35 years of age. He didn't mind the extra attention his youth got him, though. It felt nice to have people be excited to see him.

The lesson continued, and Jake started to get the hang of the steps. As the time approached the start of the after-lesson party, more people began to filter into the dance club. Most of them were other regulars, all Japanese people. He waved and smiled at the people he recognized. As Jake scanned the people trickling in, a foreigner with bright red hair stood out from the crowd. Jake didn't recognize the guy, so he turned back to focus on the lesson.

Once the lesson ended and the party started, Jake thanked his practice partner and glanced to see what the other man was doing. The redhead was in the middle of approaching a woman, a regular named Aiko, and inviting her to dance.

Kenneth arrived as the lessons were approaching their ending. He was surprised to see a new foreigner. It was rare to see, since the place wasn't as popular as some of the other salsa clubs. Still, one new face wasn't the end of the world. The Scotsman glanced around and recognized everyone else. He smiled. It turned out not much had changed. Just as he had hoped. Knowing everyone already meant he could relax. After he found an opportunity to check the new guy.

"Oh, Kenneth. Long time no see." One of the more seasoned dancers walked up to him. She had danced several songs with Kenneth the last time he was around.

His smile widened. It was always nice to be remembered. Out of the corner of his eye, he kept track of the curly-haired man. "Long time no see, Aiko. How you been?"

"I've been fine. Where have you been, though? I haven't seen you since last year."

"Work's just been busy. Finally got some time to myself." Kenneth noticed the other foreigner staring at him and instinctively felt defensive. His shoulders stiffened for a moment before he forcibly loosened them again. He stood out; he knew this. If he stayed calm and wary, he would find an opportunity to introduce himself later.

Aiko smiled. "Well, since you're here... let's dance."

Kenneth nodded, taking her hand and walking onto the dance floor where other people had already started dancing. Out of the corner of his eye, he noticed the other guy grabbing a partner as well. Kenneth turned most of his focus back to his partner, but he kept alert.

As the redhead started dancing with his partner, Jake remembered himself. He went to his favorite dancing partner and started dancing with her. While they danced, Jake tried the new pattern he had just learned. The dance floor was packed with people, and Jake ended up jostling against the redhead from earlier as he moved to avoid crashing into somebody else. He turned to nod his head in apology before focusing his attention on his dancing. Jake paid special attention to the other dancers around him, which led him to notice how the new guy moved. The redhead stepped confidently, and his moves were different from what Jake had learned. For a moment, Jake wondered where the man had learned to dance.

Swinging through the dance with Aiko, Kenneth felt rejuvenated despite his heightened awareness. His spirits lifted, and the weight of his work felt lessened. That peaceful bliss was interrupted as Kenneth felt the foreigner bump into him mid-dance. While a bit of jostling wasn't unusual, the wave of energy that came pouring from the other man definitely was.

Kenneth already knew who it was, but he turned to look to pretend he didn't. Of course there was someone magical on his one night off—the only new person out of the whole group. Kenneth nodded in response to the other man's apology before turning back to his partner. Despite himself, Kenneth wanted it not to be true. He cursed his luck as he recognized his duty to double-check. His one sanctuary from work. The place he went to leave work behind. And work had found him. Still, he didn't have an opportunity to do anything until the song ended. Kenneth shook off the tension of the moment and threw himself into the dance, savoring what was left of the moment.

All too soon, the song was over. After thanking Aiko for the dance, Kenneth made his way toward the potential mark and extended his hand. "Hey, nice dancing. Name's Kenneth."

"Thanks, I'm Jake." Jake shook his hand, faking a smile. He hoped Kenneth wasn't looking for a foreigner to help show him around Japan. When their skin touched, Kenneth felt his body tense involuntarily, and he quickly withdrew his hand. The reaction made Jake pause, but he quickly shrugged it off. "I haven't seen you before. Is this your first time here?"

In that moment of contact, an intense throb of power had surged from Jake. Kenneth reoriented himself. Whoever this Jake person was, he was either a threat Kenneth couldn't safely deal with or a potential ally worth investing time into. He couldn't tell which without further investigation.

As Jake continued the conversation as if nothing happened, Kenneth wondered for a moment if the human was truly unaware. Had it been unintentional? Or was this an elaborate ploy? He had to tread carefully. "No, but I'm usually so busy I don't get the chance to come. It's probably been a year or two since last time."

Jake blinked in surprise, and Kenneth felt a moment of anxiety at the human's surprise. "A year or two? How long have you been in Japan?"

Kenneth had been prepared for something more intrusive. Did the human not know anything? He let a tendril of his own power leak out and brush against his conversation partner's mind. There was no reaction. There were no natural defenses, either. He was dealing with someone that wasn't part of his world, even if the man had the potential for it. It was time to put on the appropriate mask. Kenneth shrugged, adopting a casual tone. "Not that long. I came from Scotland around… three years ago. How about you? You seem comfortable here. Do you come often?"

"I moved to Japan from the States a bit ago. Trying to strike out on my own." Jake took a sip from his drink and gestured with his other hand. "I've been coming every week for the past couple of months. Salsa's my favorite hobby, so this place is great."

"Cool stuff." Kenneth smiled. This one seemed like it'd be an easy mark. They shared a hobby, so it wouldn't be hard to forge a friendship. Simply inviting him to dance would make him easy to befriend. "Hey, you seem like a nice guy. I know some other great salsa clubs. If you're down for some exploration sometime, want me to introduce you to them?"

Jake took a moment to consider the offer. He wondered why Kenneth was inviting him out when they had just started talking, but he quickly chalked it up to a difference in culture. The Scottish were friendly, right? It wouldn't hurt to have other salsa clubs to visit sometimes. A tingling sensation ran up his spine as he smiled and nodded. This was the right choice. "Yeah, sure. Let me know the date and time, and I'll see if I can make it."

With that, Jake called out to one of the other regulars, Mayu, and invited her to dance. He wasn't going to stand around talking all night.

Jake had not been as eager as he had expected, but Kenneth knew better than to rush things. Kenneth decided to follow Jake's example and invite a partner, but the mood had changed. In his mind, the wheels were turning on a plan to secure Jake's trust and perform his duties. The joy of the dance was a sidenote at best.

The night kept on as Jake continued dancing and having a good time.

As the night started to run late, Kenneth struck up a conversation with Aiko.

"So, Aiko. I noticed the new guy. How long has he been coming here?"

Aiko smiled, casting her eyes to glance at the topic of conversation. "Jake? Oh, maybe a month or two. Why? Has he caught your eye?"

"Well, he can dance, and he seems nice enough. Do you know much about him?"

"He doesn't talk much, but I heard he's writing a blog."

A blog. Kenneth immediately recognized the opportunity to get to know Jake in more detail, turning to notice that Jake and Mayu had just finished dancing. He gestured toward the pair. "That sounds interesting. How about we join those two and talk about it?"

Kenneth smiled internally as he managed to arrange for him to talk with Jake, Aiko, and Mayu.

Eventually, the party started to wind down. Jake, Kenneth, Aiko, and Mayu ended up talking with each other.

"Hey Jake, Aiko said you are writing a blog. I'm a bit of a writer, myself. What's it about?"

Jake shyly scratched the back of his neck as he answered Kenneth's question. "Oh, you know. It's just about things I've done or seen in Japan. Kind of a travel blog. Hoping it gets popular, but we'll see how that goes."

"That's so cool. I wish I could travel around and blog about it." Mayu smiled. "You still haven't shared the link with us because it's in English. Maybe you can share it with Kenneth and see what he thinks?"

"I guess." Jake hesitated. He didn't really feel comfortable sharing his blog with someone he had just met, especially when he hadn't been getting much of a viewership. Still, an extra reader was an extra reader. Besides, what was the worst that could happen? "Sure, if Kenneth's interested, I'll send him the link later."

Kenneth glanced at his watch. He didn't expect they would stand around much longer, given the time, but he needed to extend the conversation for at least a little while longer. "Speaking of late, it's practically morning already. I don't know about you three, but I could use some food. Anyone up for early breakfast?"

Jake usually went home after the party ended, but a sick feeling started in his stomach as he contemplated making an excuse and leaving. He quickly changed his mind and agreed to go with them. The tingling in his back returned. Kenneth had noticed Jake's indecision and was surprised by how quickly it vanished. Had Jake been faking the internal struggle? The thought gave Kenneth pause as he followed Aiko and Mayu out of the club.

It was Jake's first time going out to eat with anybody from the salsa community. It wasn't something he would like to do regularly, but it made for a nice change of pace. Toward the end, Jake and Kenneth exchanged contact information, and everyone said their goodbyes. Jake knew from the way his body had reacted to his choices earlier that Kenneth was somehow involved with his future. He did not understand how or why, but he felt better that night than he had in a while. He trusted it. The future looked like it held the promise of more fun to come.

The conversation at the restaurant was mostly small talk that didn't give Kenneth any more information about Jake. He had hoped to get the website where Jake was blogging as well, but Jake had changed the topic. It didn't matter. Kenneth felt confident he could find it with a bit of searching. He was not entirely certain that Jake knew nothing of magic, but he was certain that Jake was a magical human of significant power. Any such mark would be of great value to his people. There was only one way to find out.

And so the path was set.

Chapter 2

Jake flopped over lazily on his bed and checked the clock. It was ten minutes before classes started. Jumping out of bed, he rushed to put on clothes and grab his bags. He was going to be late again. Mumbling to himself about being irresponsible, he ran out the door to the station. Jake once again wondered why he had made the mistake of arranging for morning classes. His class went by without much trouble, though it was mostly a blur. He had made sure to study in advance to make up for his usual exhaustion. Once classes ended in the afternoon, he quickly packed up his bags, said his goodbyes, and went around the corner to eat lunch. While he waited for his food, Jake thought about his blog.

The concern he had felt the previous day about his audience wasn't there anymore. He had time, after all. Things were good. His mood was brighter than it had been for months, and the future seemed bright and brimming with possibility. Looking back on his previous concerns, he almost felt like laughing. There really wasn't anything to be so concerned about. There was more than a year left before the blog had to have enough of a following for him to use it as a reason to stay in Japan. The viewership would come as long as he stuck with it, surely.

With that done, Jake finished the rest of his meal and went home. Once he arrived, he sat in the futon that he had moved out of his bedroom and into his living room for the latter's better insulation. He never felt as comfortable writing at his desk as he did in bed, but for some reason, his bedroom was so drafty that it never got to the right temperature. This forced him to drag his futon into the other room to stay at a comfortable temperature.

He decided to try and write his next blog post about salsa dancing, as he had planned the previous night. He wrote notes down until he had a document full of details from his experience. Once that was done, he started writing his article about salsa dancing in Japan. Since it was a travel writing blog, he tried his best to keep his excitement out of his writing. It was meant to be somewhat professional.

His first draft ended up as a retelling of what happened. It was an okay blog post, but it wasn't satisfying. Using that as his base, he slowly removed the pieces that were personal to him, such as his positivity about the future. While removing the personal information took a while, Jake felt better about the post. He had used his writing as a way to organize his thoughts about the evening. He had done several things that his gut told him set him on the right path. The excitement of finding a direction was not something he could explain to his readers, especially since he hardly understood it himself.

Jake shook his head. He was letting himself get distracted again. Glancing around his living room, he grabbed a bag of chips he had left on the table and started eating. He returned his focus to the document in front of him and added more information about the lesson. As he started to run out of material, Jake looked back over what he had written. Removing his bias and the names of people he had met, there wasn't enough to make a complete post. If he didn't have enough information from going to one club for a while, then it meant he would have to go out again sometime. The post could wait until then.

Jake threw himself backwards into his futon and stared at the ceiling. The peace of the moment surrounded him as he looked at nothing. Everything was okay. He was at home within himself. Perhaps that was the secret. Home wasn't a place. It was this peace he could only find inside. The thought made him smile. After a bit of rest, he forced himself to sit up and open an unfinished blog post he had started about exploring temples and shrines in Nagoya and other parts of Aichi. He had made sure to include the most famous one, Atsuta Shrine, but he also listed a few of the small shrines that he sometimes found by walking around after school. He described as much of the history that he could remember for each shrine, relying on internet searches to fill in the gaps. After adding a few pictures and fiddling with his opening and closing lines, he started to feel like the article was coming together nicely.

He jumped as his phone rumbled against his leg. Picking it up, he realized that it had been a couple of hours since he started writing. He saw that it was a message from Kenneth.

"Yo, Jake. Are you available Friday night? If you are, let's go dancing. Meet me at nine outside Sakae station exit six."

Jake stared at the message. It was about what he had expected. For a moment, he considered saying no. Kenneth seemed a bit strange. While he was still halfway unsure about the decision, he texted back. "Sounds good. See you then."

In the end, the value for his blog was the tipping point. He wouldn't have to go on his own, and he'd have a chance to talk with Kenneth about his experiences dancing in Japan. That could bring new life to Jake's writing as well. Jake returned his focus to the nearly finished article. He'd have to wrap this up so he could fully enjoy the next night. And so the sounds of a keyboard filled the air once more.

Kenneth woke up in the middle of the afternoon. His body was still on the Japanese time schedule even though he was groggily staring at his quarters in Scotland. He let his eyes wander while his mind worked itself into full gear. His bed took up a fifth of the space, with the majority of the rest of the room filled with desks and chests containing everything he needed for his work. Large books of languages and clothes that were appropriate for a variety of different disguises were haphazardly thrown over the chests or onto desks. Like every other morning, he promised himself he would take the time to clean things up and sort them. Just as soon as he wasn't busy. If doing it magically didn't take a long time because of the large number of small parts, he could have just done it that way. Part of him wished that the servants would clean it for him, while the other was happy that operatives like himself were considered staff. He kept his privacy, even if it did lead to things being messy.

The Scotsman stood up and stretched, feeling his body pop and complain about his night of dancing. He needed to do more practice in his spare time. It wouldn't do to be sore like this the day after he had fun. Kenneth walked over to the closest desk and dropped the books he had put on it onto the floor next to him. He'd clean that up later, too. Focusing his mind, he thought over what he needed to write in the report to his superior. Last night's events were definitely the most pressing concern. Kenneth estimated that Jake was at least as powerful as an A-class mark. The wave of energy Kenneth felt reminded him of a similar mark that was deemed too dangerous to let live. It had taken Kenneth a month to set up a way to fulfill that mission. Jake was definitely far more powerful than the c-class marks that could barely muster the magic to make minor changes to their hairstyles. A human of Jake's magical power was a potentially serious threat to their cause or a potentially valuable ally, depending on how events took their course. But he still didn't have a plan of action. It was best to leave it unannounced until he had made some decisions about what to do with Jake.

Kenneth decided to save the information about Jake for another time. His boss didn't need to know everything he was doing. Not until he'd made steps to force it down the path he wanted. He waved his hand in the air. The pen floated above the paper as he mulled over the words. He had to start by summarizing the known marks and their statuses first. Words formed on the parchment as the pen danced smoothly through the loops and curls of the letters. Kenneth did his best to keep things short. His superior had to handle half of the agents operating in the entire continent of Asia. She wouldn't have the time to read something with too many useless details.

After finishing with the written report, he went through the verbal report in his head. This was much harder than the written report since Kenneth had a tendency to disagree with his superiors. Making sure none of his dislike filtered through when he spoke to them was part of his job. Still, it was just another mask. Another role to play.

Since he had some time to spare, Kenneth searched for Jake's blog on the internet. After a bit of searching, he eventually managed to find the website. As he read through several blog posts and Jake's introductory page, he felt like he understood his mark better. If nothing else, it was clear that Jake didn't have anyone that he'd call a friend. There was no specific mention of any people, and none of them seemed to be the same person. Jake was a drifter. Kenneth felt confident that he could use that to his advantage.

Kenneth gasped as he glanced at the clock. He was going to be late for his debriefing if he didn't hurry. Flicking a hand, he grabbed the documents for his report and hastily changed into proper clothing while swapping the parchments from one hand to the other.

Tearing down the hallways of the castle, he was gasping as he knocked on his superior's door.

"Enter."

Kenneth took a moment to wipe the sweat from his brow and straighten his clothes before walking into the room and bowing his head. Even without looking, he knew Anissa was glaring at him through her glasses from behind the large oak desk that dominated the room. She hated it when reports were late. "Anissa, Ma'am, I'm here to deliver my report."

"Please do."

"First, here are the written documents." He barely caught himself before he commented on how she was as terse as ever. Placing the papers on the desk in front of her, Kenneth firmly gripped his hands behind his back to keep them still. "The thirty-two A and twenty-four C marks have been safely transferred to our local handlers with no issues. There was a scuffle between myself and Locke when the fifty-six A and sixty-two B marks crossed paths in an unfriendly fashion. We managed to avoid revealing the existence of magic, but it was... difficult."

Kenneth's hands squirmed behind his back as he restrained himself from complaining about Locke. The two of them had never gotten along but now was not the time.

"Is that all?" Anissa reached out one hand and flipped through the written report to look for anything of note.

"Yes, ma'am. No other significant things to report at this time." Kenneth did not even bat an eye as he lied to her.

His superior scanned the written report. He wasn't sure what she was looking at. "And you've filed everything with accounting?"

"Yes, I have." He nodded, clenching a fist. Of course he would know to do such trivial matters.

"Hmmm." Anissa's fingertips clacked loudly in the silence of the room as she stared at Kenneth.

He held her gaze for a minute but eventually turned his head away. He tried to take his mind off the anxiety by staring at the potted plants in the corners of the room behind her. The basil plants looked particularly healthy, despite missing a few leaves. She must have used some recently. Her voice snapped him out of his reverie.

"Very well." Anissa's voice was sharp and cold as she gave him his new orders. "You are to continue with your current course of action. Make sure to reach out to Locke and coordinate with him to avoid any future problems. Understood?"

Kenneth sighed. "Yes, Ma'am."

"Make sure the appropriate documentation is filed and submitted for your discussion with Locke. You are dismissed."

"Understood."

Kenneth walked out of the room before forcing his hands to unclench. His fingernails had left marks in his palms. He had a gut feeling that she knew something was going on. They knew each other for too long for him to hide it completely. He would have to move fast with Jake. Kenneth pulled out his phone, intending to make a call to Locke's phone. Remembering how badly their last conversation had gone, he decided against it. Instead, he opened up his contacts and sent a message to Jake.

"Yo, Jake. Are you available on Friday night? If you are, let's go dancing. Let's meet at nine outside Sakae station exit six."

He waited a few moments before Jake responded with a yes. Perfect. Since it was his responsibility to keep Jake under management, he was obligated to push the 'friendship' forward. Kenneth smiled to himself. He could build the groundwork for bringing Jake in while following orders. It seemed best to keep such a powerful human closer to them than further away. He texted back his reply.

With that, he suddenly felt the urge to stretch his legs. Kenneth walked to the section of the castle that held the secretarial departments and filed the paperwork himself instead of phoning it in. This way, he could leave himself with more wriggle room by approximating his superior's orders. Things hadn't gone perfectly, but he would make the most of it. For his people. For whatever the future held.

The light from the sun shone through Jake's window and woke him up. He rolled out of his futon and swiped the blinds closed. It wasn't the most reliable alarm clock, but sometimes it worked when his actual alarms didn't. Having woken up with plenty of time before school, Jake took the opportunity to eat breakfast at a leisurely pace. Waking up in the morning wasn't that bad when his outlook on life was as bright as it had been the past couple of days. Things were going just right.

After another uneventful school day, Jake arrived home, plopped back onto his futon, and opened his laptop. He had finished his article about shrines in Japan the previous night, but the article wasn't doing any good sitting in his documents folder. Jake pulled up his website and worked through putting the post into place. He double-checked that his writing matched what he had wanted to express, then uploaded it. That made one. The blog required a lot more effort than he had expected going into it, but he didn't feel the same pressure to go on social media and grind as he had before. Taking it slow was fine sometimes.

He absentmindedly ran his hand through his curls and accidentally messed up the style he had set after showering that morning. A rumble in his stomach reminded him that he hadn't eaten anything since breakfast. Thankfully, he had rice still sitting in the rice cooker. He heated up a pre-made packet of curry sauce and mixed it with the rice. There was something to be said for easy meals. Jake wondered if he could write an article about settling into Japan now that he had been in the country for a while. It was a popular topic. He remembered reading through a dozen different websites about Japan and the difficulties and challenges people faced. A lot of them came down to expectations. He didn't realize until coming to Japan that he had held a lot of expectations about how life would be. Japan had grown to symbolize positive change, satisfaction, and happiness all because of his strong feeling that it was the right place to be. For a time, it hadn't been. And now it was. The patience to wait was paying off.

Jake dropped his empty bowl into his sink and filled it with water. He'd clean it later. As Jake turned over the "Settling in Japan: A guide" article over in his head, he decided to skip it. It required him to explain his instincts and his views on life. It was too much work. Jake checked the clock. There were still a few hours left before his planned meeting with Kenneth.

He looked up his train route to Sakae and tried to guess where Kenneth planned on taking them. From what he remembered, there were two salsa clubs near the station. It would have to be one or the other. He smiled to himself and looked in the mirror. Noticing the part in his hair that he had made earlier, he quickly pushed the hair back into the right style. It took so long for his hair to dry that his hands were slick with moisture. He wiped them clean on a towel and picked out his outfit for the evening.

With preparations done, Jake spent the next while watching dance videos on his computer and practicing the steps. He wanted to have some new moves for this new group of people. Every new group of people was a chance to change a bit about yourself and have that be the new you. It was a bit difficult to pretend to dance with an imaginary partner, but Jake managed to haltingly make his way through a couple of new variations. In the back of his mind, he wondered how the night would go. He had to do research for his writing, but he also planned to get to know Kenneth better. It was obvious from the tingling sensation running up through his back that becoming close with Kenneth was important somehow. He didn't understand how the Scottish man related to his future, but he shrugged it off. Whatever the reason, he was sure it'd be revealed in time. And he had time aplenty, now that he had a direction. Even if it wasn't much of one, it was enough.

Eventually, it was time to leave. Putting on his fresh outfit, Jake smiled at himself in the mirror. He looked good. He felt good. And now he was on his way to have a good time.

Chapter 3

Kenneth wiped the sweat from his brow as he thought about his schedule. Normally, he wouldn't be so stressed about time. But he had invited Jake for that evening. He didn't have time to be lazy about his other duties. He scratched at his beard. Since he was going to be keeping Jake away from magical influences, it meant he had the responsibility to reach out to potential leaks in advance and make sure they were aware of the circumstances. Before he could do that, he had to wait for the information department to compile a list.

In the meantime, Kenneth was left with most of the day to himself. His other marks didn't need his attention until Saturday, aside from light communication that could be handled remotely. He made his way back through the castle to his room. After the tense interaction with Anissa, he felt on edge. Kenneth shook his head. He couldn't let himself brood over it. She would either figure him out or not. To help himself calm down, he decided to clean his room a bit. Doing it by hand would help give him time to center himself.

Rolling up his sleeves, Kenneth set to work sorting through his books first. Some of them were ordinary novels that he read for fun and could talk with Jake about. Anything that talked about magic was off-limits, along with all records kept about his people. Kenneth put in the extra effort to create neat, orderly piles ordered by how mundane they were.

After opening up a decent amount of space, he started tossing clothes into two piles; to be washed and to be closeted. He would have been embarrassed by the size of the wash pile if anybody were around to see it. He really needed to keep himself more together, even if he spent little time at home.

"This is taking a while. This should be enough for now, right?" He muttered to himself. As if in response, his stomach grumbled. "Ah, that's right. Food."

Walking through the castle, Kenneth admired the stonework while his feet traveled automatically toward the mess hall. It was around afternoon in Japan, but it was still early morning in Scotland. Thankfully, the cooks worked in shifts to make sure food was available for operatives coming and going from around the world. The mess hall was mostly empty when he arrived. A few of the other people working in Asia were talking amongst themselves. Kenneth would have joined them normally, but he didn't have the time. He would have to eat and prepare himself for the evening with Jake, which meant changing out of his dusty clothing and putting together a suitable outfit.

He filled his plate with bacon, potatoes, and salad. Once that was done, he grabbed a few slices of pie to top things off. Kenneth ate quickly, but he enjoyed every moment of it. He rarely let himself gorge on food. It dulled his senses. But it was bound to be a long night, and he wouldn't have the energy to eat when he came back.

Once he finished, Kenneth walked back slowly through the castle. He smiled and nodded at people as they passed. Most nodded back as they hurried on their way for one errand or another. Laying a hand against the wall, he felt the cool stone beneath his fingertips. He had lived in the castle for so long that he had forgotten what it was like to live anywhere else. He wondered how Jake would fare if the human were to ever be brought into the fold. Adjusting to the lifestyle wasn't easy. If Jake struggled with life in Japan, getting used to magic would likely be even more of a challenge. Kenneth made a mental note to learn more about how Jake's life was going. It was a crucial insight toward his decision about whether the human was truly a possible asset.

The door to Kenneth's room was ajar when he arrived. Inside, a stack of papers had been placed on his bed. The secretarial staff had left the list someplace away from the chaos of the rest of the room. Picking it up, Kenneth read over the list, jotting down notes about the most likely threats to Jake's isolation from magic, and pulled up his computer to send the necessary messages. He made especially sure to send a message warning Locke, with all of the appropriate by-the-book wording to suit the annoying law-abiding operative on the other end. His distaste for Locke's mindless obedience made it chafe, but he needed to avoid Anissa's attention if he was going to handle Jake's situation without any interventions. After a short while, he glanced at the time and realized he was scheduled to meet with Jake in half an hour.

Kenneth didn't have the time to take a proper shower, so he hurriedly changed clothes and used a spot of his energy to make his hair style itself and fix the smell of his body odor. Thankfully, such small adjustments didn't take much time or effort. Then it was time for the main thing: teleporting without being seen on arrival. Focusing his mind, Kenneth located a bathroom in Sakae station with an empty stall. He harnessed his will and transferred himself from one place to the other.

Smoothing his clothes, he opened the stall and headed to the proper exit. It wouldn't do to arrive late to meet a mark.

The train ride to Sakae gave Jake time to think about the evening. He wondered what kinds of people would show up to this new club. Would he see anybody familiar? How large was the salsa community, really? He half-expected it to be mostly the same people with maybe a couple of new faces. Not that it mattered. As long as he got to dance, he was going to have fun. Jake's foot tapped to the tune of one of his favorite songs as he mulled over the possibility. Besides, if there weren't many new people, then he would write about that in his blog post. It would be interesting for people to know how close-knit the community was. For the remainder of the train ride, he reminded himself of the steps he had practiced earlier.

At last, Jake got off the train and walked with the crowd to the wicket. Sakae was a central downtown station, so it was almost always busy. Once he was free of the crush of people, Jake set off to exit number six.

Kenneth had arrived ten minutes earlier despite his late departure. For a moment, he wondered how he would get by in the world if he ever lost the ability to teleport. He didn't understand how anyone could bear losing so much time just to get around. After doing a quick scan of the crowd to make sure Jake wasn't nearby, Kenneth pulled out his phone and checked his messages from the other operatives in the area. He wanted to make sure there would be no chance happenings between Jake and any other marks. It was easier to contain Jake that way. Who knew what effect someone of his power would have on another uninitiated magical person?

With that done, Kenneth pocketed his phone and resumed scanning the crowd. He noticed Jake when the human was still halfway down the hall, but he pretended to be staring off into space. He didn't want to display his powers of observation just in case the human was faking his ignorance. If Kenneth could pretend to be easily distracted, it would be that much easier to gain Jake's trust. People didn't like being inspected too closely.

Jake arrived at the exit. Spotting Kenneth, he waved.

"Yo, Kenneth."

The Scotsman turned and waved back. "Hey, Jake. How's it going?"

"Pretty good. I'm excited for tonight." Jake grinned and demonstrated one of the new steps he had learned. "Can't wait to show off my new moves."

"Let's get going, then." Kenneth smiled and started walking up the exit steps. Jake's confidence and calm were in stark contrast to the unsure man Kenneth had seen last time. He didn't understand why Jake had bothered learning anything new or why he was so happy and carefree. Kenneth both wanted to pry and also didn't feel their connection was strong enough to do so. It irked him to still be so uncertain about a mark's way of thinking. They were usually more predictable.

As if to underscore his newfound confidence, Jake said, "can't wait to show off my new moves."

Jake followed Kenneth up the stairs, giving him a chance to look closely at his new acquaintance. He couldn't see what would make Kenneth important. He was a decent looking guy, but that wasn't a reason for Jake to feel the tingling he did in his spine. After a few seconds of thinking about it, he gave up. He had no clues to figure out the puzzle.

Kenneth could feel the eyes on his back. The Scotsman had to force his shoulders to relax as his body instinctively stiffened under the scrutiny. Normally, being stared at like this wouldn't be so unnerving, but Kenneth had a hunch that Jake wasn't as air-headed as he seemed. There was some purpose behind his behavior, even if it wasn't magically related.

They reached the top of the stairs, and Jake quickened his pace to walk alongside Kenneth. "So, what's the club like? Is it similar to the other one?"

"A bit. It's got more space, so more people tend to show up. You might recognize a few faces. I know Aiko likes to come here sometimes." Kenneth scratched at his beard, resisting the urge to shrug. "Other than that, it's pretty similar. You go, you dance, you have fun."

"Cool, cool." Jake nodded and glanced around. He had to come to Sakae for his Japanese classes, but the school was in a completely different direction from the station. It felt strange to think that a place could be familiar yet have so many new things. The restaurants and clothes shops were all well-lit, with groups of people in their teens and twenties regularly flowing in and out. It was a stark contrast to the large groups of businessmen who walked together during the morning commutes Jake took to school.

Kenneth couldn't help but wonder what was going on inside of Jake's head. Was the human simply unused to the area, or was he looking for something specific? For his own peace of mind, Kenneth shifted his gaze to the people around them and did a check of the crowd. There were a few magical entities nearby, but they weren't approaching. If any of them were observing, they were doing it more subtly than Kenneth could notice. With that done, Kenneth glanced and followed the other man's gaze. The excitement in Jake's eyes seemed genuine enough, and he wasn't looking at anything out of the ordinary. It didn't seem like an act. He wished he had the confidence to believe his own observations. "Well, here we are."

Kenneth's voice startled Jake out of his reverie, and he had to resist the urge to laugh at Jake's almost jump.

Jake turned to look at the building. It had several signs indicating the restaurants, bars, and clubs inside. Kenneth pointed to one of the signs for the upper floors.

"It's up on the sixth floor. The elevator is over here."

Kenneth led the way in and pushed the button. Once they reached the floor, Jake felt welcomed as several people immediately called out greetings. Kenneth walked forward, smiling as he accepted hugs from a few people. Jake followed him and glanced around. There was a surprisingly large number of new faces. Kenneth turned and gestured at him. "Everyone, this is my friend Jake." He didn't want the human to be too uncomfortable.

A chorus of voices called out, "Hi, Jake."

The warmth of their welcome made Jake smile. "Nice to meet all of you."

So far, things seemed to Kenneth to be going well. All he had to do was keep it moving forward. He smiled at Jake as he opened the door and led the human into the club.

Jake's eyes widened as he entered the club behind Kenneth. It was larger than the other one, and there were already quite a few people dancing. It was surprising since most people showed up at his usual haunt later in the evening.

Jake's surprise confused Kenneth. It was just another salsa club. Still, it seemed only to make Jake more excited. Kenneth could almost feel the desire to dance coming off of Jake. He put a hand on Jake's shoulder and leaned in to be heard over the music.

"I'm going around to the bar to get a drink. Everyone's friendly, so go ahead and dance without me."

Jake blinked as Kenneth turned to walk around the dance floor to the bar visible on the other side. He wondered how the Scotsman knew he was eager to get on the floor. Kenneth was more observant than he let on. Jake smiled at the thought. It wasn't a bad thing. He strode over to a woman and held out his hand. The woman took it, and he moved onto the dance floor with her.

At first, Jake did simple steps so he could get used to how she followed his lead. After he had a feel for her movements, he started branching out to more advanced steps. Once they were into the swing of things, she leaned forward to talk to him as they danced.

"Your dancing is so good."

Jake smiled, spinning her through a turn before responding. "I'm still learning. You're a great dancer, though."

"No, no." She shook her head. "It's all thanks to your leading. Where are you from?"

"I'm from America. I'm studying Japanese for a bit. Kenneth brought me here."

Her eyes lit up at the mention of America. "Ohhh, I always wanted to visit America."

While Jake danced, Kenneth ordered a glass of water from the bar.

With his water in hand, Kenneth turned to watch as Jake strode over to a woman and held out his hand. The woman smiled and took it, and he smiled back as he moved onto the dance floor with her. The Scotsman took a moment to remember her name. Ma...

Mayu? No. Mai. That was it. Because the club was larger, there were typically more new faces that Kenneth had to spend time remembering. The task of never forgetting anybody eventually took its toll on his memory reserves.

Kenneth watched how tentative Jake was with his initial dancing. If Jake hadn't been a magical human, Kenneth had a feeling they could have gotten along decently as dance acquaintances. He let out a sigh. Life had its twists and turns. Once they were into the swing of things, Mai leaned forward to talk to Jake as they danced.

While he couldn't hear what they said, he had learned to read lips and got the gist of the conversation. It was fairly standard. Kenneth continued to observe Jake's dancing until he caught the other man staring back at him. When their eyes met, he immediately turned to look at something else. He would have to be more careful.

As the next song was about to start, Kenneth sought out someone he had never danced with before and invited them. They started dancing, and Kenneth could feel Jake's eyes on him. It made him uncomfortable to realize that his mark was staring at him almost as much as he was staring at them. What was going through Jake's mind? Did he find Kenneth's behavior strange? Or was he just a guy looking out for his friend?

Kenneth forced himself to put those thoughts aside. If he didn't seem like he was enjoying himself, that would definitely arouse suspicion. He threw himself into dancing with his partner. He overdid it slightly on a series of steps and had to readjust quickly to avoid an awkward pause.

Jake had noticed Kenneth watching him and couldn't help but think Kenneth was keeping some secret. No normal person could ping so strongly on Jake's instincts, right? The thought had come and gone quickly. Jake had spent little time thinking about it. He had let himself live in the moment, dancing and getting to know his dance partners a little.

Most of Jake's conversations were similar. He'd invite someone to dance, talk with them while they danced, then move on as the song changed. Another song ended, and this time a woman approached Jake to invite him to dance. Being invited was pretty common for him since he was young and decent at dancing.

He accepted and started dancing with her. Out of the corner of his eye, Jake noticed Kenneth was also dancing with somebody. That was good. Jake had started to wonder if the other man enjoyed dancing as much as he had seemed the first time they met.

As the song came to an end, Jake looked around for Kenneth and walked over to him. "Hey."

Kenneth smiled, though the smile seemed different from the one Jake had seen outside. It didn't reach his eyes. "Hey, having a good time?"

"Yeah, these people are just so friendly. And there's so many good dancers that it's even fun just to watch." Jake paused for a moment. Jake didn't know how open Kenneth was to talking about himself. The questions were on the tip of Jake's tongue, but he chose not to vocalize any of them. Not yet.

Kenneth could see Jake had questions and decided it was better to err on the side of caution and not wait to find out what those questions were. "Well, there's going to be more people later in the evening. Also…" Kenneth leaned in conspiratorially. "I saw you dancing with Mai earlier. She said you're kinda cute."

Jake scratched his head and wondered which of the women it had been. "To be honest… I haven't gotten anybody's name. Can you describe her?"

"Mai's the first girl you danced with."

"Ohhh, her." Jake wondered what he should say in reaction. He was flattered, but he wasn't out looking for a relationship either. He chose the safe option of saying something positive about her in response. "She was… nice to dance with."

Kenneth laughed. "Jake, you're so easily flustered. She's married. I'm just teasing you." He was surprised that Jake hadn't gotten anybody's name. He always made sure to do so. It was important to have people recognize him. It made him seem like a fixture in the community.

"Why you…" Jake felt embarrassed by how seriously he had taken it, but he smiled. Kenneth was a surprisingly good actor. Jake heaved a theatrical sigh. "And here I thought you were an earnest and honest guy. How could you?"

"I am. You're just so innocent." Kenneth grinned, walking off to invite another person to dance. He wondered about Jake's complete lack of interest. The man seemed surprised at the mere mention of people finding him cute. Kenneth felt as if Jake rarely thought about others' opinions. It was a useful piece of the puzzle that was Jake's personality.

Jake decided to take a break and watch as new people shuffled in and the party started in earnest.

Kenneth grinned, mentally high-fiving himself for smoothly handling the delicate situation as he walked off to invite another person to dance. He didn't want to stick around Jake for too long, or it would seem strange.

Jake danced and talked with so many people that, by the end of the night, most of them had become a blur in his memory. He didn't understand how anyone managed to remember everyone that they met. When Kenneth greeted every new person by name, it was as if the Scotsman had magic powers. While the two of them were relaxing to the side as the dance floor grew too crowded to dance properly, Jake turned to ask him.

"Kenneth, how do you remember everyone so easily? I can barely keep three or four people apart. Are you a wizard or something?"

Kenneth stiffened and hurriedly waved his hands in the air. "What? No, nothing like that. There's no such thing as magic. I just have a good memory."

"Must be nice, huh… being able to remember everything."

"It can be a pain sometimes, you know. People don't like it when you remember too much." Kenneth shrugged. From Jake's reaction, he didn't seem to have really noticed. That was fortunate. "Not sure why, though. Jealousy, maybe?"

Jake smiled. "Who wouldn't be jealous of that? I can't imagine any real downsides."

Kenneth shrugged, but he didn't say anything more. He really did have a good memory. It was trained through years and years of drilling from his instructors when he had just started doing this kind of work. He couldn't go into too much detail without it being awkward, so he just leaned back against the wall and took a sip of his water. He watched as Jake scanned the crowd. The human's eyes stopped on the Latin dancers that frequented the club. Kenneth didn't get involved with them much. They were a clique, and they left him alone if he left them alone.

Jake took that opportunity to let his eyes scan the crowd. There were a surprising number of non-Japanese people. A handful of the dancers were Latin American. It had been awkward when a couple of them tried to speak to him in Spanish earlier. He had instinctively responded in Japanese to say he didn't know any. He turned to look at Kenneth. "Do you know any Spanish?"

"Not really. Why?"

Jake shrugged at Kenneth's quizzical look. "Just wondering. It is salsa dance, after all."

Kenneth nodded. These interactions confirmed to him that Jake was not a very good liar. "Do you speak Spanish, then?"

"No."

"Why ask if you can't even speak it?"

Jake shyly scratched at the back of his neck as Kenneth chuckled at his expense.

Kenneth glanced down at his watch, grabbed his glass, and downed its contents. Much longer, and they would have to stay out all night, again. He couldn't afford that, given his schedule. "It's getting late. I've got work tomorrow. How about we call it a night?"

Jake glanced at him in surprise. "Wait, what? You work Saturdays?"

"I work almost every day. My job keeps me busy." Kenneth shrugged. "It pays the bills, though. I can't complain."

"What kind of work has you out on a Saturday morning, though?" Jake stared at Kenneth in surprise.

The Scotsman shrugged again. Better to not say anything that could be confusing and just be vague instead. He hoped Jake had enough tact to avoid prying. "The kind that pays well. I like it, so I don't mind the extra hours."

Jake sighed and gave up. No point in continuing that line of conversation. Still, it did make him more curious about Kenneth's life. What did he do aside from dancing? As the two of them walked out of the club and back toward the station, Jake glanced at Kenneth. He seemed well off. And he didn't seem stressed out, so it wasn't a normal businessman job with bad overtime. Jake decided he'd find out by spending more time with Kenneth. For that purpose, he would need to meet him even more. His instincts told him it was the right path to take.

"Say, what do you do other than dancing? If you've got something going on Sunday, mind if I join yah?"

Kenneth thought about his options. He was supposed to do some scouting at a fair that happened regularly at a shrine. He'd never found any magical humans before. It would probably be okay to bring Jake. His superiors couldn't complain about keeping an eye on him at least, right? Assuming he ever had to report it to Anissa, to begin with. Kenneth snapped his fingers as if he had just made a realization. "Ah, right. There's a festival on Sunday. Want to visit that with me?"

"A festival? Sure, why not." Jake smiled as they approached the wicket for the train.

Kenneth stopped and gestured in the other direction. "My train's actually that way. How about I text you the info?"

"Sounds good. Thanks again for hanging with me. See yah on Sunday."

The two men smiled and waved at each other as they walked their separate ways.

Kenneth ducked into a bathroom and found an empty stall. He teleported and sighed with relief when he was once again in the comfortable surroundings of his quarters.

Chapter 4

Jake groaned as he woke up. It was already noon, but he still wished to go back to bed. Two nights of dancing so close together had left him more tired than he expected. Still, he had work to do so that he could have a relaxed time on Sunday hanging out with Kenneth. He forced himself out of the comfort of his bed and into the shower to help himself fully wake up. He spent half his time in the shower staring into space while the water ran over him. His mind kept going to the tingling sensation. Why was it stronger now than it had ever been in his life? He felt on the verge of something. It left him feeling that any moment could lead to a revelation. As if there was a presence behind a hidden curtain. Waiting. Jake shivered as he pinpointed the sensation. There was more to this than he could see. He was sure of it.

Once he eventually left the shower, he sat on his futon and turned on his laptop. While the excitement of his realization in the shower was enticing, he knew himself well enough to know it wouldn't lead anywhere deeper. He had hit the limit of what he could perceive for one day. To keep his mind off of it, he decided to do his Japanese homework from Friday and write his blog post about dancing. After having experienced two different places, he felt confident that he could write the post effectively. While his computer booted itself up, he grabbed his homework out of his backpack and stared at it. He still remembered everything they had studied the day before.

He stared at his computer screen as it popped up with an "installing updates" screen and sighed. He would have to do his Japanese homework first, then. There was no point waiting around for what could take half an hour. Forced updates were always a pain. Jake turned his focus back to the papers he had been given. He pulled out his textbook and used it as a hard surface to write in his answers. He didn't bother checking his answers against the book. He felt confident he could get good grades without the extra effort.

After finishing the grammar homework, Jake was left with the kanji homework. This was more difficult for him. He had a hard time remembering the shapes and meanings of the symbols unless he wrote them down repeatedly. He had always been better at things when he experienced them than when he tried rote memorization. When he was halfway finished, Jake glanced over at his computer. It was still downloading the update. He decided to wait the last bit of time before it finished to eat a quick meal.

He told himself that making food would give him time to test if he really remembered the symbols. The truth was that he just didn't like doing the work. Jake stood up and stretched his arms until he felt one of them pop. He felt too impatient to make a real meal, so he grabbed some bread, toasted it, and spread peanut butter over the slices. Jake stared at his computer as he chewed his food without tasting it. He was already focused on the blog post and forming it in his mind.

Jake pulled open his unfinished document about salsa dancing. Reading back over what he wrote before, he started to make tweaks to the information. He wanted his writing to be consistent. Jake then started adding things from his experience the previous night.

He reemphasized how friendly and welcoming the community was, wrote about the variety in people's dancing styles, and shared the joy he experienced moving his body with other people.

Once he was done writing down the different details that had made his dancing experiences unique and fun, he started editing things properly. Jake went through cleaning up his language and removing some of his rambling thoughts. With that done, all that was left was to add photos. With a start, he remembered that he had forgotten to take any photos the previous night. For a moment, he felt frustrated with himself, but the positive feeling that had suffused him for the past few days buffered him against the negative thoughts. With a small shrug, Jake settled on using the internet to find pictures.

Jake sat back and stared at his finished product. It was a mixture of images and text that he hoped would flow well for the readers. Nodding with satisfaction, he uploaded the post to his blog and scheduled for it to drop the following week. He had set up his blog so that one post was uploaded every Friday. Since it was Saturday, that gave him a lot of time until his next one.

He finished the last of his toast and stood up to place his plate in the sink. Staring at the mess of dishes, he decided to clean them while he thought about his future blog posts. He grabbed the sponge and gave it a generous squirt of dish soap. His hands went to work while the gears in his head turned. The first order of concern was deciding on the topic. What could he cover that he hadn't already? Jake's thoughts turned towards a trip out of town. Writing about a different city would give him plenty of opportunities to write something new. The more he considered it, the more uncomfortable Jake felt. His back and neck slowly started to hurt. A headache was forming from his body's tension, which did not go away when he consciously relaxed his muscles. As he finished a dish, he placed it to dry on the rock above the sink. It seemed his instincts disagreed with the idea. He quickly dismissed the plan to travel and, instead, Jake thought about his plans for the upcoming week. The only out of the ordinary thing that he had planned was going to the festival with Kenneth.

The thought struck him as soon as he made that connection. So far, Kenneth had introduced him to two new things. Perhaps through Kenneth, he could find a way to bring new life to his blog. He just had to hang out with the other man regularly and try different things. It seemed like a manageable goal, and the headache quickly went away as he thought of plans that kept his bond with Kenneth. Jake placed the last dish on the drying rack and wiped his hands on his hand towel.

As long as Jake kept hanging around Kenneth, everything seemed to be working out nicely. Jake returned to his computer and closed his documents. Now that his work was done, he could relax. He opened up a movie and set it to play. He pushed his laptop to the side of his bed and laid down to face it. He drifted to sleep mid-way through the movie, his thoughts focused on the festival that was happening on Sunday.

Kenneth checked his watch. It was about the right time. He walked into the modest-looking restaurant just a few minutes after it opened. The serving staff walked up, all polite smiles.

"Welcome. Smoking or non-smoking?"

"Non-smoking, please. Also, is Rivera here? Tell him Kenneth wants to see him." Kenneth followed the waiter to his table while a waitress went into the back to relay his message to Rivera. Taking a glance around, Kenneth noted that the restaurant had a handful of other people already. It wasn't even the prime lunch hours yet. He decided to stick around and see how the rush hour looked.

"Kenneth, my friend." The bright-eyed Spaniard yelled as he approached the table, his arms wide open. "It has been some time."

"Rivera. Lively as ever, I see." Kenneth stood, walking over and embracing the larger middle-aged man. He tried his best to match the strength of the bear hug, but Rivera all but picked him up off the ground in his excitement.

Once Rivera sat Kenneth back down, the Scotsman smiled and took a seat across from his host. "How has business been going, friend?"

"Very well, Kenneth. In the months since our opening, we have made many loyal customers. I couldn't have done this without your help." The Spaniard smiled and gestured around. "You are a blessing to me."

"Not at all. It was your skills that did it. I just gave you the opportunity." The Scotsman waved a hand dismissively. It had taken him a while to build up enough of a friendship with Rivera to get the man to attempt opening a restaurant. And even longer still to pull enough strings to make it happen. It was better that the man used his magical talents for putting things together on cooking rather than something more nefarious. It had helped that Rivera was already interested in cooking. Kenneth's mind wandered to Jake. What did that human's powers enable him to do? It would take some time to figure out, but it was important. "How is your wife?"

"Oh, she is wonderful. Beautiful as the morning sunrise and wiser than I could ever hope to be. As always, the light of my life."

"And still as stubborn as an ox, right?" Kenneth grinned as Rivera laughed. He was always happy to come here, even if it was for work. The food truly was delicious, and Rivera was a vibrant host. If Kenneth didn't come and take special efforts to make sure Rivera's Palace never became too popular, it would have likely been talked about in magazines. As long as Kenneth could keep it a gem known only by the locals, there was less risk of Rivera learning about the real magic in his cooking. Just one more person that his superiors had not allowed him to bring into the fold. It irked him.

Rivera stood and clapped his hands. "You've come all this way to see me again. I can't let you leave without putting food in your belly. What would you like?"

Kenneth glanced at the menu for a few moments, then made his order. As Rivera sauntered back to the kitchen, Kenneth glanced around at the restaurant. Two of the people he had noticed earlier had left, only to be replaced by a couple of others who were still perusing the menu.

He leaned back in his chair and tried to look casual as he started making a mental chart of the flow of customers and what they ordered. While he couldn't look at Rivera's books, Kenneth had been involved in the process of starting up the restaurant. He knew enough to determine how much he needed to intervene and how much could be dealt with by the local handlers. Kenneth pulled himself out of his calculations and put it in the back of his mind as his food arrived. He ate slowly, savoring each bite as the tingle of magic sharpened the existing flavors. He sometimes wondered how normal humans experienced cooking of this kind. They weren't aware of magic, so they couldn't feel the tingling rush as their body absorbed the energy. All they would get was the flavor. It was at times like these that he pitied those without any power.

Half an hour later, the rush hour started. Groups of businessmen came and went. Kenneth resumed his note-taking. As the crush of people started to die down, Kenneth stood up and grabbed his bill. Taking a glance, he saw that Rivera had written "Free" across the paper. Ever the generous one, that man. Despite his attempts to stay dispassionate and disconnected, Kenneth found that he truly liked Rivera. It was a shame that he had to work so hard to limit the man's success. Kenneth wondered if he could ease the workload on himself and help his people by changing the circumstances a bit.

Kenneth asked one of the wait staff to extend his regards to Rivera before walking out the door. In his mind, he was already writing up a report for the current situation and potential threats that he noticed. He would have to check in with the director of the local handlers to compare notes. It would be a bother, but it was a necessary one. He turned a corner, ducking out of sight as he transported himself directly to the director's office.

The director jumped out of his chair, immediately throwing a pencil at Kenneth's face. The Scotsman caught it mid-air and placed it on the desk. "Is that any way to treat an operative, Wilbur?"

"You know I hate when you do that, Kenneth." Wilbur adjusted his tie and sat back down. "Not all of us are used to teleporting as casually as you are. Now, what do you want?"

"I'm here to report on the state of affairs for Rivera's Palace and the gossip I picked up while I was there." Kenneth sat down heavily into one of the chairs opposite Wilbur's large, wooden desk. "As you probably already know, he's growing in popularity again. At this rate, I feel he will garner too much attention. Local intervention seems the best choice."

Wilbur twirled one end of his mustache. It was one of the things he did while he was thinking that made Kenneth feel uncomfortable. "And what would be your suggestion?"

"The wait staff you have planted should be able to handle that admirably, as they have in the past. Is there a problem with using them again?" Kenneth tried to keep his tone casual, though he knew Wilbur understood the question as a probe for more information.

"Hmmm. You know, I recently ate at Rivera's Palace. To try it out for myself." Wilbur leaned back into his chair, still twirling his mustache. "The food was amazing. And reports have said that his abilities are only growing. Watering down the magic in the food is not enough anymore. His cooking skills are improving, not just his magic."

Kenneth had a feeling he knew what was coming next.

"I believe it may be time to simply recruit him and send him to be a chef at headquarters in Scotland." Wilbur reached out and straightened a line of pencils on his desk. "We have been putting a band-aid on the situation. It is time to cure the sickness, not treat the symptoms."

"With all due respect, I disagree," Kenneth spoke before he had finished thinking. Following up on his own words, Kenneth thought about the man in question. He knew from multiple conversations with Rivera that the man loved his life in Japan. There was no guarantee that he would accept moving to Scotland. As he followed the train of thought to form his argument, the silence stretched between them.

Wilbur waited a few moments in silence, then placed his hands on top of the desk. "Agent Kenneth. I understand you disagree, but that is not enough to convince me that an alternative exists. Unless transferring Rivera poses a greater risk to our operations than keeping him here, I will be forced to move forward with a recruitment plan."

Wilbur's mention of risk gave Kenneth an idea. He stood up and walked over to the whiteboard that Wilbur kept in his office. Grabbing a marker, he wrote down "Rivera's Palace" and a circle around it. From there, he started drawing lines and connections. "Currently, Rivera's Palace is a popular location among locals. This includes the magical among us. As a hub for information, it is well-suited for the job. I am not against recruiting Rivera, but I do feel there is too much risk involved with attempting to transfer him to Scotland. The man loves Japan. If the plan is to separate him from his home, we are less likely to be successful."

Wilbur watched silently as Kenneth wrote more lines and outlined the steps to working Rivera into their system for Nara. Kenneth noticed out of the corner of his eye that the director of Nara's handlers was smiling. He realized that Wilbur had planned for this the whole time and stopped talking for a moment. In the silence, Wilbur clapped his hands.

"Very good work, Kenneth. You have laid out a wonderful recruitment plan that also takes advantage of the benefits Rivera's Palace can bring to us. I will have our local handlers work toward putting it into effect, and I will reach out to you when your assistance is required. Thank you."

Kenneth scratched at his beard for a few moments. He had been tricked, but it had turned out well for both Rivera and for his people. There was very little risk of blowback from the plan he had set out. It furthered their cause as best as he thought possible. In the end, Kenneth could only nod in acceptance. "Very well. I will send a written report of other minor matters to your secretary."

With that, Kenneth teleported himself back into his quarters in Scotland. Wilbur was always taking opportunities to teach Kenneth a lesson. Kenneth respected the man, even as he hated being humbled. He shook his head and sat down at his computer to type up the written report. It was a short message, and he promptly sent it to Wilbur's secretary. Kenneth leaned back in his chair and thought about the next day's plans. The plans he had made with Jake were an immediate concern. If they came across another magical human, things could get messy.

He shook his head. That was the wrong way to think about it. Instead of hoping that nothing bad would happen, he had to plan for the worst. With that in mind, Kenneth thought about how best to handle different levels of magic being revealed or performed in front of Jake. In the worst case, an argument between two magical creatures could have flared tensions. Festivals served as good cover since performers did many kinds of outlandish tricks. He would have to distract Jake and use performance art as an excuse. Just in case, Kenneth grabbed a couple of books that explained the "trick" behind some of the more common magical techniques. He read through them so he could seem like an expert. He also flexed his magical muscles, warming them up with some simple exercises to help hone his mind and increase his focus.

With his preparations complete, Kenneth went to the mess hall to eat. He had a few more reports to send out, then his day would be done. All in all, he had been very productive. He hoped he wouldn't have to be as on-point on Sunday.

Chapter 5

The sound of his alarm startled Jake out of his sleep. He flailed about until he realized his phone vibrating against his table was the source of the buzzing sound. He stood up and turned off his alarm. Still half-asleep, he didn't remember why he had set the alarm for Sunday when he usually slept in. While he woke up and got ready for the day, he remembered his plans with Kenneth. They had agreed to meet at 11:30 at Osukannon station.

Jake never knew that festivals were held around that area. He had heard that the area around Osu was popular for cosplayers and anime fans because there were specialty stores in the shopping area. Since he wasn't a big anime fan, it had never appealed to him. He wondered what was going to happen at the festival. If it was like the other ones he had experienced in Japan, then there would be a lot of food stalls and attractions for children. Would there be a parade? Or cool street performances? He smiled at the thought. Magic tricks and acrobatics were always a fun experience.

With his shower done, Jake thought about eating before the festival. He didn't want to go the entire morning without food, but festival food in Japan was too good to pass up. Aiming for a middle ground, Jake made a couple of slices of toast for breakfast. It wasn't much, but it was enough to tide him over until later. He checked his train route on his computer before moving on to think about his blog.

To plan in advance, Jake pulled up a word document and jotted down an outline of the types of things he was going to seek out; food stalls, interesting performers, and more. He also made a mental note to ask Kenneth some questions about the festival itself. If his new-found acquaintance could provide information about the festival's history, it would save him the time of searching for it himself. With his shopping list, as he liked to call it, of photographs, he felt confident that he could make a solid post when he got home. He finished off his toast and brushed his teeth.

He didn't have anything left that needed doing until it was time to leave. Setting an alarm on his phone, Jake plopped down in front of his computer and started playing some games. He considered writing messages to a few of his friends back home, but he decided it could wait. Just like he did the last few weeks. It was strange, but the distance in his heart felt like it matched the physical distance between them. They seemed less real now that he didn't see them often. He felt almost disconnected from his past. It was so normal and ordinary. It contrasted with the excitement of moving to a new country and discovering someone that felt important to his future. It made it clear to him that his old friends were part of his old life. The future waited for him. Jake resolved to push forward into the unknown. It was the only way he could live comfortably. While he was lost in thought, Jake made a mistake and died in his game. Swearing under his breath, he looked at his last save. It was from last week. He sighed. Of course he had forgotten to save before the boss fight.

Before he could do anything else, the alarm beeped. After he picked out and put on his clothes, Jake grabbed his bag and walked out the door. The subway ride was uneventful. He arrived at Osukannon along with a large crush of people that all flowed to the same exit. He had forgotten to confirm the correct exit number with Kenneth, but the crowd was enough of a hint as he made his way through.

Kenneth woke up an hour before his alarm. He felt unusually tense. Swinging out of bed, he turned his clock off before he disrobed, focused his mind, and scrubbed his body clean with his magic. It wasn't quite as effective as a proper shower, but it meant he didn't have to wait in line or join the others in the communal showers. He had never gotten used to the shared bathing area concept, despite all his time spent in Japan - the land of the hot spring bath. Looking in the mirror, Kenneth appraised his facial hair. It grew unnaturally quickly whenever he used magic to clean himself, and this time was no exception. He still hadn't figured out why it happened. Grabbing a pair of scissors, he went to work trimming the wild mane back into a tamer cut.

With his personal hygiene finished, Kenneth's mind was fully awake. He immediately thought about his duties for the day. The first was meeting Jake and scouting the festival. He had already worked out the contingencies for that, so it was no longer a significant cause of concern. Probably. Hopefully. Kenneth ran back through his list of options for the various potential disasters that could happen at the festival. After going to the event, he would have to file the report of his findings from the festival. Then came meeting with one of his informants among the normal magical populace around Nagoya. Kenneth never felt comfortable around their kind. They were essentially spies with no allegiance. The information had never been faulty, but Kenneth always took the extra few steps to confirm its authenticity before relaying it to his superiors.

Thinking about his timetable, Kenneth realized that he wouldn't have any time to collect the funds to pay the informant after the festival. It was fortunate that he had woken up early. Slipping into some clothes, he rushed out of his room and down the hallways to the financing department. He had already filed the expense, but it took time to get the money. Half an hour after his arrival, one of the employees handed Kenneth an envelope sealed in wax with no insignia. He never really understood the old-fashioned use of wax, but he also never asked any questions about it.

As he walked out into the hallway, Kenneth almost crashed into one of the serving staff. The nervous young man stammered out an apology while Kenneth dusted himself off.

"Oh, don't worry about it. No harm was done."

The servant nodded and then gestured back down the hall. "Ani... Lady Anissa has requested your presence. In her office. Post-haste."

With that said, the servant charged off in the other direction. Likely for some other errand. Kenneth sighed in irritation. Why was Anissa summoning him just before a scouting mission? He was going to report to her after, anyway. He slipped the envelope into his jacket pocket and set off through the corridors to Anissa's office. He didn't bother knocking. Instead, he pushed the door open, letting it swing shut automatically behind him, and sat down in the chair opposite his boss. She held up a finger while the other hand scrawled notes out onto a piece of parchment. Kenneth stared and wondered how she managed to write so neatly while working at such a furious pace. Not even magic could explain everything. The pencil clattered as she threw it down on top of her desk and looked up at him.

"Kenneth. How good of you to join me."

"Not like I had a choice. What do you need, Anissa? I'm due to leave on a scouting mission in twenty minutes."

"Yes… about that." Anissa leaned forward, her eyes narrow. "I would like a written report afterward of every individual you've met in the past week that you have determined to be worthy of my attention. Both magical and non-magical humans. Written on truth parchment."

Kenneth leaned back in the chair and sighed. Of course she had figured out he was hiding something. He had hoped he would have a bit more time before she acted on her suspicions. "Yes, ma'am. I will get that list to you as soon as I am able, after performing the appropriate post-scouting procedures."

Anissa clacked the long, perfectly manicured fingernails of one hand against the top of her desk. Her impatience was palpable. He knew she wanted to order him to spill the beans, but she couldn't without openly expressing distrust, which put her at risk of losing face. She had nothing she could do. He resisted the urge to smirk. With a sigh, Anissa wordlessly waved her hand in dismissal. Kenneth stood up, made a mocking salute, and then walked to his quarters. Checking his watch, he realized there wasn't much time left.

He wished he could teleport freely within the castle grounds, but the security measures restricted transportation. While he walked, Kenneth scouted for a blind spot near the place where he agreed to meet Jake. Having found one, he opened and closed the door to his room, then immediately transported himself there. Raising one hand to wipe the sweat from his brow, he walked out of the alley and into the crowd. The day had already been more stressful than he had expected.

Kenneth preferred to always be the first person to arrive. It made him feel more comfortable. If Anissa hadn't taken up so much time, he could have. Yet another reason to dislike his boss. Kenneth faked a smile as Jake noticed him and gave a small wave with one hand.

"Yo, Kenneth. This place is bustling. Is the festival today that popular?"

Kenneth nodded as the two of them started walking toward one of the streets that had a flow of people in it. He took those first few steps as an opportunity to center himself. "It's a cool festival. And Osu already has a shopping area that gets lots of people on weekends."

Looking around, Jake realized that there were signs indicating the different locations for some of the bigger shops. Despite the press of people, there weren't any festival stalls in the area they had entered. The two of them walked for a couple of minutes down a walkway flanked on both sides by stores offering goods ranging from accessories made of silver to cosplay goods to kimono shops. He was surprised by the massive variety. Most of the stories he heard only told one side of Osu's shopping area. He made a mental note to come back another time to inform himself more and get pictures for a blog post.

Kenneth watched as Jake stared in wonder at the normal shops that were open along their walking path. It was obvious that Jake had never visited Osu before. Since that was the case, it made things easier for Kenneth. As long as Jake was easily distracted, Kenneth could scan through the crowds and do his job without being noticed.

"This place is really different from how I had imagined it." Jake's head swiveled around. For a moment, he seemed like any other gawking tourist.

"Yeah, it has a weird reputation." Kenneth gestured at the stores. "It's got some really cool stuff and even some arcades, but all you hear about are the cosplay shops."

As the two of them made their way further, with Kenneth leading, they approached the outskirts of the festival proper. The first food stall Jake noticed was offering one of his favorite snacks - grilled corn on the cob covered in miso, butter, and soy sauce. Jake lightly tapped Kenneth on the arm and gestured to the stall. "I'm a bit hungry, lemme grab one of those real quick."

"Go ahead. I'll grab some takoyaki over there." Kenneth walked to a nearby stall. Kenneth left Jake to stand in his own line and walked to a nearby stall. Kenneth let his senses expand as he observed the people nearby for anything out of the ordinary. Everything seemed fine here as the line progressed until he was at the front.

Jake couldn't help but stare for a few seconds at Kenneth's back. He had tried the doughy balls of octopus, pickled ginger, and spring onion before but didn't enjoy them. It was interesting to find out Kenneth liked that type of food. He returned his attention to himself as he walked up to order and pay. His stomach rumbled a bit as he reached out to grab the stick holding his corn. Biting into it, Jake immediately winced as he burned his tongue and mouth on the still-hot corn. He knew from experience that his impatience would leave his mouth in pain for the next few days as well. It was still worth it for the warmth mixing in with the flavor of the corn. Jake walked over just as Kenneth was walking away from the stall with his takoyaki.

"How's your corn?"

"Hot but good. How's the takoyaki?"

Kenneth speared one of the balls with the toothpick he had been provided, watching the steam roll off it. Unlike Jake, he wasn't interested in burning his mouth over food he could enjoy in a couple minutes. "Too hot for me to try yet."

The two of them chuckled as they made their way along. Down different streets, there were performers vying for attention. Here, a comedian pretending to be a magician, making promises and failing to deliver in amusing fashion. There, a duo performing acrobatic tricks with each other. Jake pointed out some of the neater tricks, and the pair stopped at times to watch one or another act for a couple of minutes before moving on. When they paused to watch performers that caught Jake's interest, Kenneth took the opportunity to scan through the crowd again. So far, things had been silent. Which was good, since Jake was also around. They continued wading through the festival and repeating this process until Jake became enraptured with a magician's performance.

Jake stood and marveled as a magician started performing tricks with Japanese folding fans. Kenneth waited several minutes for the human to grow bored. When Jake kept watching, Kenneth decided it was a perfect opportunity to scout ahead without him. He tapped on Jake's shoulder.

"Hey, I'm gonna go keep looking around. Enjoy the show, I'll catch you later."

"Oh, yeah. Have fun." Jake nodded distractedly as he tried to focus on the performance. He enjoyed magic tricks because they were ultimately always just people being very clever and skillful. It was refreshing, and he always felt somewhat clever when he could spot things in a trick. This magician was too good for Jake to notice any of the sleights of hand as she made the folding fans change color, vanish, and twirl in her hands. It was awe-inspiring.

Kenneth wandered between the different stalls in the flea market, barely paying attention to the goods on sale. As he walked into the Osukannon temple grounds, the crunch of gravel underneath his feet was strangely satisfying. The sound of people calling out to passersby to sell their old children's toys, clay pottery, and home-made necklaces filled the air. They were mostly worthless to Kenneth. His eyes constantly scanned the crowd. A shimmer caught his attention. As he glanced down, the Scottish man noticed the art pieces on sale. Taking a closer look, it became obvious. These enchanting works were, in fact, enchanted.

"Oh, do you like? I paint them!" The Japanese woman spoke to him in passable English.

Kenneth smiled at her. It was convenient that she had done them herself. He wouldn't have to go looking for the person who had worked the magic. "They're beautiful. Do you have more?"

His fluent Japanese surprised her. The woman took a few moments to process it before nodding shyly. Making a full recovery, she gestured toward the stacks of painted and sketched art and spread them out to give him a better view. "These are all that I have. Do any catch your eye? These two are my favorite."

"Hmm. This one, please." Kenneth pointed toward a traditional Japanese rendition of hell. He mirthlessly considered giving it to Anissa as a gift. She started the work of carefully wrapping it in protective paper before slipping it into a bag. Now to press her for information. "It's so beautiful, I have to ask. What is your secret to this… luster? Do you do this all by hand? Do you have help? I am truly fascinated."

"Oh, you are too kind. I'm not so special." The woman waved away his praise. Typical Japanese modesty.

Kenneth kept pressing. He had a time limit, since he couldn't risk Jake interacting with her. "No, I really think it is amazing. Could you teach me how to do this? I've always wanted to learn. What's your name, by the way? I'm Kenneth."

"My name is Yuri. Thank you for being so nice, but I am not good enough to teach." Yuri covered her mouth with one hand, thinking for a few moments. "Maybe… I am part of a sketch group. Would you like to practice with us? We meet every Monday."

Smiling encouragingly, Kenneth pulled out a pen and paper. "I would love to. Could I come to the meeting tomorrow, then? What time is it?"

Yuri wrote down the location and time for the meeting onto the paper and handed it back.

Once the magician's performance had ended, Jake turned to see if he could spot Kenneth. He saw no sign of where the Scotsman had gone. Shrugging to himself, Jake continued to walk down the path he had originally been traveling with Kenneth toward Osukannnon temple. Along the way, he stopped at a box where a man was replaying famous songs using only a trumpet. Jake chuckled at some of the song choices, and he eventually dropped a couple of one hundred yen coins into the hat near the man's feet as he walked away.

Jake gasped in surprise as he walked through one of the gates into the courtyard of Osukannon temple. The entire courtyard was filled with small shops people had set up to sell various odds and ends ranging from old clothes to handmade accessories. It was as he was walking through the area that Jake caught sight of Kenneth talking to a young Japanese woman who was trying to sell some vibrant and cool paintings and drawings. He came up behind

Kenneth and lightly clapped a hand on the Scotsman's shoulder. "Finally found yah, Kenneth. I didn't know you liked art."

Kenneth's shoulders tensed for a moment. He hadn't noticed Jake's approach, and the contact reminded him of how much power the human held within. Forcing himself to relax, Kenneth turned to Jake with a smile on his face. "Oh, you spooked me there. Yeah, I do. In fact, Yuri here was just suggesting I join a sketch group so that I could practice with her and some other artists."

"Wait, you actually draw? Man, you've got to show me sometime." Jake smiled encouragingly and turned to face Yuri. He switched to Japanese and gave a very small bow of his head. He didn't see anything out of the ordinary about her, but he still had a feeling that she wasn't normal. "Nice to meet you, Yuri. I'm his friend, Jake."

"Nice to meet you too. Do you also do art?"

"No, not at all. I'm terrible." Jake shook his head and laughed, resisting the urge to scrutinize her. "I can't even draw stick figures well."

Kenneth stared as they talked, wondering why Jake seemed unaffected by the raw display of magic in front of his eyes. Internally shaking himself, Kenneth held out a hand with the exact change for the book. "Anyway, thanks for the talk, Yuri. Here's the money for painting."

"Ah." Yuri looked down at the bag she had already slipped the painting into as if she had completely forgotten about it. With her free hand, she accepted and counted the coins while holding out the bag for Kenneth to take with the other. "Thank you very much. See you tomorrow, Kenneth."

Bag in hand, Kenneth led Jake away from Yuri. He resisted the urge to walk quickly. His mind mulled over the events that had just happened. Jake had been exposed to magically enhanced paintings and seemed unaware. And there were no visible changes to him, or Yuri, either. Could Jake have not been influenced despite his raw power? It seemed unusual. Most cases of humans with such untapped potential just needed small nudges to have the mental barriers unravel. Perhaps Jake was already slipping closer to his magical origins than Kenneth had thought?

Jake walked slightly ahead of Kenneth with a grin on his face. "Tomorrow, huh?"

"Huh?" Kenneth's face was blank as he took a moment to bring himself back to the present. His face lit up when he realized what Jake was talking about. "Oh, yeah. She's got a group that does sketch practices on Mondays. I figured I'd join tomorrow's and see how it goes."

"Oh really?" Jake's grin grew wider. He wasn't sure if Kenneth was playing at misunderstanding or if it was intentional, but he decided to keep trying to tease the other man. "That's all, huh? You weren't just pretending to do art because you're interested in the girl?"

For a moment, Kenneth's expression seemed to go dark. Had Jake really been unaffected, or was he simply faking it? Noticing the shock in the other man's face, Kenneth quickly smoothed his facial expression and faked a smile. "Of course not, Jake. I have many things about me you don't know yet. After all, we just met."

The two walked in silence. Jake wondered whether Kenneth was just shy about getting caught flirting. Something inside him told him that Kenneth was no artist. That combined with the strange sensation he had around Yuri told him something was going on, even if he didn't understand what it was. Jake couldn't place the feeling, but it was too strong to ignore. Even so, there wasn't any reason for him to keep pressuring Kenneth about it. Kenneth's romantic life was his own business, and if it was something else, Kenneth probably wasn't going to share. No point worrying about things he couldn't control. Jake resumed smiling and enjoying the festival as if nothing had happened.

Kenneth tried to guess what was really going through Jake's mind. The fact he was thinking was obvious. Eventually, Jake shrugged and resumed smiling and carousing like normal. Kenneth decided to be more careful in the future, even as he pretended to have fun alongside his false friend. There might have been more to Jake than Kenneth had initially estimated. He would both have to be more careful and try to frame his interactions with Jake in a way that wouldn't make Anissa call him off the mark.

Eventually, the festival started to wind down. People were leaving, as were some of the performers.

Jake turned to Kenneth. "Looks like things are wrapping up. Wanna do the same?"

Kenneth nodded and stretched, yawning loudly. "That sounds like a plan. Catch yah next time, then?"

Jake shook hands with Kenneth and smiled. "Of course. Thanks again for inviting me."

The two parted ways. Jake arrived home and smiled to himself. The festival had been a lot of fun, and there were so many things to include in his post that he wasn't sure if he could fit it all. He decided to let it wait until Monday after school before working on it. Turning on some YouTube videos, Jake settled in for the night.

Kenneth pulled out the paper he had received from Yuri as he ducked down an alley, walking into the shadows and arriving in the dim lights of his own room. He spent the rest of his time before sleeping, formulating a plan for the woman and writing the associated reports from his day's activities. It had almost been a mess, but he had managed. His report only communicated half of the story. Once he was done, Kenneth remembered the report he owed Anissa and decided to put it off until the morning. He needed time to sleep on how he was going to maneuver through the conversation. And so he slept, with the image of Anissa's scowl filling his mind.

Chapter 6

Monday rolled around, and Jake resisted the urge to hit the snooze button on his alarm. Every time he made that mistake, he overslept. He forced himself out of bed and went about his morning routine. With that done, he took some time to crack open his textbook and review what the class had studied over the past week. Every Monday, there was a quiz on what they had learned. There were no grades or points in class, so it was simply for the students to know how well they had learned the material. Even so, Jake hated the idea of getting a bad result.

He kept an eye on the clock as he muttered the grammar structures to himself under his breath and formed his own sentences in his head. When it approached time to leave, he scooped up the books, dropped them in his bag, slung the bag over his shoulder, and left his house.

In class, Jake nodded to his fellow students and greeted his teacher before it was time for the lesson to start. Despite it being a test day, the lesson still started off with the day's new kanji. Jake never managed to remember them right away, so he zoned out during half of these sections of the lessons. Unless he reviewed them at home, it just never stayed in his mind anyway. While Jake struggled to deal with the kanji, he didn't mind it. He accepted the fact that he just didn't think about things in a way that let him learn like the rest of his classmates. Once the kanji review was over with, the teacher took out the test sheets and passed them around the room.

Jake went through the test at a quick pace. He remembered everything, so picking out answers during the multiple-choice sections or writing in the proper form for one or two words took little time. As usual, he was one of the first to turn in his test sheet, even though he took the time to double-check his answers after filling everything out.

While he waited, Jake pulled out his textbook and checked a couple of the questions he had been uncertain about. He smiled to himself when he found the section that explained those answers and realized he had written the correct ones. Jake took small pleasure from his success, but it wasn't very motivating for him. In the end, whether he succeeded in this class or not, he needed to figure out the next stage of his life. After the experiences with Kenneth, he felt confident that learning Japanese was not truly his way toward the future that was right for him. He was merely going through the motions, now. One by one, his classmates all turned in their sheets to the teacher. When the last sheet had been handed over, the teacher announced the test was over. They moved on to the grammar lesson for that day. At the end of class, everyone received their graded tests back. Jake frowned when he saw that he had missed a couple of the questions but quickly dismissed it. This wasn't as important as it had seemed when he first started.

Once class was over, Jake and a few other students walked out together. After test day, the five of them typically ate lunch together and talked about the class. He wasn't sure when it became a scheduled thing, but Jake enjoyed the experience. They were a mixed group; one other, like Jake, almost always did well on tests while the others were less consistent. Every time they got together, a different person suggested a restaurant and led the way. This time, the Vietnamese student in the group led them ten minutes away from the school to a Vietnamese-style restaurant.

Jake was surprised that a Vietnamese restaurant was so close by. It was just barely outside the normal area that he explored when he ate food on his own, but it was completely different from what he had been finding. The miniature adventure of exploring just a bit past his horizon was satisfying and part of why he had previously enjoyed eating with the group. It was a small adventure that he had found satisfying. And it also provided an opportunity to practice speaking Japanese with other people trying to learn. This time, it felt different. It wasn't an exciting adventure. Exploring food wasn't bad, but it failed to give him the satisfying sensation of the tingle in his back and the feeling of rightness. After ordering based on his friend's recommendations, Jake and his classmates all talked about their results.

"Jake, what'd you get on the test?"

He pulled out his paper and showed it to everyone. "Almost perfect, but I messed up a couple that I was sure I had gotten right."

They all nodded. It was his usual problem.

"What about you guys?"

One classmate pulled out her paper and showed that she had missed about a third of the questions. "I just really didn't understand chapter fifteen and sixteen's grammar at all."

"Oh, that stuff? It's easy once you get used to thinking about it in terms of direction. Person A tells this to person B. Person B was told this by person A." One of the others explained.

Jake tried to avoid joining the explanations unless he was asked a question. He felt uncomfortable when the others trusted him to be right about everything because his scores were better on tests. Unless he completely disagreed with an explanation, he preferred to stay silent or talk about other things. To change the subject, he brought up his weakness: kanji. "So, how are you guys feeling about the kanji test this Friday? I'm worried I'm going to fail it. It's covering everything from the start of class."

"Me too. There's so many to remember."

"I'll be fine. I remember all of them, after all." One of the two Chinese students in the group waved a hand.

The other one laughed and poked him in the side. "But don't you always mix up the Chinese and Japanese readings? You should be studying harder than the rest of us, if anything."

They all exchanged questions and talked about the coursework while joking around until the food arrived. Jake and two of his other classmates pulled out their phones and took pictures of the food while the other two just rolled their eyes. It was practically a routine for all of them by now.

With that done, the group was mostly silent as they ate. Even though he had been warned, Jake was still surprised by the spiciness of his food. They rarely ever ate anywhere spicy, so it was a nice change of pace. The food was delicious, too. Jake made a mental note to come back to the restaurant in the future. One more option for his daily lunch spots. Once they were done eating, everyone hung out for a while longer to talk about life and their plans for the week.

The Vietnamese student smiled. "This week, I'm going skateboarding."

"You do that every week." Everyone else responded instantly.

"Yeah, but this week I'm going skateboarding in Osaka. Boom, different place, different experience."

Jake laughed. "Osaka's not even that far. Not that I'm one to talk. I don't even have any plans this week."

"What? You usually have one thing or another to go to. What's up with you, Jake?"

"Oh, I don't know." He shrugged. "I think I'm just worn out after this past week. I went out to a festival yesterday, and I went out dancing twice."

"Whoa, whoa. You went to a festival and didn't invite me?" The Turkish student jabbed the air with his chopsticks. He went out to festivals and fairs as often as he could. "I expect you to tell me all about it sometime."

"Yeah, yeah. Sometime."

The conversation turned to other people's plans and slowly died down. Everyone had very different interests outside of class, so they rarely ever hung out more than their weekly post-test meetings. Even so, Jake was fine with it. They were different people, after all. Everyone said their goodbyes, and Jake went straight home afterward.

Even though it was only early afternoon, Jake felt sleepy. Something about socializing with his classmates left him feeling tired even though he enjoyed it. The contrast with how he felt the previous few days only made his exhaustion affect him more. Setting the alarm for two hours later, he plopped himself down into his bed and took a nap without even bothering to take off his clothes.

He woke up ten minutes before his alarm went off. The nap had restored his energy. He thought, for the hundredth time, about how strange it was that someone as young as him needed to take naps after spending time with friends. Flipping open his computer, Jake wondered about how to spend the rest of his day. Thinking back over his list, he remembered that he still needed to write a blog post about the fair he had visited the day before. He could write about the restaurant he visited on a different day. That would put him two posts ahead of schedule, and he could spend some time doing whatever he wanted without any problems after those were done.

Normally, he would have had homework from class, but there was no homework on test days. It still felt strange to start each week off without any homework, but the heavier workloads during the week more than made up for it. Jake reoriented as he clicked open a word document on his computer and started writing about the festival.

A couple hours of intense typing later, he was done. Jake saved the document and put some water on to boil for his pasta. While he waited, his phone buzzed. He picked it up off the table. One of his friends, Matt, had sent him a message inviting him out to a party on Thursday. Normally, he would've gone out on Wednesday, but this seemed like a better opportunity. Plus, there was nothing wrong with spending his Wednesday afternoon and evening doing nothing. The past week had involved a lot more outings than he was used to anyway. Jake messaged back with a request for the details before pouring some pasta into a pot of boiling water.

His friend responded with the details a few seconds later, and Jake sent back a thumbs-up. He then opened up his phone's calendar and put the event's details into the program. He tended to forget that he was invited to these types of events unless he had some way to remind himself. Jake thought over the rest of his evening and the next couple of days. For the night, he planned to watch a movie then sleep. He needed to do his other blog post on Tuesday, then Wednesday could be a lazy day after he went to school. The next few days passed without incident.

Kenneth scratched his beard as he thought over his report. He had come across a magical human while keeping track of Jake. He needed to word his report carefully so that Anissa couldn't do anything to the process. If he made it seem like he performed poorly in his duties or was unable to handle the situation at all, she could take advantage of it. He also still owed Anissa the blood-oath list. He had no way out of that. Leaning back in his chair, he let out a long breath. No matter how he looked at it, Sunday had been a mistake. Jake and another magical human had come into contact with each other. Even if there had been no visible effects on either of them, Kenneth had failed to keep Jake away from magical sources while forming a plan of action. He gave up on trying to frame it positively. Attempting to make it look good had the potential to give Anissa more ammunition instead of less.

Having made that decision, Kenneth made quick work of the report. Only his trepidation made it take as long as it did. Kenneth checked the time and noticed that there was only an hour left before his planned visit to Rivera. And after that, he had to go to that sketch meeting Yuri had mentioned. He rubbed his right hand. There was a bit of pain left over from the time he had taken to prepare for that meeting. Kenneth grabbed the small notebook where he had drawn his sketches. He slipped it into his pocket to make sure he didn't forget it while he made his preparations to see Rivera.

According to the plan Kenneth had proposed to Wilbur, he would have to start coaxing Rivera into the concept of magic and the idea of coming under his people's employ. Most magical humans didn't take to the idea easily, so it was going to be a multi-step process. Kenneth's job was mainly to open the man up to the people Wilbur planned to send. Kenneth thought about what to say. The angle of the approach would determine how smoothly the rest of the process went. Even though he had confidence in the plan, Kenneth felt a great deal of pressure to start it properly. He checked the clock. It was time for him to head over, or he would definitely not make it to the sketch group on time.

Kenneth smoothed out his hair in the mirror and straightened his clothes before willing himself to cross from his room to an alley a short walk from Rivera's Palace. He ignored the homeless cat that scampered away from his sudden appearance and made his way down the street to his destination. The wait staff recognized him, and one of them immediately went to tell Rivera of his arrival.

Rivera was all smiles as he walked out of the kitchen. "Kenneth, my friend. You honor and surprise me with another visit so soon. What fortune brings you back to me?"

"There's no luck with this. Only the result of your hard work." Kenneth smiled back and followed Rivera to the nearest table to sit. "You remember that I helped you receive backing for this restaurant, I'm sure."

Rivera nodded silently. Kenneth clasped his hands together underneath the table to keep them from shaking. This was the moment of truth.

"The people I contacted to support you have been keeping track of your restaurant, and they are happy with and amazed by your progress. The quality of the food and the quality of service as a whole has improved since you started. They suspect you could become much more popular with just a little bit more support. Which they wish to offer."

"Why, this is fantastic news." Rivera smiled for a moment, but his face turned serious after a moment. "There is a catch, isn't there? What do they want me to do? I will not sacrifice the soul of my restaurant for anything, even the chance at greater success."

Kenneth shook his head quickly. "No, no. They don't want anything like that. I explained to them how much you love this place and the people here. They wish to hire you to work as part of their network. I am part of it as well. Your career as a chef will be almost entirely unchanged. That, I can promise."

"Hmmmm." The Spaniard drummed his fingers against the table as he considered the offer. "I can make no promises without more information. Did you bring a contract or something I could look at?"

"I did not. I'm not the person they have do that kind of work. We know each other, so I requested to be the first person to approach you with the offer." Kenneth smiled. "If you're open to it, I'll let them know, and they should send people with more details another time."

"Nothing you've said would make me say no. I am interested. Please, tell your friends that." Rivera stood up and clapped his hands together. "But first, you must eat. I will never let you go on an empty stomach, my friend."

Kenneth didn't have the chance to object or respond as Rivera quickly bustled over to the kitchen, already barking orders to his assistants inside. Fortunately, he had planned for this to happen. Rivera was nothing if not a generous host. Kenneth checked his watch. There was just enough time to eat, say his goodbyes, and still make it to the sketch group's meeting spot. Perfect.

The meal was as delicious as it always was. Kenneth and Rivera embraced each other and said their goodbyes, and Kenneth nodded in affirmation to one of the wait staff that had signaled they were working for Wilbur. The process was underway.

Kenneth walked into the elevator, grateful for the brief pause it provided. He had to change personas between marks, and moments of silence helped him focus. Glancing at his reflection in the wall of the elevator, Kenneth made his clothes slightly messier and adjusted his posture to match how he had been when he first met Yuri. The sketch group was renting out a meeting room, so Kenneth had to walk down several more hallways after exiting the elevator. There were too many cameras in buildings like these to simply teleport inside.

He pulled out his sketchbook and gave it a quick look. Kenneth hated drawing, but he had spent the entire previous evening making dozens of attempts at sketching various people, scenes, and animals to prepare the illusion of interest. His hand still hurt from the effort, and he rubbed his wrist again. He wished there was an easier way to create the identity of an art hobbyist. Kenneth slipped the notebook into his pocket once more as he opened the door and entered the group's meeting room.

"Oh, you came." Yuri stood up as soon as he walked in, gesturing to the open chair next to her while also speaking to the assembled members. "This is Kenneth, the man I was just telling you about. He really wants to learn and practice with us."

The other five people in the group introduced themselves, and Kenneth followed suit with the formalities. He was surprised so many people had already arrived. Once they were finally seated, everyone brought out their sketchbooks to show their most recent work. Each member swapped their book with someone else. Kenneth swapped books with Yuri first, noticing the shimmer across each of her works. "Who taught you how to draw like this?"

"I practiced by myself. I like drawing and painting, but until recently, I was too shy to show other people." Yuri glanced around at everyone.

Kenneth was surprised by her shy demeanor. It was a stark contrast from the confident girl selling her art at a festival. Not wanting to push her too far, Kenneth smiled and nodded. He talked a bit with her, asking questions about shading and other art techniques. He then moved on to trade books with the next person and repeat the process. He quickly confirmed from looking at everyone's art that, while some of them were very good artists, none of them shared Yuri's gift. Kenneth thanked his luck. It was difficult enough to handle one mark in a group, let alone more.

After everyone had exchanged personal tips, one of the more skilled artists, a middle-aged man in a business suit, stood by the whiteboard and did a presentation on art fundamentals. Kenneth guessed the man was the "teacher" of the group since he was the most senior of all of them by far. Kenneth opened his sketchbook and took notes alongside the rest of the group. If he was to maintain his cover, he needed to practice these fundamentals before the next meeting.

Eventually, the group ended their time. Each person had received notes and tips from their fellow artists, and everyone had started a sketch that they planned to finish and show at the next meeting. Kenneth had watched Yuri out of the corner of his eye as she sketched, but he did not manage to notice any signs of magic from the couple minutes of work that she put into it. The sketch itself wasn't even of the same quality as the sketch she had shown earlier. He would have to make an opportunity to watch her process more closely.

Everyone in the group walked out together. When they asked, Kenneth made sure to say his house was in the same direction as Yuri's. The rest of the group waved them goodbye.

"Thank you for inviting me. It was a real learning experience." Kenneth scratched the back of his head. "I'm not very good, but maybe someday I can be like you and the other talented artists in the group."

Yuri smiled encouragingly as they walked. "You're already good. I think you could be amazing. It just takes practice."

"You flatter me." Kenneth smiled back. "Still, I have a lot to learn. Maybe you could help me practice sometime?"

"Me? But surely Tanaka would be better. His teaching is always so easy to understand."

Kenneth shrugged. She wasn't wrong. The man's presentation was surprisingly clear, even for someone as untrained as Kenneth. Still, he couldn't admit that. "I appreciate his effort, but…. I think he's probably busy with work, you know? I wouldn't want to put that kind of pressure on him. Plus, I kind of like your style more than his."

"Oh, uhm." Yuri nodded. "I guess you're right. He is probably busy. Though I think his style is really cool. The lines are always so neat, and the perspective is so good."

He nodded and listened as she continued to talk excitedly about Tanaka's art style. It was strange that she could be so energetic about this topic when she had been so reserved about her own art earlier. He wondered if there was some history that he was missing. Perhaps she was simply shy about her process? Kenneth had seen inside her sketchbook before they all packed up, and she had barely drawn anything in comparison to everybody else. Or perhaps she knew about her magic and was trying to hide it? The idea made Kenneth wary. He didn't know the limits of her powers yet, so there was some risk involved with that.

Yuri eventually went silent. They continued walking for a few minutes before Kenneth spoke up.

"Ah, wait. I'm actually going that way from here. Thanks again for inviting me. I'll see you next week."

"Okay. See you then. Thanks for coming."

The two of them smiled at each other, and Kenneth ducked down a side street. Once she was out of view, he waited a few minutes then teleported himself back to his quarters.

He let out a sigh, pulling the sketchbook out of his pocket and tossing it onto his desk. He had made progress with the girl, but it still felt like he was scratching the surface. He would have to spend Tuesday doing the sketches and writing up the report from the day. Kenneth disrobed and slipped into his bed, flicking the light switch along the way. On Wednesday, he had to check in with Wilbur to make sure things were progressing properly. He also planned to check in on some other low-maintenance marks afterward. Kenneth decided he would visit Rivera again on Thursday. It made the most sense to check in again at that point. The information he received from Wilbur would help him adapt his approach to rope Rivera into their world. Having the patience to tease the truth out of people like Yuri or introduce the truth to people like Rivera felt like a magical power in and of itself.

He just hoped things kept on their current track. If all went well, he would be able to stabilize his schedule and build up a routine for his work again. The thought put a warm feeling in his chest and lulled him to sleep.

Chapter 7

The beeping of his alarm broke Jake out of his reverie. He had fallen asleep sitting up. Despite spending most of Wednesday relaxing, he still felt tired. He double-checked his route to the party, then grabbed his bag and swung out the door. It had been a while since the last time he went to a party that wasn't about dancing. The place was a bar run and owned by foreigners, and most of the staff had been American the last time Jake was there.

While he made his way over, Jake wondered about the types of people that were going to show up. He wasn't as active in the bar scene, so he didn't know much about it. When his friend sent him the information, Jake was surprised by the mention of trivia games and prizes being handed out. He wasn't very good at trivia, so he just hoped he was on a team that could win it for him.

Once he arrived, Jake kept an eye out for Matt. Jake usually arrived early, and Matt had a tendency to come later, so he wasn't surprised when his friend was nowhere to be seen. He shrugged to himself and took stock of the crowd that had already gathered for the event. Even though the party was hosted in a foreign bar, there was a surprisingly large number of Japanese people mixed in with the rest. Off to the side, some of the bar's regular customers were talking amongst themselves and mostly ignoring the party attendees. Jake recognized them from the last time he came to the bar, but he didn't remember their names.

Jake grabbed a drink at the bar and moved around different groups of people having conversations, listening in to bits and pieces but not getting involved with anybody. The atmosphere was friendly and bustling, but he still felt a bit shy. Something about events like these always put him on edge until he had gotten a feel for the people. A tap on his shoulder caused him to turn around. He smiled as he recognized Matt.

"Hey, Matt. You're early for you."

Matt smiled back and clapped him on the shoulder. "I got off work early. It's been a while. How you been?"

"Good, good. Just dancing and studying. The usual." Jake waved a hand dismissively. "What about you? How's life treating yah?"

"It's not bad. Getting better, hopefully." Matt turned and gestured to the three people that had been watching the exchange behind him. "Oh, I almost forgot. Jake, meet Hirayama, Sylvia, and May."

"Nice to meet yah." Jake smiled at each of them in turn. He was impressed by Matt's ability to always have a group of friends to introduce. Every invitation Jake received from Matt usually mentioned something about helping Jake get to know some 'cool people.'

Just as they were finished with introductions, the host of the party announced that the food was ready and invited everyone to eat up while it lasted. Most of the crowd shuffled into line, and Jake and his newly made group of friends squeezed in as well. The party had been set up with an "Italian" theme, so the food was a mixture of spaghetti, different kinds of pizza, and bread.

"They really committed to the theme, didn't they?" Jake eyed the food with a mixture of surprise and hunger. He loved pasta more than he cared to admit.

Matt laughed. "They always do. The trivia game later will also be about Italian stuff, you know. Last time, it was sports-themed, and I crushed it."

"But the prize last time was a dehumidifier or something, right?" May turned toward Matt. "Did you even keep that thing?"

"Well… no. But that's beside the point. The point was I was awesome. Recognize me, dangit."

May rolled her eyes. "Praise be, sir Matthew of Florida."

Jake smiled and started to relax as the banter continued. The group seemed friendly enough. They were more talkative than he was, but that just meant he could join the conversation when it felt natural rather than having to try and keep up with everyone. The talk slowed as the line progressed, and everyone had their food. The previous din of conversation in the entire bar died down while people ate.

The host spoke through a microphone about the trivia quiz later and listed the prizes for the group with the most points at the end. The stuff they listed didn't interest Jake. Wine, discount coupons at clothing stores, and other random pieces. He tuned most of it out as he focused on his spaghetti. Despite being at a bar, the food was actually decent. It was better than some of the cheap restaurants he visited for lunch after class.

The conversation picked up again once the five of them had finished eating, and Jake took the opportunity to get to know them more. While talking with them, he found out that Silvia and May were both English teachers and coworkers of Matt's. Meanwhile, Hirayama was an engineer.

"And what about you, Jake?" Sylvia gestured toward Matt. "When you were talking to him, you mentioned something about dancing?"

"Oh, I'm not a professional." Matt chuckled as Jake hurriedly waved his hands in denial. "I just do it as a hobby. I'm here studying Japanese, that's all. Not sure how long I'll be here after, but I love it so far, so… hopefully a long time."

"That's cool. I wish I had time to study, but work keeps me so busy."

May nodded. "Yeah, our schedules get pretty hectic. But hey, we enjoy what we got, right?"

"I'll drink to that." Matt downed the last of his beer and put the glass down with a soft thud onto the table. "And now to get more. Anyone want anything while I'm ordering?"

Everyone responded with their requests, and Matt gave them a thumbs up. While Matt went to wait in line, Jake excused himself to the bathroom. Once inside, he sat down and rubbed his eyes. He was enjoying the time with the group, but he also wished he could split off to talk with other people. It felt awkward to leave the group and find another one after having spent half of the evening with them. He hoped the trivia game would provide a chance to get to know some other people. After washing his hands, Jake glanced at himself in the mirror and straightened his clothes. He took a deep breath and walked back out.

As he was making his way to the table his group had commandeered, the trivia game time was announced.

"When you came in, you were handed a piece of paper with a color. Please group up with other people of the same color."

Jake finished walking over to grab his drink off the table, then pulled the slip of paper out of his pocket. He had forgotten all about it. The color was blue. His favorite. On the opposite end of the bar, there was a tall guy holding up a blue sign, so Jake nodded to Matt and the others then made his way over. He showed his blue slip and joined in with a group of six others.

"Let's do this." The tall guy was nearly shouting as he looked around at the group. "We're gonna win. Let's get a game plan, everyone huddle."

Jake grouped up in a circle with the rest of them, confused by how seriously a trivia game for trivial prizes was being taken. "Do we really need a plan?"

"Of course we do, uh… what's your name?"

"Jake."

"Of course we need a plan, Jake. How else are we going to win?"

Jake turned to look at the other people in the circle and saw varying degrees of amusement on everyone's faces. He shrugged and turned back to the de-facto leader. "What's the plan, then?"

"That's the spirit." He grinned and clapped Jake on the back. "Today's about Italy, so anyone who knows stuff about Italian history or things like that should be the person to pick the answers. That's the plan."

As he finished the explanation, the host announced the first question. It was something about the century that tomatoes became popular in Italian cuisine. Nobody in the group had a clue. Jake suggested an answer and somehow got it right. The next question, nobody knew the answer yet again. Everyone turned to look at him, and Jake simply shrugged and made another guess. He was wrong. Trivia games were never his strong suit. With each answer, the tall guy responded dramatically. His intensity made the game a lot more fun than Jake had expected it to be.

When the questions were over, the host tallied the points, and Jake's team had somehow managed to come in second place. When it was over, the tall guy put an arm around Jake's shoulders.

"You did great, Jake. My name's Donovan, by the way."

Jake tried to gently pull out of Donovan's grip, but quickly gave up. Instead, he gave a thumbs up. "Thanks, Donovan. It was all because of your leadership."

Donovan smiled in response, giving Jake a smack on the back before going to the bar to get more alcohol. Friendly drunks like him made Jake smile despite himself. They were endearing, despite everything. While Donovan was waiting in line, Jake took the opportunity to look around at the other people and noticed a familiar face. He slipped between groups of people, smiling as he approached Mai.

"Hey, Mai."

Mai turned, her look of surprise quickly giving way to a smile. "Jake? You come to these events too?"

"Not often, but a friend invited me. What about you?"

"When the mood strikes me." She looked around. "Which one's your friend?"

Jake gestured over to Matt and the others. "That's my group over there. Did you come alone?"

"No, I came with my friend, Sana. She's in the bathroom, though."

"Oh, okay."

"I'm too shy to come to these by myself. Oh, before I forget." Mai pulled a paper out of her bag and handed it to Jake. "We're throwing a birthday dance party this Saturday for Takeda. If you've got time, you should come."

He nodded and slipped the paper into his pocket. He would read it later. As he did so, a woman walked up to them and looked him up and down. "Hey Mai, who're you flirting with while I'm gone?"

"I'm not flirting with anybody. Sana, this is Jake. I met him last week while I was out salsa dancing. Jake, this is Sana. She's my friend from college."

"Nice to meet you, Sana." Jake nodded.

"A pleasure." Sana smiled and turned to Mai. "So this is the cute foreigner you told me about?"

Mai hissed out a breath. "Sana, I told you that in confidence."

Jake resisted the urge to laugh at Mai's obvious embarrassment. Instead, he gestured toward Matt. "It was nice talking with the both of you, but I see my friend gesturing for me to come over. I'll see you on Saturday, Mai. Thanks again."

"Take care." Mai smiled before turning to pout at Sana as the two of them continued their friendly conversation. It occurred to Jake that he maybe should have offered to introduce them, but he gave up on the idea since he was already walking up to Matt.

As Jake approached, Matt grinned and raised the wine glass he won in the trivia game. "Hey, Jake. Congrats on second place."

"Yeah, thanks, mister first place. Did you cheat?"

"What? Of course not." Matt turned to look around conspiratorially, then leaned in. "Yeah, we looked up the answers on our phones. Easy prizes."

"Of course you did. Those questions were crazy." Jake smiled.

"They're always really tough. I don't know how they decide to come up with these things, honestly."

Jake shrugged and looked at the bottle in Matt's hands. "You going to drink all that by yourself?"

"Actually…" Matt put the bottle on the table next to them and made a show of slicking back his already smooth hair. "I have been seeing someone. I'm going to share it with her."

"Hey, congrats. When do I meet her?"

"You already did. Sylvia's amazing."

Jake smiled and nodded. That explained their glances in conversations earlier. Jake held back a response as the rest of their small group rejoined them, and they all exclaimed about Matt's team winning. They joked about Matt sharing the wealth with them and caroused for a while longer until the party eventually ended.

The group talked briefly about doing an after-party, but Matt and Sylvia both said they had work and couldn't do it. Nobody commented on the obvious, and instead, they all agreed to go their separate ways.

Looking at the time, Jake realized it was still rather early in the night. He wasn't feeling tired after what was essentially just a night spent standing around and talking. After double checking the directions on his phone, he went to his favorite normal club. On the way home, Jake pulled out the paper Mai had given him. There was a dance party being held this Saturday at a park. The flier mentioned things about food and drink. Since it was a dancing event, Jake's mind turned to Kenneth. It only made sense to invite him after he had introduced Jake to a new place. Pulling out his phone, he sent Kenneth a quick message.

"Hey Kenneth. I was invited to a birthday dance party this weekend. Wanna join me?"

Kenneth responded quickly, asking for the details. Jake decided to wait until he got home to take a clear photo of the flier and send it to Kenneth. It was easier than trying to type out all the information himself.

It wasn't very long before Jake arrived. He liked this club because it had multiple floors with different types of music; hip hop on one, pop on another, and so on. Many of the other clubs only had one dance floor, and they all played the same kind of pop club music.

After going through the entrance security and paying, Jake packed his bag into a locker and made his way up to the hip-hop floor first. There were always fewer people on the hip-hop floor than the others, so it gave Jake time to relax into his club dancing style. He used his drink ticket so he could have something to drink as he warmed up to the current DJ's style. For a few minutes, Jake simply swayed back and forth to the beat.

He put down his glass when the DJ started playing a song that had a rhythm he liked. Twisting and turning in his steps, he enjoyed the freedom of the mostly empty dance floor to fully enjoy the range of motion. A smile lit his face as his feet hurried to match the quick pace of the drums in the song's beat. Sweat started to bead down his forehead as it picked up speed, and he quickened his steps to keep up. Once he had danced a few more songs on that floor, Jake made his way up the stairs to the electronic music floor.

While he enjoyed listening to hip-hop, Jake enjoyed the freedom of dancing to electronic music more. He enjoyed alternating between the slow, swaying movements of the beginning of the songs into the sharp, fast-paced drops that pushed him to his dancing limits. Jake let himself lose focus on the world around him as he focused only on the beat and moving his body with it. He kept his movements tighter because of the other dancers but still managed to feel freer than he did while dancing to hip-hop. He felt no pressure to perform any set moves, even though he imagined there were some patterns for electronic dancing.

Jake danced until his breathing became labored, then went down to the pop music floor. The pop floor had the largest crowd, and the dance floor had no room for actual dancing. Jake grabbed a drink at the bar with his remaining drink ticket and sipped it slowly while he let himself recover. In the meantime, he watched as the mass of people on the dance floor jumped almost in unison according to some code he didn't know. Every time a song people knew started playing, there were shouts of excitement and joy. Jake smiled at their enthusiasm.

Before long, he had recovered enough to continue dancing. Taking a sweat towel out of his pocket, he wiped himself dry before moving to a somewhat empty area near the dance floor where he could move around a bit along with the song. Jake didn't know many of the pop songs, so he had to guess how they would rise and fall. Once he got a feel for the song, he started changing his dance steps to match the lyrics as well as the music. Jake felt eyes on him as he danced and turned to scan the crowd without stopping his body's movements.

Off to the side, a pretty woman was smiling as she watched him dance. Jake smiled back and slowed his pace, dancing as he moved through the crowd to approach her.

"Hi, wanna dance?" He tried to shout over the noise.

She pointed to her ears and shook her head, shouting back at him. "My name is Chie."

Jake reached out a hand to invite her to dance. Chie moved away from the wall and followed him to where he was dancing. They started dancing together. Jake moved cautiously at first. He wasn't used to dancing with a partner outside of salsa. As she smiled and moved with him, he grew more confident and comfortable. They moved closer to each other then further apart, swinging back and forth along invisible lines. When they were close to each other, Jake took the opportunity to try speaking to her.

"I'm Jake. I'm from America."

Chie nodded. "Nice to meet you."

They swung back apart. Jake smiled and took her hand to lead her into a turn, and she accepted it in stride. He wasn't sure what to say in those brief moments, so he stopped talking and simply danced. Chie smiled with him, dancing through two songs with him.

As the second song ended, Jake gently took her hand and led her away from the noise of the crowded dance floor. He leaned in, so he didn't have to shout.

"Do you want to grab something to eat with me? It's a bit noisy here."

"Sure."

The pair went to the locker area and grabbed their bags. Jake led the way out of the club to a nearby restaurant that was open till the first train, sitting across from her.

Chie twirled her hair with a finger as she browsed the menu, glancing up at him. "Jake, right? How long have you been in Japan?"

"Oh, not that long. Half a year or so, maybe. Your dancing was really good, by the way."

"Why, thank you. Same to you." Chie blushed a bit.

The waiter came by, and the two of them ordered drinks but no food. Neither of them were really hungry.

"Do you live around here?"

Jake shook his head. "I live over by Ozone. You?"

"Yeah, I can walk home from here. Otherwise, I wouldn't be out so late on a weeknight." She giggled.

"I guess so."

The two of them sipped their drinks in silence, staring at each other and smiling. Jake wasn't sure what to say. He found her attractive, but he wasn't usually the type to pick people up. He put down his drink and gestured toward the door.

"If you want, I can walk you home."

Chie tilted her head slightly as if pondering it, then nodded her head. "Please, do. I'd like that."

Jake stood up, paid for the drinks at the register, then walked out with her. His heart pounded in his chest as he reached his hand around to place it on her back as they made their way down the street. When she didn't pull away, Jake smiled despite his nerves.

"So, Jake, what do you do?"

"Oh, I'm here studying Japanese. I'm aiming to live here for longer if I can."

"That's cool. I wish I could speak English, but I'm terrible at it."

He laughed. "It's not that big of a deal. I can speak Japanese, after all. Which way is it to your house?"

"Oh, this way." Chie led him down a side-street. "How long have you been studying Japanese?"

"Since before I came to Japan. Two years now, I think? I lost track."

Eventually, they made it to Chie's apartment. She turned to look at him and gestured toward the door. "You're welcome to come in for some tea. As thanks for bringing me here."

"That would be appreciated." Jake followed her in as she opened the door. They took off their shoes and entered the apartment. At first, the two of them simply talked. Jake slowly grew more confident and leaned in closer to kiss her. Chie kissed back, and Jake kissed her again. She paused, whispering into his ear.

"Wait, my room." She grabbed his hand and led him into her bedroom.

Jake and Chie spent some time getting to know each other. Once it was over, the two of them slept in a bed made for one. Jake was reminded of how hard it was to breathe with another person's weight added to the mix as he slowly drifted to sleep after Chie was already at rest. In the back of his mind, he remembered that he had class in the morning. But it was too late to set an alarm. He let out a sigh. It was what it was.

87

Chapter 8

The call to Anissa's office was not a surprise when it came. Kenneth figured it was going to happen after the events on Sunday. Even so, he wasn't happy about being woken up early for the meeting with his superior. He growled his understanding at the servant. Once he heard the click of his door closing, Kenneth stood up and did a short, somewhat messy fixing of his hair. He wanted to be presentable, but he also wanted to signal his displeasure with being forced out of bed. A few minutes later, and he was out the door headed to her office.

In his mind, Kenneth was already thinking about the possible ways she would try to bring him under her thumb. He considered their history and other conflicts of opinion they had had in the past. Anissa's style tended to be more direct than anything else. He started planning out exactly what he'd say when she tried to pressure him. Kenneth had no intentions of letting Anissa bring him to heel on the issue of Jake's management. His intuition was pointing too strongly at Jake being important to let it go. Kenneth paused to take a deep breath as he arrived outside of Anissa's office. It was time.

"Shut the door." Anissa was, uncharacteristically, standing up behind her desk instead of sitting. She did not have any of the usual signs of frustration that Kenneth had come to expect when it came to situations like these.

He closed the door behind him and stood awkwardly. He wasn't comfortable sitting down if she was standing. "You called for me, boss?"

"Yes, I did. To discuss your recent report about the Jake mark." Anissa reached down and grabbed one of the folders on her desk, opening it up. "It says here you brought him with you during a scouting mission. And that your decision accidentally caused two magical humans to come into contact with each other. On top of that, I am only just now hearing of this mark that you've been watching for over a week now."

"That is correct."

Anissa sighed and tossed the file back onto the desk. "Normally, I would try to take the reins from you and force you to stay away, but I know that look in your eye. You'd just find some way to disobey me without disobeying, and I would be back to square one."

Kenneth blinked slowly. This was not the reaction he had expected. There was no fire in Anissa's voice. She didn't plan to fight him. Had she figured out a different way to win? One that Kenneth hadn't thought about?

"Instead, I'm going to give you what you want. With conditions." She held up one hand and started counting them off. "One, all reports are to be in full—no missing details. Two, I want you to follow my orders if I order you to back off at a later point in time. Three, no more shenanigans. This is your last time."

The list was short, but Kenneth still felt it was unreasonable. He had to give up control in order to keep it. "And what if I say no to the conditions?"

"Then I can simply put someone else in charge of Jake's case. I'm your superior, Kenneth." Anissa's glare was intense. Kenneth felt a shiver run down his spine. "There are other options aside from you. You're simply convenient. Remember that."

Kenneth shook his head in consternation. If that had been a possibility for her, why didn't she simply do that? He was sure there were plenty of agents that would have followed her commands without argument. It was then that Kenneth realized it might not have been an option for Anissa. She was half-bluffing. She could remove him from the case, but they were probably too short-staffed to replace him. Kenneth smiled and sketched a bow. "As you wish, Lady Anissa. Under the condition that what I say goes when it comes to the handling of my mark."

Anissa nodded and finally shifted to sit down in her chair. Kenneth stayed standing in the hopes that the meeting wouldn't last much longer.

"Well? What are you waiting for? Get back to work."

"Right. Dismissed. I got it." Kenneth turned and left. He was still unsure of where he stood with Anissa, but it seemed as though she had accepted his place in everything. The reason for it didn't matter. Kenneth took what he could get.

Checking the time as he walked, Kenneth realized he had some time before he went to check in on another mark. It was about time for him to head out, so he quickened his pace to arrive in his room and teleport to a side alley near the performance hall. He bought a ticket and made his way toward the seats furthest from the stage. As more people came in and seated themselves, Kenneth checked the time again. If things went properly, he would arrive at Wilbur's place in time to discuss the progress they had made for the Rivera integration plan.

A small man came out to announce the start of the magic show. The audience didn't know the truth, but the magic they were seeing was genuine. Kentaro made a decent living as a magician, but his shows attracted the attention of all kinds of magical entities. Kenneth's job was to keep him protected without revealing himself. While Kentaro was performing his act and doing his build-up chit-chat, Kenneth closed his eyes and leaned back. Focusing his will, he scanned the crowd for dangerous magical creatures. There weren't many, but there were enough for Kenneth to be proactive in removing them.

He channeled energy down through the floor and directed it at each of the supernatural threats seated around him. With the surge of power, he transmitted a message to each creature that Kentaro was under protection. The beasts flinched as they smelled the type of magic that Kenneth possessed. Pixies were rarely if ever, working alone. One by one, they stood up from the crowd and headed out the door. None of them decided to risk an outright confrontation in such a public space. Kenneth performed a final scan around the room and the crowd. All that were left were small-time magical beings, if they could be called such. Their powers were insignificant.

Kenneth stayed through the entire show, continuously performing a check in the area. The air reeked of magic as Kentaro's performance approached its climax. It was a wonder that the youth had survived so long doing performances of this kind before Kenneth ever discovered him.

The show ended, and Kenneth joined the rest in applauding before maneuvering so that he was walking out with a group of other people leaving rather than by himself. He didn't blend in well with the mostly Japanese audience, but it was better than doing nothing. Once he was free of watchful eyes, Kenneth shook himself to wake back up as he transported himself to Wilbur's office.

Wilbur jumped in his chair as Kenneth appeared. "You really must stop doing that. One of these days, I will have a heart attack."

"I'll be more careful, then. You are important, after all." Kenneth smiled as he slipped into a chair. "Still, I'm here to get a quick update before I visit Rivera. How has progress been with introducing him to us?"

"Good, so far. We have not broken the magic concept to him, but he has been amenable to being sponsored by us and supplying us with information in exchange for funding and publicity. It may be best if he hears what kind of information we're seeking from you. As you have his trust, after all."

Kenneth nodded and stood up. "Sounds like a plan for today's meeting with him, then. About what I expected, really. Off I go, then."

"Swift success to you." Wilbur turned his eyes back to the documents that he had been signing as Kenneth shifted himself to his next destination.

He walked into Rivera's Palace just a few minutes before closing time. Rivera looked up from where he had joined his staff in cleaning tables. "Kenneth, my friend. You are here again. I guess you come at this hour not looking for food."

"You would be correct. Can we talk somewhere more private than this?" Kenneth glanced meaningfully at the staff.

"Of course, of course. This way." Rivera walked over to a door and pulled out a key, unlocking it and gesturing for Kenneth to go in first.

Kenneth walked into Rivera's office. It was small and plain in comparison to the rich decor of the restaurant. It showed Rivera's humble nature better than anything Kenneth could have imagined for himself.

"So, Kenneth. Your friends visited, and we spoke of information and deals. Nothing seemed wrong. I am thinking of signing the agreement with them." Rivera spoke as he seated himself behind the desk.

Kenneth sat as well and nodded. "Yes, I heard that as well. I am here to discuss the finer points of the information they are seeking."

"Please do."

"We are looking to use your restaurant as a hub for us to gather information about magical entities, both human and otherwise. This makes the most sense because your cooking, which your magic enhances, will attract many that are not aware of the reason for their interest. And many more that are."

Rivera stared at Kenneth, confusion plain on his face. "What?"

"Perhaps it would be easier to show you." Kenneth raised one hand, palm facing the ceiling. After a moment of focus, he formed a small statue of ice in his hand. After yet another few seconds, the statue began to dance in his palm before jumping off and vanishing completely. "Magic is real, Rivera. And you use it in your cooking without even knowing it. Your powers leak through because they exist even if you don't recognize them. We can keep you safe, and we can help you channel those powers. You are not alone, after all."

"That... I...." Rivera's eyes were wide. His hands clenched the arms of his chair. A minute passed before he took a slow, deep breath and relaxed his body. "I can't believe it. What kind of joke is this, Kenneth? You do a parlor trick and try to tell me magic is a real thing. Are we on candid camera?"

Kenneth let out the breath he had been holding. He had not been sure how the gambit would work out. It hadn't quite gone as well as he had hoped, but it was still workable. "It is no joke, my friend. Trust me when I say that you have a magic for creation that exceeds simple cooking. If you want proof, I can give it."

"Proof? How can you provide proof of something that isn't real?" Rivera frowned, standing up. "If you're not going to speak honestly with me, Kenneth, I'm going to have to ask you to leave. We do not joke about business."

The pixie stood up as well, shifting his focus and pushing his own magic into Rivera's mind. Kenneth pushed at Rivera's thoughts and forced his unprotected mind to wrap around the magic the Spaniard possessed. By forcibly guiding Rivera's power, Kenneth made the other man create an entire plate of chicken and salad, with utensils, on the table next to them. "There you are. Proof."

Rivera stared down at the plate of food, then stared at Kenneth. His eyes darted back and forth for several long seconds before they rolled up in the back of his head, and he fainted. Kenneth reacted quickly, catching the larger man and propping him up in his chair. Things had gone quite horribly compared to his hope, but at least Rivera had seen the truth. Even if he hadn't accepted it yet. He still had to leave the magical chef in the restaurant and go back to report the results of things to Wilbur.

Kenneth walked out of the room and gestured to the staff that had been cleaning - both of them sent by Wilbur. "Rivera's passed out. I revealed magic to him, and it was overwhelming. When he comes to, you're going to have to make sure he's sane. And keep him that way. The initial shock is a lot, but he's likely to be open and work with us. I believe he's strong enough to make it. Understood?"

When they both nodded and moved into the room, Kenneth made his way back home. As he arrived, he received a message from Jake.

"Hey, Kenneth. I was invited to a birthday dance party this weekend. Wanna join me?"

He frowned slightly as he texted back. "Sure. Send me the details."

It broke from the established pattern for the human to be inviting him. Kenneth wasn't sure if this indicated that Jake was starting to open up to him or if the human was simply impulsive. There had been signs indicating either, depending on how he looked at things. Regardless, Kenneth felt confident he could make things work. Anissa had all but given him free rein of Jake's handling. The future seemed bright, despite its uncertainty. It was unusual.

"Jake, wake up."

He groaned, turning over in the bed and reluctantly opening his eyes. Chie was standing over the bed, looking down at him. He appreciated being woken up but at the same time was unhappy about how exhausted he still felt. He smiled tiredly at her and gave a small wave. "Good morning, beautiful."

"Sleep well?" She smiled back before going to her closet and beginning to get dressed. "Want some breakfast?"

"One second." Jake curled up for a moment in the bed. His entire body felt sore from sleeping someplace new. He took a few seconds to wake himself up more fully before reaching into his bag and grabbing his phone. According to the clock, he didn't have much time before class. "I slept okay. As much as I'd like to spend the morning with you… I have to pick up my school supplies back home before I head to Japanese class. I've gotta head out."

"Aww, that's too bad. Next time, then." A look of disappointment passed over Chie's face for a mere moment before she was smiling again.

He paused in putting on his clothes to give her a hug. "Next time, for sure."

"Sounds good. My mother sleeps in late, so I usually cook."

"Wait a second." Jake turned to look at her. "You live with your mother?"

Chie continued getting dressed as if she had said something completely normal. "Yeah."

"And me being here isn't… some kind of problem or anything?"

"Why would it be? It's not like I brought you here to meet her."

"That's true, I guess." Jake swallowed his surprise and forced himself to move past it. The entire concept of having spent the night with Chie's mother next door was beyond his ability to process so early in the morning. He focused on remembering the way back to the station instead. If she wasn't bothered by it, he didn't need to be either. As strange as it was. For now, there were more immediate concerns, like getting dressed and out before her mother woke up. He did not want to have an awkward meeting like that, especially when he was in a hurry.

After Jake finished gathering his stuff, the two said their goodbyes. He resisted the urge to hum to himself as he made his way to the subway and, from there, to his home. He had a tendency to hum when he felt uncomfortable, and the thought of having stayed the night at someone's house that was still living with their mother was having that effect. Once he was finally home, Jake checked the time. He rushed to pack his bags, gathering his scattered homework pages and notebooks. Once they were packed, he hastily made his way back to the subway.

The lesson for the day was an easy one for Jake. Despite being tired, he managed to participate enough in class that his teachers weren't upset with him. During their ten-minute break, one of Jake's classmates came up to him.

"Hey, Jake. You alright?"

He forced a smile and nodded. "Yeah, just tired. Didn't sleep well last night."

"Okay…" She gave him a skeptical look then went to talk with some of the others.

Jake couldn't focus well during class, and he ended up spending his time remembering the events of the night before. He had a good time with Chie, but he wasn't sure if spending the night at her house was a good idea. For some reason, Jake simply couldn't relax unless he slept at home. It didn't feel the same. He pushed the thought out of his mind as he was called to read a passage in the textbook.

In between participating in class, his mind eventually turned to the invitation from Mai. He wondered how the dancing event would go. He had not been to a birthday salsa party before. Did they just dance like normal, or were there special rules? What would dancing at a park be like? He had only ever danced indoors, where the floors were designed to be easier to dance.

He moved on from the party without thinking too deeply about the questions that had come up. It was a party, so things would make sense once he got there. He wasn't going to worry when it was out of his control. All he had to do was approach the event with an open mind. He shrugged, which drew a questioning look from his conversation partner that he had just been assigned.

Once class ended, Jake rushed home. He packed his bags and was out the door before any of his classmates could invite him out. Having spent the entire day without bathing, Jake's skin itched uncomfortably. The first thing he did when he arrived home was disrobe and jump into the shower. The feeling of the night and day's worth of dirt being cleaned off in combination with the warmth of the water made him sigh with relief. After he finished cleaning himself off, Jake spent a few extra minutes simply relaxing before getting out.

He didn't feel like getting dressed to go out again, so he made himself some pasta with tomato sauce. After eating, putting on pajamas, and finishing his homework, Jake pulled open his computer and opened a document. He wrote up a brief article about his night's experiences, leaving out the personal details, and titled it "More Nagoya Night-life." Once that was wrapped up, Jake leaned back and stared at his ceiling. He tried to focus his thoughts but struggled. He felt an itch to move despite having spent the entire previous evening being extremely active.

To satisfy his urge, Jake turned back to his laptop and opened an old game he hadn't played for a while. It was an easy game that didn't require any focus, so he enjoyed playing it when he was thinking about other things. His hands could move and fulfill the need to be active without doing anything intensive.

Inevitably, his thoughts turned to Chie. The evening with her had been nice, and he was interested in meeting again. He knew next time he would invite her when he didn't have to get up early the next day. On top of that, he had to make sure to invite her to his place. The idea of staying in her house and potentially meeting her mother by accident made him far too uncomfortable to repeat the experience.

It wasn't unusual for Japanese women to live with their parents until they married, but Jake hadn't thought he would be invited to someone's home if they didn't live alone. Did it mean she was interested in him? Or did she not expect her mother to be awake while he was there? He shook his head and forced himself to take a deep breath. He was probably overthinking things again. She probably didn't care. How she used her time wasn't her mother's business. Jake nodded to himself. The simplest answer was usually the best. And that answer also took all the pressure off of him to behave in any particular way. All he had to do was be himself. Easy.

He thought over his schedule in his mind while his hands moved his character across the screen, dodging attacks and counterattacking with ease. His best chance was inviting her for something next week over the weekend. That way, he could plan for things to finish closer to his house to have an excuse to invite her back instead of going to her place. Having made a decision, he finished the level, picked up his phone, and wrote a message to Chie.

"Hey, Chie. I had a great time last night. Are you free next weekend to hang out some more? Dinner and a movie, maybe?"

With that done, he plugged his phone into the charger and looked back at the game. It was a good distraction for his hands, but it wasn't as fun now that he had mastered the game. He shut it off, having made the same decision as the last time he played it. Turning from his computer, Jake grabbed the flier that Mai had given him. Looking up the station nearest the park, he found the train routes online. A few minutes later, and he had made a schedule for himself on Saturday that would give him time in the morning to be lazy while still arriving to the event on time to meet Kenneth.

He spent a few moments thinking about his plans with Kenneth. Not remembering if they had set a time, he grabbed his phone to check their recent messages. It was then that Jake realized he hadn't actually sent Kenneth a picture of the flier. They hadn't set a time because he hadn't given Kenneth all of the info yet.

Jake felt like a bad friend for forgetting, but he was sure Kenneth would have understood if he knew the circumstances. He hurriedly put the flier on his table and took a photo before sending it off. Jake hoped Kenneth didn't ask any questions about why he had taken a full day to respond with one picture. Jake wasn't sure how he would answer if he had to explain things. His love life wasn't Kenneth's business, after all.

"Yo, Kenneth. Here's the flier. Sorry, forgot to send it last night. You still good for tomorrow?"

To follow up the photo, Jake suggested meeting five minutes before the starting time since the station opened up directly into the park. Kenneth had mentioned being free all day, so he assumed the suggestion was fine. Kenneth's reply was quick.

"Sounds good. See yah then."

Once that was done, Jake let himself relax into the evening. All of his social obligations were done.

Jake spent several minutes staring at his computer. He went down his list of games, trying to decide on one to play. For each game he looked at, he tried to remember why he had stopped playing it in the first place. Jake didn't know why, but he had the habit of starting a lot of different games and then never finishing them. He loaded up a couple of them to try playing, but he had forgotten the controls so completely that he died very soon after getting into his first fights. He closed them and moved on. He checked online for new free games to play and messed around with a few without paying much attention to them. He felt strangely idle. His life was active, but he felt like he was waiting for something to happen.

After arguing with himself for a while, Jake gave up on playing games and decided to catch up on one of his favorite TV series instead; a murder mystery program. Positioning himself in his bed so that he could watch while lying down, Jake tried to figure out the killer before the detective. He was still hit or miss when it came to the correct answers, but it was a fun game to play. He managed to get through several episodes before he felt the weight of his exhaustion hit him with surprising force.

Jake checked the time and realized that it was already two in the morning. He felt like it had only been half an hour ago when he had checked the time and saw it was nine at night. He chided himself as he hurried to turn his alarms to the time he had planned earlier.

Once that was done, Jake set a video series up on his computer to play through the night. One content creator made hour-long videos that helped him sleep better than anything else he had tried. Closing his eyes, Jake let his mind wander. Eventually, he fell asleep with the show still playing in the background.

Chapter 9

Kenneth woke up later than usual. It was strange for him to have a day where his work didn't need him for anything until the afternoon. But today was one of those days. After getting dressed, he made his way down to the mess hall and ate a leisurely meal. He had met with Yuri once more during the week and gotten her to agree to show him her art techniques. Since their agreed-upon time to meet wasn't until mid-afternoon, Kenneth did his best to enjoy his brief rest time.

As he ate, Kenneth thought over the preparations he needed to make before going to see Yuri. The most important one was reaching out to one of his people's contacts that operated as an art dealer in Japan. He had already filed for the man's contact information, and all that was left was to go pick it up. Kenneth chewed on a slice of fluffy, generously buttered bread. For a moment, he let his thoughts drift away and closed his eyes. Of all the food in the world, the simplicity of buttered bread filled him with the most joy. After he finished his meal, Kenneth made his way down to the information offices.

"Hey Molly, I'm here for that art dealer contact info I filed for a few days ago." Kenneth smiled. Molly was such a cheerful person that it was infectious.

"Got that right here for yah." She smiled back as she held out a small case. She clicked it open for Kenneth to see the very well-designed business cards within. "Take care and have a good one!"

He took the case and looked them over before snapping it shut and slipping it into one of his pockets. "You too, Molly."

With the pre-work managing done, Kenneth still had some time to kill before his arranged time to visit Yuri's home. He would have liked to visit her earlier and finish work early to have his evening free, but Yuri's job prevented that from happening. In the meantime, he made his way back to his room. Once there, Kenneth grabbed a book that he had started reading months ago and never found the time to finish. It was a book describing scientific discoveries about the stars and space. Kenneth felt certain from his exposure to magic that creatures had to exist beyond Earth, even if they hadn't been discovered yet. Many of his colleagues would laugh at him if he told them about his own theories.

Eventually, it came time for Kenneth to visit Yuri. He walked out of the shadow of one building and quickly ducked back into it when he saw Yuri walking down the street ahead of him. Checking his watch, he confirmed that he was arriving only ten minutes early. Sighing, Kenneth counted out a couple of minutes to give her time to get ahead of him on the street before walking out and heading in the opposite direction. He didn't like arriving late, but he had to make sure to give her enough time to be comfortable.

While he did a lap around the block, he made a point of memorizing the surrounding neighborhood as best he could. In particular, he took note of all the people he passed as he walked. There didn't seem to be anybody following him, and none of the passersby took an unusual amount of interest in him. He was used to Japanese people staring, so he could tell the difference. He checked his watch as he walked up to Yuri's apartment building. He was right on time.

Ringing the buzzer, he waited patiently for Yuri to respond. Years of experience dealing with people had taught him that impatience was simply wasted energy. Once he heard her voice over the intercom, he smiled into the camera lens. "Hey, Yuri. It's me, Kenneth."

"Oh, you're here. Please, come up." The door clicked as she pushed the button to unlock it from her apartment.

The inside of the apartment building was thankfully easy to navigate. Some places he had visited were built like mazes. He made his way to the elevator, nodding politely to other residents that were coming and going.

Once he was upstairs, Kenneth stopped in front of the door to check his sketchbook. In a last-minute decision, he used his magic to influence his creations to appear somewhat more similar to Yuri's style. It was not nearly as good, as he lacked her talent and experience, but it was a passable imitation. With that done, he knocked. A couple moments later, Yuri opened her door and gestured Kenneth into her small two-bedroom apartment. "Come in. Would you like some tea?"

"No, thank you." The Scotsman took off his shoes, glancing into both rooms. One was clearly her art room: it was filled with brushes, tubes of paint, unfinished paintings, and completed works. The other was her bedroom. Her futon was tucked into a corner of the room, with small dolls and a stuffed bear arranged carefully on the tatami mats. "I'm surprised you live alone."

"Well, I moved to Nagoya for my university studies. Though I really wanted to go to Tokyo..." A wistful look took over her face. Visibly shaking herself free of her thoughts, Yuri grabbed a chair from her dining room table and dragging it into the art room. "Please, come in and sit. I'm sorry everything is such a mess."

"It looks so clean. Trust me, my house is way messier." Kenneth smiled reassuringly. After sitting down, he took out his sketchbook. The conversation was likely to get awkward if he didn't distract her with something more in accord with her interests. "So I was doing some practicing since last time…"

Yuri visibly relaxed at the change in topic, a bright shine glowing in her eyes as she grabbed the other chair and moved it around to sit at the table with him. "Wow, you've improved so much already! But… these look kinda like my style."

He nodded. "Yeah. I tried to copy your style. I used that painting I bought from you when we met and the sketches you showed during the meetings, plus what I learned from everyone, to do it. What do you think?"

"It's… surprising. And flattering. You really should develop your own style instead, though."

"Hmmm." Kenneth sat back in the chair, pretending to think about what she had said. He had expected her to be embarrassed. But this method opened up the next part of his plans better, if his assessment of her personality was correct. Once enough time had passed, Kenneth flipped the sketchbook back to some of the other attempts he had made. "You're right. I should develop my own way of doing art. But first, I need to learn the techniques great artists like you use so I can be better, right? Style means nothing without technique."

"That's not true." Yuri leaned forward, her voice aflame with passion. "A person's personality and soul comes out on the page. Technique means nothing without style because style is just another way of saying the soul. A painting or drawing without that piece of humanity is just colorful paper."

As Kenneth sat there quietly, Yuri's face slowly grew red as she caught up to what she had just done. Before she could get upset, he raised his hands in surrender. "You're right again. Art is deeper than the paper. I just am not sure how to express my soul. I've seen your work. It captures an essence to it that I envy, and I wish I could pour myself onto the page like you. That's why I am copying you and wanted to witness you creating a piece of art today."

Her expression had calmed from the intensity of a few moments prior, but the tension still hadn't left her shoulders. "That's right… I agreed to do a piece of art while you watched today…."

"Don't worry, I'm not in a rush. If you're not ready, we can talk for a bit first."

"No, no. It's okay. Let me get everything ready." Yuri stood up and immediately began going back and forth across the room, grabbing different art supplies until a miniature pile of organized chaos had formed on the table. Kenneth sat still the entire time, doing his best not to stare as she whisked about in a flurry of activity.

Once she had gathered everything, she moved an easel over to the table so she could sit near the supplies as she worked. Dipping her brush in ink, she began painting. Initially, her hands shook. With each stroke, she calmed and became more focused. Her eyes shifted between him, the various paints, and the easel. Kenneth watched every movement with an eye for when her magic would reveal itself. By seeing it in action, he could finally determine the extent of it.

The minutes dragged on, and Kenneth finally began to see the small sparks of energy flickering from her hands as she worked. It was enough to sharpen lines or improve the colors, but the magic was merely a trickle. It was clearly unintentional, but Kenneth could not see if that trickle was natural control or the full extent of her powers. Focusing his own energy, he reached out a tendril of his magic to gently touch hers. Despite the contact of their magic, Yuri's focus remained unbroken. Kenneth, on the other hand, became aware of the pool of potential within her. With that, he had a clear assessment of her limits.

She would never be more than a particularly talented artist, but she had the reserves to become great in that field with training. Kenneth nodded to himself. As he had suspected, she was not a threat. He wouldn't have to kill her, and she didn't need to be brought into the know about magic. He would include this information in his request for a handler to be transferred. As he had expected, the art dealer's contact information would be of use.

Once Yuri had finished her painting, Kenneth took a look. It was a very handsome rendition of his own face, and it made him smile despite himself. "Truly, your work is stunning. You know... I actually know a man who works as an art dealer. Please, let me set up a meeting. I insist."

Yuri shook her head. "No, please. I'm not good enough. I haven't even gone to art school."

"Yuri, Yuri. It's okay. Trust me, he'll love your work. I've known him for a long time, and your style is perfect for him. This is your chance at your dream. Please, take it." The mixture of truth and lies flowed as easily as the inks from her brush just minutes before.

"Okay... if you think it is a good idea. Please, let me set up some of my work for photos for a portfolio." She was still clearly nervous, but she still set about putting her best works into place for Kenneth to photograph. With that done, Kenneth thanked Yuri and headed out.

Once he had left her home, Kenneth pulled out the business card case in his pocket and contacted the art dealer who operated as one of their local handlers. After a few brief conversations with the handler and later Yuri, the meeting was arranged.

Kenneth arrived back home to find Jake had contacted him with information about the next day's event. He replied back, confirming that he was good to go, then settled in for the evening. He had a feeling he needed all the rest he could get for the next day.

Kenneth haphazardly tossed the book he had just finished on top of a pile of other novels. Eventually, he had to return the books to the library. His latest read had been an interesting story to start with, but the ending had left him feeling unsatisfied. It was almost as if the author had planned for a longer book then cut it short for no reason. Kenneth turned to check the clock, reminding himself of how much time he had until his meeting with Jake. A part of him wondered if there would be another magical human at the event.

With so many people, it wasn't an impossibility. If Jake were exposed to more people like Yuri, there truly was a risk of something unexpected happening. Kenneth ran his fingers through his beard as he considered the problem. Judging from Jake's lack of reaction before, as long as there was no direct magic involved, things seemed likely to turn out okay. He nodded to himself. If that was the case, all he had to do was make sure to keep things normal. Simple enough. Since he still had more than an hour until the event with nothing important to do, Kenneth took the time to scoop up all of the books and scrolls he had read on loan from the library. Once he had an armful of volumes, Kenneth willed the unsteady collection of reading materials to be still as he made his way through the castle.

The library was dead silent. It was one of the few places in the castle that didn't have a set staff or consistent hours. He knew they had a librarian, but he had only met her once. The books thudded against the desk as he sorted the business of recording their return on his own. Years of experience had taught him that the books would stay on the desk for days if he didn't handle the paperwork himself. Once he was done, he slipped them into the book return slot and hummed as he made his way back to his room.

Checking the time again, Kenneth saw that he had around twenty minutes before the event was scheduled. Jake had mentioned wanting to arrive early. With that in mind, Kenneth dressed himself quickly and once again sent himself to Japan. Walking out of the bathroom, he waited outside of the wicket gate that matched Jake's train route. Kenneth saw Jake before Jake noticed him, moving to be easier to see as he noticed Jake scanning the crowd.

Saturday had finally arrived. Jake sleepily reached out with one hand to turn off his alarms, feeling excitement but lacking the energy to do anything with it. Dragging himself into the shower, Jake turned the water to a temperature just a bit hotter than he liked to force himself to wake up faster. When he came out, he hurriedly dried himself off and dressed to avoid shivering too much from the difference in temperature. Having forced himself awake, Jake remembered that he had set his alarms early so he could relax in the morning.

With a sigh, he slumped into one of his chairs and stared at his phone. Turning it on, he saw he had no new messages. He put it back on the charger and thought about his plans for the day. He didn't know how long the salsa event was going to last or if there was going to be an after-party. Most of the people he'd met tended to be very spontaneous about these types of things. His best bet was to be open to the prospect of an after-party without expecting there to be one. This left him with very little room to plan anything other than the party itself, which was fine. He wasn't sure if he had the energy to do anything else, given how late he had accidentally stayed up the night before.

He stood to stretch before grabbing his laptop off of his bed and moving it to the table. Not wanting to spend his time doing nothing, he looked up some videos of intermediate salsa dance patterns. It always felt nice to have a new move or two that he could try out with people he knew. Since they were already comfortable dancing with him, if he made a mistake, it wouldn't make a lasting impression. They already knew he could dance. He refused to try out new things with new partners out of concern about first impressions. He found a couple of new moves that he liked and practiced them until he felt confident he could try them with a real partner.

While he still had some time to spare, Jake double-checked all of his train routes and transfers. With his timetable memorized, he still had a few minutes left before he had to leave. Looking at himself in the mirror, he did some finishing touches to set his hair the way he wanted it. After brushing his teeth and grabbing his bag, Jake strode out the door with confidence. He was in a surprisingly good mood despite the unfortunate start to his day. He wondered if he was better off waking up early every day.

Jake arrived at the station and saw Kenneth was already standing outside the wicket. He waved as he approached. "Hey, Kenneth. Ready to go?"

"Yup, let's do this." Kenneth smiled, and the two of them walked through the station's tunnel toward the park exit. Not wanting to walk in silence, he said the first thing that came to mind. "So, were we supposed to bring presents?"

Jake realized he hadn't even thought about it. He hesitated, then shrugged. "I think we'll be fine."

"Oh, good. I hate trying to think of presents for strangers. It's so awkward." Buying presents had always been one of Kenneth's least favorite activities. In a community where magic was normal, most mundane objects lost their appeal.

The two of them laughed in agreement. Jake immediately relaxed. Kenneth hadn't brought anything either, so it was probably not a big deal. Besides, neither of them knew the person whose birthday they were about to celebrate. Kenneth hadn't realized that Jake was nervous. He made a mental note to keep it in mind. A nervous magic user was a volatile one. As they walked out into the sunlight and the park itself, Jake stared in surprise at the number of people that had shown up. Most salsa events he attended had only around thirty people at one time, but there were easily over eighty people already grouped together. There was no way any place he had been to so far could have held this many people. It made sense why the event was happening at a park instead.

Kenneth shifted his gaze and started to scan the crowd for both familiar and unfamiliar faces. He did his best to remember details about every person he recognized, which took most of his focus as Jake led the way. One of his responsibilities was to make sure he was well-connected in the communities he engaged with.

Two grills were positioned on either side of the throng of people. One person attended each grill, both with serious looks on their faces as they watched their cooking meats. Jake tried his best to catch a glimpse of Mai in the crowd. He didn't manage to find her, but he did notice several people that he had met at previous dancing parties. He wasn't sure if he should bring Kenneth to one of those groups or seek out the person that had invited him.

Jake walked slowly in front of Kenneth, trying to figure out where to go in the mix of people standing and others sitting on tarps that had been set out across the ground. He kept skirting along the outside, peeking through the people for some sign of Mai. He had figured she'd be easy to spot, but it was turning out to be a challenge. He was eventually saved from the awkward lurking by a familiar voice calling out to him.

"Jake! Kenneth! Hey!"

Jake and Kenneth turned to see Mai walking toward them from a patch of people that Jake could have sworn he had just checked for her. He noticed from Mai's expression that she was in the mood to talk a lot, which was common for her. He just hoped that her attention would be focused on Jake instead of on him. The conversation had a chance of distracting Jake from his nerves, and it would give Kenneth time to filter people. They both smiled as she approached. Once she was finally in range to speak normally, Jake turned to Kenneth.

"Hey, Mai. I invited Kenneth along, hope you don't mind."

Kenneth chuckled. "Hey, Mai. How's your husband doing?"

"He's good, thanks for asking. I'm looking forward to dancing with you later." Mai smiled, then turned and gestured for them to follow. "Come on, I'll introduce you to some of the others."

Mai led them through the crowd, introducing the pair of them to what felt like every person they crossed paths with. Most of them already knew Kenneth, so he was spared having to repeat the same conversation with a different person repeatedly. Jake wished he was as lucky. In between introductions, Kenneth continued to check Jake's body language. While his magical mark seemed uncomfortable, it appeared to be more of a problem with Mai's tendency to talk than anything else. Mai shared gossip about some of the people, made exclamations about her excitement for the dancing later, and barely let either of them speak. After several minutes and several dozen introductions, they finally arrived at a tarp that only had a couple of bags in the center. "… and this is the tarp I've claimed for us."

"Well, I'm beat." Jake plopped his bag next to the others on the tarp before sitting down at the edge and looking at the crowd. "There's so many more people than at the normal salsa events."

Kenneth nodded, putting his bag down. "Yeah, people have preferences when it comes to the normal party locations. Events like these are just about friendship, and the whole community gets along pretty well."

"Yup. And Taiki is super popular because he's nice to everybody." Mai glanced back and forth between Jake and Kenneth. Her eyes suddenly lit up. "Oh, I almost forgot. This is a barbecue. You guys need plates and food. Come, come."

"Actually," Jake opened his mouth to protest having to get up when his stomach growled loudly. "… that sounds great."

Mai led them in a much more direct path to the nearest table with plates and wooden chopsticks set out. On a separate set of tables towards the center, several platters of different barbecued meats and vegetables were in various stages of being cleaned of food by other party-goers. Mai, having already eaten, left them to go back to socializing.

Jake turned to Kenneth. "She's quite the talker. I didn't realize last time because we were dancing."

"Trust me, I know." Kenneth smiled as he placed some sausages onto his plate. The first time he had talked with Mai, the conversation had been so one-sided that he had to resist the urge to tune her out. She had a knack for identifying when people weren't paying attention. "Still, this is a lively event. I'm sure we'll have a great time."

"Very true. Let's do it."

The two men opted through unspoken agreement to split up, each of them joining the crowd and striking up conversations. Jake learned so much information about so many different people that he already knew that he was going to forget at least half of the people he had spoken with. He figured they wouldn't notice as long as he greeted them next time. The other conversations he joined were surprisingly difficult for him to follow. People referenced previous events or other dancers, leaving him confused and nodding his head politely.

He began to realize how long everyone in the salsa community had known each other. They hadn't been joking when they said they needed more young blood and fresh faces. He wondered if he could convince any of his classmates to try dancing. Maybe he could try selling it as a Japanese learning experience. He was sure he could convince one or two of them, and it'd help him feel a little bit less left out if he was sharing the experience with someone else.

Kenneth angled toward people he hadn't met before and introduced himself. He made sure to shake hands with everyone he met. None of them were magical. With each person that he confirmed was normal, Kenneth felt himself relax a little bit more. The day was low-impact, overall. Most of Kenneth's responsibilities involved dealing with eventualities instead of directly managing events. If Jake was having a good time, and Kenneth seemed like he was enjoying himself, then their friendship would grow stronger.

Despite his best efforts, there were simply too many new people for Kenneth to make his way through all of them at a reasonable pace. He had to move slower than he would have liked, since he needed to not only check each one for magical potential but also make sure he remembered facts about them for future reference. He was in the middle of introducing himself to another person from out of town that was visiting for the birthday party as the event started to get more fully underway.

It wasn't long before people had put down their plates and a few portable speakers were placed in the open grass of the park. They were all synced to the same device, and the dancing portion of the party was soon underway. Unlike what Jake expected, the party didn't have any semblance of a birthday party. It seemed like a normal social event, instead. As he danced with partner after partner, he pulled out his moves that he had practiced, messing up and laughing or doing them successfully and smiling when his partner was impressed.

Kenneth did his best to dance with as many strangers as possible. While he went through his duty of checking for other magical humans, Kenneth kept an eye on Jake. The other man was laughing and having fun. The discomfort from earlier seemed to have vanished as soon as he started dancing. As he danced with partner after partner, he pulled out the moves that he had practiced, messing up and laughing or doing them successfully and smiling when his partner was impressed. Kenneth nodded in satisfaction.

After a while, the music changed to a birthday song in Spanish. Taiki took center stage as women lined up to dance with him. The others in the crowd clapped in rhythm with the song, and some even sang. Jake watched as Taiki danced with each woman in turn. One of the event organizers conscripted Kenneth into helping bring out the cakes that people had brought for the event. While he was helping with the setup, the songs eventually ended. As it ended, someone produced a cake seemingly out of thin air, everyone wished Taiki happy birthday, and Jake turned to realize that several more cakes had been prepared for the event.

As the party drew to a close, Kenneth noticed Jake searching the crowd and made himself more visible by standing up straighter and walking into Jake's line of sight.

Jake was just finishing a slice of cake as he walked over. "That was unlike anything I could have expected a birthday party to be."

Kenneth laughed. It was strange to think that Jake knew so little. In so many ways. More and more, he began to believe that Jake truly was as ignorant as he seemed. "Yeah, it's fun. Low-pressure, dancing with each other. Thanks for inviting me along."

"No problem. Least I could do after you introduced me to a cool place."

"Well, hopefully, we'll both be introducing each other to more fun experiences in the days to come." Kenneth forked the other half of his slice of cake and shoved it into his mouth.

Jake grinned. "I don't know how many places I'll know that you don't, but we'll see. Do you do things other than art and dance? Are you a musician, perchance? Opera singer?"

"Oh, I'm not really an artist. It's a small hobby at best, really." Kenneth dismissively waved his hand in the air. "I always enjoy a good hike or camping."

"Sounds good. I'll let you know if I ever get invited to something like that."

The two of them made their way back to the station. Kenneth gestured toward the far end, and Jake nodded. Kenneth waited until Jake had passed through the ticket gate before quickly making his way around a corner, out of anyone's line of sight, and out of Japan. Jake turned to glance back after crossing the ticket gate, but Kenneth was already gone. He was surprised at the other man's walking speed. He hadn't seemed like he was in a hurry. Over the next couple of months, the two men grew closer and spent plenty of time dancing and drinking together.

Chapter 10

Kenneth waved as Jake approached. He had taken the time to free out his schedule in advance of the all-night event, though he was still nervous at the idea. There was a risk of coming across more triggers for Jake's power. But, he didn't have a choice. The human had invited him, after all.

"Hey Kenneth. Ready for the all-nighter?"

Kenneth nodded, though in his mind he was shaking his head. "Ready as I'll ever be. Let's go."

At the first club, it was just Jake and Kenneth dancing. Early in the evening, most people were still eating dinner or heading home from a busy afternoon. This gave Kenneth time to relax into the pattern of socializing with Jake while analyzing their surroundings. He had learned Jake's patterns well enough to balance the two more easily than before.

Kenneth kept a watchful eye on the other people who had decided to start their clubbing early. Whenever someone new drew too close, the pixie tried his best to position himself between them and Jake. His training had included dancing to a variety of music, so it wasn't hard for him to do. Jake often wondered how Kenneth had gotten so good, though he never asked.

After they had gotten warmed up, Jake and Kenneth looked through their phone contacts to invite people to meet them at the next place. Kenneth pretended to be sending more messages than he really was. He contacted a few people he noticed Jake missed out of their mutual friends and left the rest to Jake. This made sure most of the people invited were already safe to be around the human.

Even with Kenneth's limited number of invitations, the group grew much larger as people met them at the next club.

The group grew and shrank as people came and left, with all of them venturing to various places. Jake was surprised at the number of clubs and bars that he had never known existed. Kenneth worked to keep track of everyone that spoke with Jake. Whenever it seemed a new person was going to approach, Kenneth made sure to be the first to greet them. The strategy gave him the appearance of being very friendly while still providing the opportunity to check each person before they had a chance to do anything.

With his active behavior, Kenneth became the de-facto leader of the band of party-goers. Whenever people suggested a bar or club that he knew was risky, he asked for other options and took ones that seemed less dangerous to his mission. Kenneth mentally cursed Jake's stamina as the night continued. Most of the others had gone home already, yet Jake was still in the partying mood. Kenneth's exhaustion was catching up to him. Screening and socializing took their toll eventually.

In a smaller, back-alley club, a woman caught Kenneth's attention. Maeva. Even though she looked different from her last recorded sighting, it didn't matter. He recognized her aura as soon as he saw her and had to resist the urge to panic. If he did anything drastic, he only risked attracting her attention. His mission was to keep Jake away from magic, and she was one of the biggest threats to that mission he could have imagined. He turned to suggest a different location only to see Jake already walking toward her.

The cigarette smoke from other patrons was so thick it was visible, adding a haziness to the already dim lighting. Like a fog or mist. Jake squinted as he focused on the woman. She was drinking alone. Her hair cascaded in beautiful locks, and the ruby-red of her lips was tantalizing as she pursed them to drink from her glass. Despite her beauty, something else urged Jake to approach the woman. The sight of her sent a shock through his body. A voice in the back of his head told him that he'd always regret it if he didn't take the chance to approach her.

Kenneth mentally cursed his slow reaction time and rushed to grab Jake's shoulder before he got too far. "Yo, Jake. She's bad news. Let's go somewhere else."

Jake waved off his warning. "Come on. It's just a woman in a club. I'll be fine. Besides, I've got a good feeling about this one."

Jake turned to keep walking, and Kenneth had to resist the urge to wrestle him to the ground. Kenneth took a step forward. "You don't get it. This isn't a good idea. We need to leave."

Kenneth grit his teeth as Jake shook his head. "I'm going to talk to her, that's all. There's something about her. I feel like I'll regret this if I don't do it."

"Seriously, Jake. Let's go somewhere else." Kenneth grabbed Jake's arm again, pulling him toward the door. He didn't want to wrestle Jake to the ground since it was sure to grab Maeva's attention. If she saw him, she'd recognize him for what he was. Her curiosity and attention were dangerous.

Jake roughly shook himself free, pushing Kenneth away with surprising force. Kenneth was behaving strangely, but it wasn't going to stop him from doing what felt right. "What's with you, dude? I'm just going to talk to a girl. Give me some space."

Kenneth was shocked by Jake's stubbornness. He had done as much as he could without attracting attention. He swore under his breath. Even without the ability to see the future, he already knew that things were going to become complicated with Maeva's involvement.

Kenneth watched helplessly as Jake began sauntering over. Jake carefully sat in the seat next to her as she finished her drink, waving at the bartender to give her another as he turned toward her. Jake cringed internally at himself even as he tried his best to seem confident. "My friend warned me not to talk to you. Said it was a bad idea. I'd like to take the chance that it was a good one."

Her eyes flickered with what Jake hoped was amusement as she turned to stare at him. She seemed able to see through him. The woman glanced to the side toward Kenneth, then shifted back to Jake. Her voice was like velvet as she leaned forward ever so slightly. "You're both right. I am more than you can handle. But… opportunities taken are so… worth it."

Jake was so stunned by her accepting his clumsy attempt at hitting on her that his mind went blank. He somehow managed to keep things going, but the conversation was a blur for him. She laughed at a joke he told, her hand touching his arm. Her smile grew larger.

Maeva's glare burned away any hope Kenneth had that Jake might be mistaken as a random suitor to be rejected. Kenneth frantically began thinking about how to do damage control as

Maeva's predatory grin grew larger upon testing for and sensing Jake's power.

Kenneth's first plan of action was to try and stop Jake from leaving with her. If he could keep them in public, Maeva would have no opportunity to do anything serious to Jake. He followed the pair with his eyes while they danced. The gears in his mind turned as he considered his chances. Jake was almost definitely going to take her home. She played the part of the attractive and interested woman too well for it to go any other way.

Jake's smile and happiness were reflected back to him by Maeva's laughter. The two got up to dance, and Kenneth could just pick up Jake's awful jokes from his seat at the edge of the dance floor. With things seeming to go very well, Jake invited her back to his place at the end of the dance. As they were walking out, Kenneth walked up and stopped them. "Jake. You really shouldn't do this."

Kenneth sighed as Jake wordlessly pushed past him. How could all this time building a friendship mean nothing? Kenneth rubbed his face. If he had known that Jake was so easy to sway, he would have suggested a more aggressive approach to his superiors.

Jake wondered what was wrong with Kenneth. He figured his buddy would be happy to see him doing well with a woman. Was he jealous? Jake considered the possibility that something more was going on, then quickly dismissed it. Things felt too right for something to be going wrong. Jake's mind had been wandering while his mouth kept moving on its own.

Kenneth made his way down an alley before teleporting back to his quarters in the castle. He already knew that if he tried to follow them, he ran the risk of Maeva attacking him. He couldn't take her in a direct confrontation. Her power was monstrous.

Instead, he would have to monitor events from a distance. Kenneth rummaged through the mess of books he had kept for quick reference until he found the scroll dedicated to scrying. After reminding himself of the fundamentals, Kenneth focused his energy and flung his senses toward Jake's house.

From his magically-provided vantage point above Maeva and Jake, he couldn't hear the words that were spoken. Instead, he watched as they walked down the street toward Jake's residence. Maeva suddenly stopped Jake and said something.

Somehow, while Jake walked with Maeva, the conversation turned toward magic and what he thought about it. Normally, he would've been too shy to rant about it, but the words came almost in a flood as he spilled one of his secrets. "You see, ordinary life... is plain. Predictable and uninspiring. I wish there was magic, like an ocean underneath the icy, cold normal. I want to swim in that ocean. Be a fish, or even a shark. I want to take control! Live life on my own terms. I can feel it. There's something out there waiting for me."

The two of them had been walking a long while and were almost to Jake's place when Maeva stopped him, turning him to face her. Her voice sounded gentle, yet her eyes in that moment looked hungry, vicious even. "Do you really? Do you feel a... call?"

Jake felt a strange tug at the back of his mind. He couldn't put a name to the sensation, but it sent tingles through his entire body. Jake felt on the edge of release. He nodded to her, inviting her into his house. "I feel it. Yes. I feel a call."

Jake's response clearly satisfied her, as Maeva's aura flared slightly brighter. Kenneth could see the hunger in her eyes. He wondered how Jake was so blind that he couldn't see it. All the warning signs were there if Jake simply took the time to look for them.

Kenneth noticed Jake's power, which was like a visible undercurrent from his scrying, pulse in time with the flaring of Maeva's aura. It was already starting. All of Kenneth's efforts were beginning to unravel. Magic was about to become very real to Jake. Very fast.

Maeva walked in and sat on the edge of Jake's table, waving at the house. "Nice place."

He scratched the back of his head, closing the door behind him. "Thanks. Do… do you feel a call too?"

The sound of her fingernails clacking against the table was loud in the confines of the room. "No, I don't. But I understand it. I live with magic. I control it. And you can, too."

Jake stared at her. He wasn't sure if he had heard her correctly. Magic was real? It seemed ridiculous. There was no way that some chick he met while out dancing could be magical… right? He frowned, staring skeptically at her even as his alcohol-addled mind filled with hope. "Are you serious? You're messing with me, right?"

Without even a moment's hesitation, Maeva waved her hand in the air, fire forming over her fingers and dancing up her arm before turning into a snake that rose up from her skin, writhing into the air, and vanishing.

She smiled, her teeth red as if they were carved rubies. "Proof enough for you? You said you wanted to dive into the ocean of magic just beneath the surface of reality. You spoke from a connection to the magical side of things. Well, you're in the ocean now. Your choice. Want to learn how to swim or get eaten by the sharks?"

Jake stared open-mouthed at the spectacle and barely registered what she was saying. Within him was a sensation like a well overflowing. A lightning shock of pain ran through his head, making him wince for a moment. When his eyes reopened, the world around him had changed.

Kenneth watched as the river of Jake's power throbbed and flared upward. As if a dam was broken, it bubbled up and around him and suffused him. In that moment, Jake's spirit was brought into the mists. Kenneth hurriedly focused his mind to obscure his presence as Maeva entered the mist as well.

Now that they were in the mist, Kenneth could eavesdrop.

Maeva's voice seemed to form directly in Jake's mind. "This was… unexpected. Welcome to the mist."

The shock and fear on Jake's face sent a pang of sympathy through Kenneth. This could have been avoided in so many ways. Kenneth shook his head over the painful introduction. It would make his job that much harder to sway Jake to their side, if it came to that.

Jake watched in a mixture of horror and confusion as Maeva seemed to split in two. Her physical body slumped slightly as a second, more ethereal version rose from it. For a split second, Jake thought he saw her shift into something else, but she was back to normal when he blinked.

The satisfied smile on Maeva's face did nothing to make Jake feel calm as he flailed about, trying to run but making no progress in any direction. Looking down at himself, he realized that he was floating a whole foot above his body. Had he split in two like Maeva? One thought took center stage in his mind. "What the hell is going on!?"

The magical woman waved a placating hand in the air. "Calm down. You're safe. This is the magical side of the world. The mist. Your exposure to magic must have brought you into it. Here, I will help you return to your body."

Reaching out, she took Jake's hand and gently pulled him down toward his physical body. Kenneth frowned. Once they exited the mist, he would not be able to hear what they said anymore. The next part of the conversation was important to gauge Jake's reaction and plan ahead.

Jake gasped, hyperventilating in his panic and staring at the few feet between himself and Maeva. Hadn't she just been holding his hand? Taking a few moments, Jake managed to get himself under control. He wasn't dead.

Magic was real. A mixture of hope and fear filled his chest as he looked at the source of all this change. Was this what he had been searching for all his life? Now that he was aware of it, the world felt more whole. More complete. Jake stumbled, feeling suddenly exhausted. "What…"

Maeva walked over and gently led him to bed. "Your first time in the mist has drained you. Come, let's get you some rest. I'll explain everything tomorrow."

He was too weak to resist even her light touch. He shook his head, wanting to learn more immediately. Despite his urgent need to know more, he felt sleep start to take him before his head even touched the pillow. His dreams were restless, filled with images of ruby red teeth.

Kenneth felt relief as Jake stumbled and was led to bed by Maeva. If Jake was too exhausted to talk with her, this gave Kenneth time to plan. He wouldn't get much sleep, but that was what happened when emergencies came about.

As he was focusing his mind to return to his body, Kenneth felt the grip of Maeva's mind around his.

"Hello, little spy." Maeva's form materialized in the mist in front of his mind's eye. "Leaving so soon?"

Kenneth knew better than to resist her hold and instead focused on shielding his thoughts as best he could manage. "I'm afraid so. It's obvious I'm not welcome anymore."

"Quite right." Kenneth winced as Maeva's hold on him tightened slightly. Her voice was an icy hiss in his mind. "Jake belongs to me now. See to it that I do not find you or any other rats skittering around him."

"Y… yes ma'am. Anything else?" Kenneth had no intention of obeying her, but they both knew that. He wasn't sure what she really wanted by holding him here.

Maeva smiled, revealing several rows of dagger-like fangs. Her form shifted, and several tails whipped out around her. "Take a message to your queen. This stalemate will not last forever. I will win, and neither her people nor the other factions can stop it. Especially with this little gem you've just handed me."

Maeva's cackling laughter echoed in Kenneth's mind even as she let him go. He quickly brought his senses back to himself. Gasping, he wiped the sweat from his brow. He was lucky that scrying was a safe form of observing. If he had chosen another method, she would have devoured him.

After taking a few moments to catch his breath, Kenneth rushed to Anissa's office. Without bothering to knock, he burst through the door. "I know you hate sudden drop-ins, but I don't have time to wait for an appointment. This is beyond urgent."

"Wh-" Anissa had already burst to her feet, one of the pencils she kept on her desk poised in her hand to throw at him. She glared at him, processing what he had said, then calmly placed the pencil back on the desk and seated herself. "Very well. Sit, speak."

"I'll stand, thanks." Kenneth closed the door behind him. He took a deep breath, sorting everything in his mind. He had no way to word things positively. It was a disaster. Plain and simple. "I'll cut to the chase. Maeva has found Jake. And exposed him to the mist."

Anissa's eyes narrowed, and her expression darkened. She bit off each word as she slowly stood, stalking around the desk to stand in front of him. "And. How. Did. That. Happen?"

Kenneth took a step back and raised his hands. "I was on duty with him, and he forced an all-nighter on me. She was just randomly at a dive bar, and her power must have drawn him in. After that, it was simple. You know how she is. What she is."

"If Jake is as powerful as your reports have stated, this is enough of a problem to require immediate attention. Why aren't you working damage control right now?"

"Maeva left Jake to sleep at his house. His first exposure was too much for him. I am planning to visit him in the early morning and bring him to a warded safehouse. Only I know its location. At this point, I see no better options than to bring him in. Get him to align with us, instead of against us."

"I see." Anissa smoothed a lock of hair that had fallen out of place in her fury back behind her ear. The thunderous look had left her face, but her shoulders remained tense. Kenneth could feel the barely restrained rage under the facade of calm. "Seeing as we are spread thin as it is, I do not see any choice but for me to trust your abilities. Bring Jake to the safehouse. In the meantime, I will draft a report to send to the Queen. His fate is beyond my station to decide. And yours. Remember that. Dismissed."

Kenneth gave her a quick salute before walking out. He let out a sigh of relief. The conversation had gone decently: he still had his job and all of his body parts. The pixie immediately set about preparing the materials he needed to secure the safehouse more thoroughly. It had to be warded enough to avoid even Maeva's extensive reach.

As he rushed about, Kenneth had no time to lament his lack of sleep. In his mind, Maeva's words echoed. War was on the horizon. Securing Jake would slow the pace, but it wouldn't stop the wheels that were in motion. Kenneth hoped Jake was worth it.

Chapter 11

The morning after, Jake woke up to a sore everything, with an unusual headache attached. It took twenty minutes of cursing and trying to shift his body to a more comfortable spot before he gave up. The effects of last night's dancing were already showing up. Rolling out of bed, he groaned and stretched his aching muscles.

Something felt off, and it took Jake a few moments to remember what it was: Maeva! The memories of last night's events came back more clearly. He looked at the empty bed. Walking through his house, Jake searched for Maeva but found no trace. Had it been a dream? It had felt so real. After spending several minutes trying to make sense of what he remembered, Jake gave up. He hopped into the shower and turned the heat all the way up. Hopefully, the steaming water could relieve his aching muscles. He looked at himself in the mirror before it started to fog, bloodshot eyes stared back. Nothing seemed out of the ordinary, aside from the soreness. He had hoped the hot water running over his face would also scald the headache away and slowly bring the world back into focus, but it didn't help. The steam matched the fogginess of his memories.

No matter how much Jake pondered the question, he had no explanation for his memories. The door was locked, and his key was still in his pants pocket. Maeva couldn't have left and locked the door behind her, surely. Then again, if she were magical, locking a door was probably not an issue for her. Thinking back through the events of the night before, Jake pondered how he could figure out if it was real or fantasy. Maeva's words about the so-called "mist" and Jake's experience within it sprang to his mind. Perhaps he could go there again, on purpose?

Jake dried his body off, leaving his hair to air-dry as he walked into his living room and stood near the table. Hopefully, being in the same spot as last night would help him concentrate. He closed his eyes and imagined the sensations he felt: the surging energy, the shifting sensation of the world. Despite his focus, there was no sensation. No crackle of energy. Disappointment and sadness filled his heart. It was just a dream, after all. Then Jake opened his eyes. All around him, the mist churned and moved with a mind of its own. Awe and joy overwhelmed him. It hadn't been a dream.

Jake's thoughts clamored. Every idea warred for attention as reality sunk in. This was all real. Magic, everything. And he could use it. How could he use it? How did it work? Maeva had brought him into this magical world. Why did she do it?

"You shouldn't be so loud, you know. You'll attract unwanted attention."

Surprised, Jake swiveled his head to stare at the source of the voice. Hovering in the air a few feet away was a young woman. She looked to be around 22 years old, wearing the latest fashion. Jake barely had time to process the sight before she had somehow moved to be in front of him. Her pure blue eyes seemed to trap every detail of his "body" with one sweeping glance.

"You are interesting, aren't you? Maeva always did know how to find wild cards." Each word clearly came from the girl, yet the grim line of her mouth never moved.

How is she speaking? Jake couldn't help but wonder.

"Same way as you. I'm thinking out loud."

He blinked in surprise. *Did she read my mind!?*

"No, you're just speaking your mind. Shouting, really. When misting, focused thoughts or wild imaginings are expressed. If you don't focus, we hear everything."

Jake took a few moments to process what the woman had said. Such a casual explanation was surprisingly refreshing, given how unclear everything was. As she floated in a slow circle around him, Jake turned himself to keep facing her.

He found it strangely natural to move even without the normal telltale stretch of muscle. He was moving. With his mind. He could barely believe it, but it felt right. He knew in his gut that he belonged in this world. Trying to follow her advice, Jake focused his mind and asked, "Who are you, and where is this?"

"I'm Evelynn. You're in the mist. Don't worry, you're not dead or anything. And this is real."

As if her words were a trigger, Jake's physical body started to twist and writhe. Spikes of pain shot from it and up through his mist-form. The sensation was so intense, he screamed wordlessly into the mist.

"Now, now, none of that. I see Maeva didn't teach you how to breathe, yet. She'll owe me for this. Delicious." Evelynn reached out, placing a hand against Jake's forehead. Energy seemed to radiate from her, and his mind filled with understanding. His body was still connected to him, even in the mist. And he still had to breathe, even here.

"Thank... you." Was all he could manage as he focused on breathing properly.

Evelynn waved it off. "You owe me, too. I give nothing for free. With that, you can come into the mist without drowning in it. I will call in this favor later. Remember it."

Evelynn hovered there, still looking at Jake with eyes that seemed too sad, too penetrating to belong to a young girl. He couldn't make sense of what she meant. He owed her a favor? "How am I going to repay this? I don't have anything valuable. What did you even do, anyway?"

Her laughter was light, like the ringing of a windchime. Jake stared in confusion. He didn't think anything he had said was funny. Evelynn stopped laughing, spinning upside down into the air and pointing 'down' at Jake's body. "You have so much more value than you know. You will understand, in time. And I will be there to collect my due."

Floating down lazily, Evelynn poked a finger at Jake's face, only to have it phase through. "Your body can't handle being without you for a long time; it forgets to breathe. So, I taught you how to reach back and keep it breathing even while you're out and about. You would've died otherwise."

The concept of his body dying without him was frightening. Jake shuddered at the thought. Turning to look at Evelynn, Jake waved his hand at everything around them. "Could you… teach me more about all this?"

The girl's shoulders rose and fell. "Sure, I'm bored enough as is. But! If I'm teaching, I expect you to pay attention. I don't repeat myself. Capiche?"

Jake nodded, and Evelynn moved back before taking on a lecturing tone. "So, the mist is the world of consciousness. Which means everything that happens here is fast as thought, time is so much slower in the real world. I don't know how long you've been misting, but it can't have been more than a couple minutes."

The idea of time moving faster was surprising but easy enough to grasp. Jake felt an urge to know more. Yet, he didn't feel certain he could trust this stranger so easily. "Why are you here? What are you? Why should I trust you when you barged into my home? A young girl like you can't possibly know everything that's going on."

As Jake built up more steam and pushed forward with his questions, Evelynn was suddenly very still. The contrast with how animated she had been a few moments before was disconcerting. The distrust he felt was chilled by the fear of what could be coming in retaliation. He knew nothing about how to defend himself in this "mist." What if she attacked him?

Evelynn's body slowly shifted, growing older. Her hair went from a raven black to a deep white as she started to hunch forward, weighed down by what could only be decades or centuries. At the end of the transformation, the only things unchanged were her eyes. They still pierced Jake with the same intensity. "I am far older than you can understand. I have learned and forgotten more than you are likely to ever know. And you would be wise not to assume all you see is truth. The mist hides many things, and those who live in it are the same."

With those words, Evelynn simply vanished. One moment, her presence was taking up all Jake's focus; the next, simply nothing. He felt strangely empty without her there making everything real.

Jake turned to look around, not making much sense of the world. It all looked the same, mostly. Just with mist covering the edges. He then realized that he hadn't been told how to get back into his body. Panicking for a few moments, Jake tried to just will himself back in. He imagined his mind like soup being poured back into his body, along with several other sensations, but nothing worked. Jake continued to hover, pointlessly staring at himself. In frustration, he floated down toward his body and tried shaking himself.

As Jake's misty hands touched his body, the world turned, shifted, and gravity pulled him down again as he re-entered his body. Jake groaned as he felt the soreness of the previous night come back at full force. It had felt like he had been in the mist with Evelynn for ages, yet his hair was still dripping wet as he reached up to push the curls out of his face. Jake was still wrapping his mind around things when he heard a loud knocking on his door.

"Jake? It's me, Kenneth! Open up, we need to talk."

Jake was surprised by the sound of Kenneth's voice. They always met the next evening after they went out dancing to talk and relax, but they never met in the morning. Still, meeting his friend was hopefully a chance to get some normal sense back into his life. It would give him time to wrap his head around everything. "Gimme a minute. I'm putting on some clothes."

Once Jake had finished putting on a pair of pants, he opened the door to let his friend inside. "What are you doing here, Ken?"

Kenneth ignored the question, silently looking through the house and checking the rooms before turning to face Jake. "Jake, do you know what you've done?"

Something about Ken's tone set Jake on edge. He sounded completely different from normal. Was it possible for his friend to know what had happened? That didn't make any sense. How could Kenneth know about magic? Still, there was no other explanation for Ken's strange behavior. Jake pondered Kenneth's strange behavior the previous night. Kenneth had warned Jake about Maeva. Why?

While Jake was lost in thought, Kenneth shut the curtains and made sure the door was locked. When he finished, Kenneth coughed loudly. "Jake, I already know you discovered magic. If that's what you're worried about, stop it. I was hoping you'd stay normal your whole life, but that's not an option now. We don't have much time."

Jake stared in disbelief. How could Kenneth possibly know that he had discovered magic? Was it that obvious? And how did Kenneth know about magic? Too many questions ran through his mind, but one was most prominent. "Have you known about magic this whole time…?"

Kenneth's impatience was obvious as he walked over and put a hand on Jake's shoulder. "Yes, now, you need to come with me. I don't know how much time we have before it's too late."

"Too late? Too late for what?" Jake shook free of his friend's grip. "Kenneth, I'm not going anywhere until you explain things to me. You knew about magic this whole time? And you kept it a secret from me?"

Kenneth sighed, standing stock-still for a few moments before his freckled face seemed to split open, revealing a small, winged creature the length of Jake's forearm. "Look, Jake. I'm a Pixie. The Ken you've known is me, but it's also not."

Jake stared in horror and confusion. It took him a few moments to realize that, somehow, he had been pulled into the mist. Had Kenneth done that? His friend's face hadn't split apart, not really. He could just see Kenneth's true form. The knowledge came unbidden to his mind. Jake didn't have time to analyze the reason for that as he tried to wrap his mind around what he had just been told. "You're a… what? How…?"

The pixie that was Kenneth ran its hand through its still red hair. The face was the same, in miniature, as the human form. Jake could see a mixture of emotion in his friend's eyes as the creature's words entered his mind. "The how isn't so important. I've been keeping magic from you because it's dangerous. I wanted to show you what I am before I explain things. We can't linger in the mist, or we might draw attention."

With that, Jake could feel himself being pushed back into his body – he was sure this had to be Kenneth's doing this time – and flinched as the mist receded from view. His friend's human face and form stared back at him. Jake tried to see some hint of the pixie beneath but saw nothing. The shock and betrayal of it all overwhelmed him. He had trusted Kenneth with his secrets for so long. Yet there had been a secret this large hovering like a gulf between them the whole time.

Kenneth frowned a little bit, scratching at his beard. "I had actually worked very hard to keep you from this world, you know. Even last night when you went with… her. I tried to stop you. And I have good reason, trust me."

Shivering, Jake remembered the sensation of being around Maeva. How right it had felt. Why would the pixie try to stop that? "Kenneth… how can I trust anything you say? You lied to me. For years. Give me one good reason to trust you. Because right now, I feel like it might be best if you leave."

Kenneth raised a placating hand in the face of Jake's anger and hurt. "You're right to feel angry. But I kept you in the dark about all this for a reason. Once a human like you enters the magical world, you're marked for death. The tattoo on your back proves it."

"Marked for death? A tattoo? What the hell are you talking about, Kenneth? I don't have any tattoos, and you know that." Jake couldn't believe what he had just heard. Had Ken gone mad? He could feel a sense of panic threatening to take over as the words sunk in. What if his friend-turned-pixie wasn't crazy? Jake hurried to the mirror in his bathroom, turning to look at his back and crying out in horror at the sight.

There, on Jake's back, was an image of snow falling from his shoulders down his back into a jade bowl that was held up by a copy of himself. The bowl was tipped so that the snow, as it melted, would flow into his open mouth. Jake was terrified at the unexpected sight. Turning to face Ken, he couldn't keep his voice from shaking. "What is this? How? How did this happen? Did you do this?"

Kenneth shook his head, gesturing at the image. "That's part of you, Jake. Every magical human has a tattoo marking them. Magic underneath the surface. Once you're exposed to the mist, it all comes up. The tattoo… your power. I've known you were magical from the day we met."

Running his hand over his back to try and feel some sensation from the tattoo, Jake felt nothing out of the ordinary as he pondered his friend's words. So he had always had magic inside him. And his friend had worked to keep it a secret. He shook his head. It was too much to absorb right away. He needed time. Jake focused his thoughts on the future. Looking at Kenneth, Jake gestured vaguely at everything. "Okay, so you knew about all this. And kept it a secret from me. Now I'm going to die because I'm a magic human. How do I stay alive? Is there any way out of this?"

Ken nodded. "There is a way out. I can take you with me to the Pixie Kingdom. If I bring you as one of our… guests, you'll be under our protection. None of the other factions in the magical world will try to reach you there."

Jake stared at him. This was Kenneth's plan? To just… run away with him? It took Jake several moments to get over the shock. "So you're just… going to whisk me away, are you? And I'm supposed to trust you. Because you haven't betrayed my trust, right, Kenneth?"

Jake scoffed at him, turning to look at the tattoo in the mirror and clenching his fists in barely restrained anger. Why had Kenneth kept it a secret?

The pixie sighed and pinched the bridge of his nose, a habit of his when he was deep in thought. Jake watched and waited. The minutes passed without a response, and Jake grew impatient.

Leaning forward, Jake hissed, "Either you speak, or I leave."

Kenneth flinched from Jake's tone, looking hurt. "Okay, okay. I'm sorry I kept this all a secret. Things are so dangerous that I thought it would be better if you never got involved, especially with what you are. I was hoping you'd have a long, happy life without the conflict that comes with all of… this."

Jake wanted to keep being angry at the pixie, but he couldn't help but try to see things from Kenneth's point of view. Of course, his friend would want him to live. It was selfish of him to make that choice without even consulting Jake first, but wouldn't Jake have done the same thing in his position? Still, Jake wouldn't forgive Ken easily for this, even though he understood Ken's reasons. Jake gestured for Ken to keep talking.

"You know maybe it was wrong to do, but it's in the past, and I hope you can forgive me. Aside from that, I swear that things will be safer if you come with me. If you've been exposed to the mist, then us magical creatures will naturally end up being drawn to you over time. The pull is minor at first, but it grows the longer your connection remains. You can't face that alone."

Jake nodded, deciding to believe Kenneth. The words rang true. It explained his meeting with Evelynn. They were already being drawn to him. Still, there was so much left unexplained. "Before I even consider this offer, you have to tell me… where are we going? And how are we getting there?"

"Fair enough," Kenneth responded, "you should know where we're going. As a Pixie, I can take us to places by traveling through the mist. Our physical bodies will come with us. So, I'm going to transport us from here to a safe house – where you'll be safe as my guest. After some preparations, I'll take you to the land of the pixie kingdom. You will be able to learn more about magic, the mist, and everything else while you're there."

Jake stared at Ken. "So you can teleport us out of here? How long will we be gone? How can I come back home to study and live after this is over?"

Ken nodded, though his tone seemed strained. "Yes, I can teleport us. I don't know how long we'll be gone, but don't worry. I'll call your school and say you had a family emergency and won't be available. When we get back, I'll help you set your life up again. But we need to go before she gets here. We don't have time to keep talking. Make a decision, Jake."

Despite his still-existing concerns, Jake couldn't see a better way forward. If Jake stayed home, unknown and possibly dangerous creatures would find him. Jake wanted the chance to live in the world of magic mist on his own terms. To do that, he would need to learn about how to use his powers and about the other creatures that might seek him out. If he went with Kenneth, Jake had a chance to learn about the world. The idea was exciting even with all the danger surrounding it. His back tingled as he made the decision. It was the right path. Jake was smiling despite himself as he took Ken's outstretched hand.

"So, how does this wor-" Jake was interrupted by a feeling unlike any other he'd experienced before. It was almost as if he were walking forward and moving sideways instead, yet he knew he was standing still.

Kenneth's face became less solid and real, replaced by his Pixie form as he performed this feat of magic. Gradually, the mist withdrew from the spaces around them and seemed to move into place just above their skin. The mist had a strange sensation similar to touching gelatin. Jake could hear the distant thump of a giant heart, the mist pulsing in time with its throbbing. It was as if the mist were the veins of some great beast.

Kenneth tightened his grip on Jake's hand. "Don't let go, or you will end up being left behind. Are you ready?"

Jake didn't trust himself to speak, so he nodded instead. In the mist, Jake could see Kenneth's Pixie form flutter down to rest on top of his hand, even as Jake could still feel Kenneth's hand in the real world. The separation baffled him, but he did not get a chance to ask any questions. The mist turned a brilliant purple and blocked Jake's ability to see anything. The scent of tulips and chrysanthemums filled his nose as they traveled through the mist.

Chapter 12

Slowly, the mist returned to its usual shifting greys and expanded from Kenneth and Jake. As it grew, the room around them grew darker. The mist was brighter than the physical world. Kenneth panted, a thin sheen of sweat across his face. Teleporting another living entity with him was always tiring, even after his years of experience. Ken walked over to a wall while Jake adjusted, flipping the light switch on.

They were in a sparsely furnished living room with a glass wall. The moon reflected off the waters of the pool outside.

Kenneth nodded in satisfaction as he gave the room a glance over. It would do as a place to keep Jake for now. He would have to strengthen the wards and make sure Jake couldn't wander outside, but that was a trifling matter. The next stop was to give his report in person about the current events and receive new orders about what to do. He just had to make sure Jake was comfortable and didn't do anything drastic until then. Kenneth gestured vaguely toward the rest of the house. "Welcome to the safe house."

"Where are we, and how was it so fast…?" Jake had finally recovered from the journey and was looking around in awe and wonder.

Kenneth forced an encouraging smile onto his face. Pretending to be Jake's friend was slowly becoming exhausting. He wished he felt confident that telling the truth wouldn't ruin any chance he had at convincing Jake to join his people. "We are in a safe place prepared for things like this. In Jamaica. You'll be safe here while I prepare things to move you into the Pixie Kingdom."

Jake continued staring in disbelief at his surroundings while Kenneth bustled about to make sure the house was stocked on food. "How long will that take? Why did we have to come here to begin with?"

"Magical humans of your power are rare, so you catch the interest of all kinds of creatures that exist in the mist. By moving you, I can keep you hidden longer. You should only be here for a day, then I'll be back." Once Kenneth had finished checking the refrigerator and cabinets, he walked around to stand in front of Jake. "I know this is a lot to take in, but I need you to trust me. Stay here until I return. Don't try to leave."

"What about my life back in Japan? What happens to the people I knew?" Jake shook his head, moving to sit down on the couch and stare out the window.

"Don't worry about that. I already told you I'd take care of it, Jake." Kenneth waited until Jake looked up at him. He gestured expansively. "The future is filled with magic. Something you've dreamed about is real. You can have a life filled with it. You can learn to use it. And you won't have to work your life away in the mundane world from before."

Jake was silent for a time. Kenneth wondered if he was going to argue and tried to think of a more compelling argument just in case. It wouldn't do if he got this far only to have Jake change his mind.

"Fine. You're right. I want to learn more, and this is the way to do it. You're promising me a kind of freedom, Kenneth. I'll take it."

The Scotsman nodded firmly, then clapped his hands. "With that settled, I need to tell you a little bit more about the world. Maeva was… is a magical creature. She's a dangerous leader of a faction that wants to take over the magical world through any means necessary. She would have killed you if she didn't think she could use you. I want you to help us instead. The Pixies are working to prevent her and the other warring groups from taking over, and to do that we need powerful people on our side."

"Powerful people?" Jake scoffed. "Have you looked at me? I'm nothing. What can I do? I didn't even know magic existed before now."

"You may not feel it, but you have more power than you know. And we'll teach you how to use it, starting now. You already know how to go into the mist, so shift into the mist when you're ready." Kenneth shifted easily, his Pixie form hovering in the air in front of his physical body as Jake phased into the mist as well.

"Now, concentrate on the mist. Try to form an apple in your mind and think of the mist as creating that apple. Like so." Kenneth raised a small hand, the mist swirling from the air into a more solid form. Slowly, the twisting coils morphed and shifted until they matched the shape of an apple. Growing slowly more solid and taking on color, the grey strands grew red, yellow, and brown until a beautiful apple was resting in his palm, stem and all.

Jake concentrated. He was slower to focus than Kenneth. Kenneth muttered words of encouragement as Jake's face visibly strained with focus, the mist moving sluggishly as it was channeled by his untrained mind. The coils twisted and unfurled and rejoined, taking much longer to maintain a shape until, finally, a green apple was formed. Jake smiled as he looked at his creation, tossing it into the air and catching it. "Granny-smith. My favorite."

"Good job. Now, shift back." As they left the mist and rejoined their bodies, the apples that were held by their mist-forms fell to the ground, bruising against the floor. "Objects created in the mist are connected to both worlds. Mist and reality. You shift, and they will shift with you."

Jake nodded, yawning as he did so. "That… is cool. But I feel exhausted. How can I be so tired when I woke up only a few hours ago?"

"Magic takes mental effort. You've strained yourself. It'll be fine once you get used to it, but you should sit down."

Jake followed Kenneth's instruction just before the wave of dizziness hit. Groaning, he closed his eyes and leaned back on the sofa. "This is awful."

"You take some time to rest. I'm going to go ahead and get things prepared for your arrival. Can you wait here until I get back?"

The human nodded. "Yeah… go ahead. I'll be here."

Kenneth nodded to himself. With Jake tired like this, it was a simple matter to reach a tendril of influence out through the mist into the human's mind. He pushed on that feeling of exhaustion, making it stronger. Jake's eyes slowly closed. It had worked. Kenneth knew that Jake would wake up before long.

Without wasting any time to admire his handiwork, Kenneth set about the house. Channeling his reserves of power, he strengthened the wards that kept creatures at bay and set about creating barriers to keep Jake from leaving. He went from window to window, door to door, until he had created security tight enough that he felt confident everything would hold until he could return. With that done, Kenneth smiled to himself as he walked back to stand near

Jake. Now he could report back to his superiors. He prepared to teleport again, stretching his shoulders as he did so. Hopefully, he would have some time to sleep after all this.

The slight pop of air that indicated Kenneth had teleported away woke Jake with a start. He felt like he had fallen asleep for a moment, but he wasn't sure. The pain in his head was already starting to lessen as he looked around. The house was luxurious. Definitely beyond an average person's pay grade. Jake wondered what Kenneth really did for work since he was a pixie.

Determined to find some answers about this stranger who he had thought was his friend, Jake started to search the cabinets and drawers in the many rooms of the house for personal effects. Anything to indicate who Kenneth was, if that was even his real name.

After an hour searching high and low for secret compartments, Jake gave up. There was no sign that anybody lived in the place, aside from the fresh food and perfectly clean rooms. It made no sense. The place was too sterile. Jake thought back on Kenneth's lively personality and friendly attitude. Had it all been an act?

Jake spent a few minutes thinking back through all of their shared experiences. If there was a sign, he couldn't catch it. The sense of betrayal had been creeping up on him since this madness had all started, and it only solidified the more he thought about things. He decided he would have to keep Kenneth close enough to be helpful but also keep some of his feelings hidden. An uncertain ally was better than none.

With that decision made, the human also came to the realization that he hadn't shifted into the mist a single time since Kenneth had left. Perhaps there were clues on the other side. Sitting down on the sofa, he took a deep breath and felt himself flow out as he exhaled. The house looked mostly the same in the mist. The only change was still a big one; symbols in a language he didn't know were written in the mist above each of the windows and doors. Jake floated through the rest of the house to find the same strange writing on every entry and exit point. He reached out to touch one. The symbol shifted into the shape of a mouth, straining against unseen bonds and snapping sharp teeth towards his fingers. Stumbling back, Jake stared in horror as the gnashing teeth vanished and shaped themselves back into the symbol. It happened so quickly he almost thought he had imagined it.

The human could only guess that these were some form of magical security guards. He was afraid of finding out anything more about them. Retreating quickly, he re-entered his body. His hands shook as he took a sip from a glass of water. So much security for someplace with seemingly nothing in it. Jake wanted to feel safe, but it only left him feeling more exposed than ever. He truly knew nothing, and he had dived headfirst into this life.

He spent much of the rest of that day contemplating how he was going to get out of this mess, if he even could.

Anissa's nails clacked loudly against her desk. Kenneth stood as still as a statue while they both waited for word from the Queen. He felt the cold pressure of Anissa's impatience and irritation. From experience, Kenneth knew that his boss did not like to be kept waiting for any reason. He was surprised when Anissa had asked him no questions at all about Jake's status. Instead, she simply ordered him to wait with her. The silence was disturbed only by the steady rhythm of Anissa's drumming fingertips. Kenneth pondered what he would do if the Queen had him stripped of his duties. He felt sure that he deserved the punishment, but at the same time, he believed their only chance to convince Jake to join their cause lay with the friendship he had worked to create.

Kenneth jumped in surprise as the door opened. A modest-looking servant beckoned. "The Queen has requested your presence in her audience chambers."

"Finally." Anissa stood with a huff as she started walking around her desk, only to be stopped by the servant pointing towards Kenneth.

"My apologies for the ambiguity. The Queen requests only Sir Kenneth's presence. She wishes to hear the report straight from the horse's mouth, so to speak."

Kenneth did not wait around to see Anissa's reaction, though he could hear her spluttering at the servant in the background as he hastened his way toward the audience chambers. Thankfully, he knew the way by himself.

Kenneth stared at the clock on the wall and resisted the urge to start pacing. It was early in the morning, so he would have to wait a while for the Queen to be ready to see him. It had already been an hour, and the sun had just finished rising. Its rays shone against the trophies and beautiful, decorative ornaments in the waiting room, though Kenneth didn't spare them a glance. He had hoped to get this over with quickly: he didn't like leaving Jake alone. The sooner he received permission to bring the human here for safekeeping, the better.

As time kept passing, Kenneth grew concerned. He should have been summoned by now, right?. Could there have been a serious emergency happening that he didn't know about? The sound of a door opening interrupted his anxious pondering.

One of the Queen's guards gestured at Kenneth. "The Queen will see you now."

Kenneth had to resist the urge to comment on how long it took as he rushed into the audience chamber. To his surprise, the head of the Guardians of the kingdom was also there. The large, furry creature expanded its seemingly elastic body to its full height as he entered, allowing the pale white eyes in the center of its mass to see clearly. "Guardian. I did not expect to see you here."

The Queen raised her hand, and Kenneth kissed her ring before stepping a respectful distance away. "Kenneth, you have done well to keep us informed of events. Is the human safely contained?"

"Yes, my liege. He is in a safe house, sleeping. I have already taken steps to begin convincing him to join our cause."

At Kenneth's comment, the Guardian took a hissing breath and interrupted the conversation. "My Queen, I still do not think we should let such a powerful human live. How can we trust that he will really join us? Maeva unlocked his magic. This could be a trick."

Kenneth grit his teeth, resisting the urge to argue his side without permission. He didn't understand how the Guardian had picked up word of Jake or why he would bother involving himself in such matters. It gave Kenneth a feeling of unease. The Pixie Queen stared at the Guardian for a few moments before turning away. "Kenneth, what say you to this? Is the human valuable enough, and can he aid us? We do not wish to see things go wrong."

"I have worked to gain his trust for quite some time now. He has always been fascinated with magic. He's a seer. I bore witness to his mark. His discovery was bound to happen, but now I think we have a chance to use his interest. If we empower him, he could be a greater asset than we might know."

The furry beast clacked two of its claws together. "And he could be a greater threat than we know! Maeva's tricks are well known. If she has taken interest, then bringing him to us may incur her wrath.

Can we truly afford a fight? Best to kill him and be done with it. Minimize the risk."

"Quiet, we must think." The Queen waved a hand, silencing both of them.

Kenneth stared in confusion at the Guardian. The argument for killing Jake seemed so short-sighted. After all, how could killing someone that has Maeva's interest be any less of a problem? He hoped that his Queen agreed with him, even as he steeled his will to having to end Jake were she to command it.

"We see the wisdom in bringing a seer to our cause. His insight and power may yet keep the scales in our favor as we try to hold this precarious peace. Kenneth, you will bring him here and ensure that he is assigned a trainer and given appropriate access. This will be your responsibility to manage."

"My Queen, please!" The Queen waved her hand, silencing the Guardian as he started to protest and dismissing her vassals in the same motion.

Kenneth couldn't help a smile, satisfied to see the Guardian silenced. The creature had risen to its station through power, not wisdom. It showed.

Walking out of the audience chamber, Kenneth was already thinking about who would make the best teacher for Jake. He was startled when he felt the Guardian's clawed paw on his shoulder, turning quickly and moving back.

"You will ruin us, Kenneth. You may have convinced the Queen, but I do not believe. I will be watching this human. If he even seems like a threat, I will kill him. Orders or not."

Kenneth snarled, his fists balling tightly. "You have no right to interfere, Guardian. He will be my responsibility. I know the man well, and he will join us. If he plans to betray our people, then I'll kill him myself."

With that said, Kenneth stormed off. His footfalls echoed through the stoned halls of the Pixie Castle as he set about the preparations for Jake's arrival.

Jake woke up in the Jamaican safe house as sunbeams shone through the window and across his face. Casting off the sheets, he sleepily made his way through his morning routine. Once he had finished washing up and clothing himself, he stared into the bathroom mirror. He could hardly believe everything that was going on.

To prove to himself once again that this was all real, he shifted into the mist and back into his body. The slightly oily sensation of the mist clinging to his spectral form as he moved back and forth gradually decreased the more he did it. After spending a minute simply traveling back and forth, Jake nodded to himself. It was all real. Including Kenneth's betrayal.

Kenneth stood up as Jake entered the room, his face a mask. "You're awake. While you slept, I finished the arrangements for your arrival in Scotland. The Queen gave me permission to bring you into the fold, so to speak."

"Good, good." Jake nodded distractedly. "I have some questions, though. How can I know I'm actually going to be safe? How will coming with you be better?"

The Scotsman walked over to Jake, placing his hands on the human's shoulders. "I'm going to need you to trust me on this. The Pixie kingdom is safe because there will be other magical users and a great many pixies there who can keep threats out. As a guest, you're protected."

For a few moments, Jake stared at Kenneth. His instincts told him to go along with it, even if his mind still battled with the idea. "Okay… sure. And what do you expect of me once we're there? I don't believe for a second you suddenly opened up to me without some agenda."

"My hand was forced by Maeva, that's true. What I expect is that you'll obey the rules and do your best to keep from disturbing the peace." Kenneth's response was instant. "If you can do that, things should be fine."

Jake shook his head. Kenneth wasn't very convincing. Still, he couldn't go back to Japan without Kenneth's help. And Kenneth had made it clear he wasn't going to do that. Jake had to go with the pixie he didn't trust and hope it worked. With a resigned sigh, he looked up at his former friend and shrugged. "I guess I don't have a choice, do I? Go with you and live or die without ever learning about magic."

The Pixie nodded, reaching out a hand palm up. "Good. Let's get going, then. I've prepared a room for you, and I'll be able to show you around the castle."

"Wait, there's a castle?" Jake had already taken Kenneth's hand, and his words were swallowed as the mist closed in around them. The sensation felt deeper than the last. It was like putting on a pair of well-worn shoes, now that Jake had grown accustomed to the sensation of the mist. The mist fit snugly against him, and he hardly took notice of it.

Now that he was prepared for it, Jake was able to watch the process as Kenneth teleported them. Jake felt the sensation of the mist forming what seemed like a tunnel, through which Kenneth directed them. It shifted and swirled as they passed, with the colors ranging from its normal dull-grey to deep purple. He reached out with his free hand, touching the edge of the misty tunnel, and felt a great pressure on the other side, like the rest of reality was pushing and trying to break in. He imagined it as the laws of nature crashing against the mist, being bent and turned away. The idea pleased him, and he smiled despite himself while they finished the journey.

Chapter 13

The mist shifted and expanded, leaving Jake and Kenneth in the center of a well-decorated bedroom. Landscape paintings decorated the stone walls, and the light of the sun shone through windows that faced out toward a beautiful garden. Jake couldn't help but stare at the wonders around him. "It's all so… majestic."

After a couple of minutes, Kenneth clapped his hands together. "Okay, that's enough gawking. Welcome to the Pixie Kingdom's castle. Let me show you around. I've been put in charge of your care while you're here."

Jake nodded, following Kenneth out of the room and staring at everything with wide-eyed wonder. If life was going to be this luxurious, why would he ever want to go back? Magic and castles. For a moment, he forgot his worries and felt like a child living in a dream. It took effort to focus on his guide's words and warnings; not to be disruptive to other guests, to keep out of forbidden areas, a description of the daily routine, etcetera. It washed over him in a tide of information that he could barely contain. Now that he had arrived, Jake was more at ease. He was in the right place. He felt it.

Eventually, the two arrived at a stairwell leading down. Kenneth continued his explanation of the castle. "The first-floor houses servants and is also where you'll find the great hall and the dining areas."

The difference between floors was clear as soon as they arrived. The walls were less decorated, and there were more people wandering the halls. Servants worked throughout the day and night to maintain the castle and be prepared for the royal family's needs.

While leading Jake through the tour of the castle interior, Kenneth seemed to be looking for somebody. He kept glancing at every person that passed. Jake wondered why his friend-turned-guide seemed so on edge, but he wasn't sure how to bring it up. He decided to pocket the observation for another time.

After passing through the great hall and remarking once again on the beauty of the statuary, paintings, and other decorations, Kenneth suddenly called out to a woman that was hurrying in a different direction. "Good afternoon, Elspeth, it has been some time since I saw you last. Meet Jake, a new… guest here that I brought in an hour ago. He'll be working with us from now on."

"Ah, Kenneth. I hear you've been well in… Japan, was it?" Elspeth turned her eyes up from the papers she had been checking, her face a mask of calm. She turned to face Jake, performing a curt bow. "A pleasure, Jake. I hope you enjoy your stay here. If you have any needs, feel free to find me or ask any of the other staff for assistance. We value our guests, as I am sure Kenneth has already taken the time to inform you."

Kenneth and Elspeth nodded to each other. Jake couldn't help but feel that he was missing something important about the exchange. Kenneth visibly relaxed as Elspeth walked away, and Jake took the opportunity to ask a question in the following silence. "What was that about?"

"The steward handles the logs for all visitors and guests to the castle. It's part of what will keep our security from thinking you're a hostile if you are ever going through the castle without me." Kenneth waved away Jake's next question before he could start to ask it, ushering him down yet another path.

"Come, Jake. I'm sure you're hungry. Let me take you to where our guests eat lunch. You'll be eating with me today, but, in the future, you'll be alone. We're going to have to talk about some rules."

The growl of his stomach stopped the human from asking more questions as he silently followed his guide. If there was a chance to meet others like him, then maybe some of his questions would be answered without needing to be asked. He just hoped he didn't have more questions after that.

It took several minutes of walking through the castle to arrive at an archway without doors. Through the open entryway was a grand hall filled with a sea of people. Jake followed Kenneth as the Pixie led the way through the crowd, unable to stop himself from staring at people as he passed by. How many of them were actually human? Were they all pixies?

"Here, take this plate and take your pick of the food." Jake turned to look as Kenneth forced a plate with a fork, spoon, and knife into his hands. Before the two of them was a semi-circle of tables, each was piled high with a different kind of food.

Jake's eyes were drawn immediately to the bacon and sausage. Once the other meat-eaters in front of him had taken their share, he covered half his plate with crisp, salted bacon. Following the flow of the people, he went around the other tables and grabbed a vegetable broth, a bread-like food that Kenneth told him was a potato scone, and a slice of meat pie.

With his lunch collected, Jake walked away from the buffet area. Kenneth slid up next to the human, taking the lead once again. "Different magical creatures have different customs. Try not to mingle too much with the rest of the folk here until you've learned how to behave. You don't want to make anybody mad."

"Okay. Any starting guidelines, then?"

Kenneth waved a hand in the air as they continued to make their way across the hall. "For now, don't talk to anyone. And don't offer to shake hands. Follow that advice, and you'll probably not upset anyone. We'll get into the details another time."

The silence extended for a couple of seconds before Jake noticed Kenneth staring. He nodded quickly, returning his focus to the Pixie. "Sorry. I understand."

The pair finally arrived across the hall from the buffet area to a small table that could barely fit both of their plates. Jake wasted no time at all. Curious, he picked up the potato scone and took a couple bites. It was surprisingly good.

"So, your training will center around two key concepts." Kenneth's voice was muffled by the food. "First, understanding. You'll learn what the mist is and about the magical creatures in our world, their customs, and so on."

Jake nodded as he finished off his scone. He felt a strong desire to learn all he could about the world around him. A quote popped up in his head. Knowledge is power. It rang true, especially when it came to magic. It would give Jake opportunities to prepare himself for whatever may come. And, perhaps, he could learn something about Kenneth. While he relied on his erstwhile guide, Jake needed to be able to trust him.

"The second fundamental is self-control. You will have to learn to control yourself to control the mist. Power is born from your will. If you are not a master of your own mind, you will never master the use of magic." Kenneth jabbed his empty fork pointedly into the air. "From these two skills, all users of the mist find their limits and their talents. All of us have an affinity for something. For some, it is healing. For others, the opposite. Humans have stronger affinities than most. You'll learn more about that later."

"Why later? I want to get started right away." Jake put down his half-eaten slice of bacon and gestured around himself. He took a moment to describe things positively, even as he worried about the dangers of being surrounded by magic beyond his understanding. "There's so much wonder here, and I'm not able to understand it. I want, no… I need to know more."

The pixie sighed. "It's not that simple. I can't be around all the time. I have other duties to attend to as well. I need time to get certain affairs in order. We'll start your training and get you situated tomorrow after breakfast. Remember, self-control is important. If you can't be patient for one night, maybe you're not ready to learn."

"Fine…." It wasn't the answer that Jake wanted, but pushing Kenneth might just make it take longer before he could learn. He would have to wait, no matter how much it chafed. His mind wandered to think about what other duties Kenneth could be performing. What exactly was Kenneth's role in all this?

The two men finished their meal without any more conversation. Both were lost in their own thoughts. Kenneth silently led Jake back to the bedroom where they had first arrived.

The Scotsman turned to face Jake after closing the door. "Before I let you go, I am going to teach you a good habit to have when meeting other people in the magical world. Shift for a moment into the mist to look at them, then shift back. Unless they are masking their true form, you will be able to see what kind of being you're about to have a conversation with. That way, you can try to behave properly. You need to do it quickly, or else you risk being rude. Shift into the mist and watch me do it first."

"Wait, if they can tell when I shift into the mist, wouldn't it be better to just avoid everyone until I can protect myself?"

"You can't hide forever. And you'll want to get to know people here once you're more comfortable. Trust me."

Jake sighed and nodded his head. He was starting to dislike how often Kenneth told him to trust him. It just made it even harder to do. Still, he focused on doing the task set before him. Jake concentrated, shifting slowly into the mist to look at Kenneth. The Scotsman looked human, and Jake guessed that he was masking his form out of habit. It stung for a moment to see how naturally lying came to someone he thought he knew, but the feeling was quickly replaced by surprise when he witnessed a shift in Kenneth's form.

The Pixie's true form shimmered into view then vanished again in the blink of an eye. This happened several more times, just as quickly, as Kenneth demonstrated the speed of the shift. Jake returned to his body and stared at Kenneth in shock. "How… can you do that so quickly?"

"It's all about thinking. Once you get used to shifting into the mist from practice, you'll be able to flow back and forth as easily as you breathe. Come, try it."

With a nod, the human focused and stared at Kenneth. He pushed his mind outward, grasping the mist and forcing himself into it. Attempting to shift back quickly, he pulled his mind back into himself. It was nowhere near Kenneth's speed, which seemed almost instantaneous. Jake repeated the process, slowly feeling how his mind pushes and pulls against the mist and working his consciousness between the two planes of reality. Each time felt smoother than the last. Almost like slipping a foot into a well-worn shoe.

Jake panted from the exertion of rapidly going back and forth, looking at Kenneth for approval.

"Hmm…" His teacher's face was neutral. After a couple seconds of silence, Kenneth nodded. "That's good enough for now. You'll keep practicing that from here on out. I suggest you get some rest. Starting tomorrow, you'll officially begin training."

"Sir, yes, sir." Giving a mock salute, the human turned toward his room and stared at everything. Perhaps he could do some writing? He felt the strangest urge to keep a journal of his experiences. Maybe he could help bring everything into focus. He sat down to put pen to paper, trying to see between the lines of his own experiences.

Kenneth let out a small sigh of relief as he closed the door to Jake's room. He had managed to get Jake to the castle. The human had agreed to join them. As he let himself relax slightly, the exhaustion of working for so long without sleep hit Kenneth almost immediately. He stifled a yawn as he made his way back to his quarters, tallying off in his mind the things he had left to do. There were several other marks that he had to remove from his schedule. One was the recent magical human that he had scouted. He needed to handle the paperwork and in-person work of passing the man on to a new handler. Kenneth felt confident he could start the process for that one right away. He also owed Silva a visit. It had been a while since the last time, and he was due to check in with Wilbur and Silva anyway. It also gave Kenneth an excuse to eat more food. He had kept his meal light with Jake since he knew eating left him lethargic at a time that needed him to be alert.

When he arrived in his room, Kenneth checked how he looked in the mirror. He looked worn-out; his clothes were disheveled, his eyelids had started drooping, and his beard looked more unkempt than normal. The pixie sighed, stood up straight, and fixed his clothing and beard by hand. It took longer, but it saved him energy. He had a feeling as he stood there, trimming and smoothing his facial hair, that things were only going to get busier.

Once he was finally satisfied with his appearance, Kenneth closed his eyes and shifted himself back to Japan, directly into Wilbur's office. To Kenneth's surprise, Wilbur wasn't at his desk. Instead, the older pixie was standing with his back to the door, gazing at a bookcase. He was mid-sentence, speaking to one of his underlings that was sitting just in front of Kenneth, furiously scribbling notes. The pop of Kenneth's arrival interrupted both of them, causing the subordinate to turn with an audible squeak and Wilbur to simply sigh.

"Yes, Kenneth?" Wilbur continued to stare at the bookcase, his hands clasped behind his back.

Kenneth paused for a moment. He stared at the seated pixie, then shook his head and focused on Wilbur. "I'm here to discuss the changing of hands for B-class mark Yutaro, and to check in on Silva's operations."

"Very well. Sylas, you are free to go for now. We will continue our discussion later." As Sylas made his way out, Wilbur turned and seated himself at his desk. He gestured for Kenneth to sit as well. "It is quite early to be changing handlers for Yutaro. Presumably you have a reason for it."

"Maeva was in town. Might still be. She came across one of my charges, and things went an unfortunate direction. That case will be taking up most of my energy and focus, after I get things situated here."

Wilbur's expression remained unchanged as he processed the information. The silence stretched. Kenneth resisted the urge to say something. After a couple of minutes passed without a single shift in Wilbur's expression or posture, the old pixie finally spoke. "Of the operatives we have that could deal with the Yutaro case, only Madison is available right now. She will be waiting outside once we finish our discussion here. Did Maeva notice you? How much did you learn?"

"She caught me when I tried to scry her interactions with my mark from a distance. She gave me a warning that we can't keep the balance forever. She's going to start a war, in time. It's a matter of when, not if." Kenneth paused to think. He could reveal more of his concerns with Wilbur, but it seemed unwise. Even if Wilbur was above him in the chain of command, there were still some things his superior didn't need to know.

"I see. So Silva's information about increased conflicts between the other factions and Maeva's heightened activity was mostly accurate, then. The engines have started rumbling." Wilbur sighed once again. "This peace was never bound to last anyway—too many hotheads going around trying to be head honcho for that. You are dismissed. Talk with Madison about a plan. I trust you two can figure it out without my presence."

Kenneth hesitated. Silva had gathered information? Kenneth knew Silva's operation was performing well, but he didn't realize how well things were going. He would have to ask Silva for details later. He walked out of the room, closed the door, and turned to see Madison staring at him. "Hello, Madison. Do you have somewhere we can talk about the mark without awkwardly standing in front of Wilbur's office?"

"This way." Madison made her way down the steps that led up to the office, through the maze of cubicles, to a communal lunch and rest area that had some others hanging about and carousing. She seated herself at one of the open tables and leaned back with her arms crossed. "What're the circumstances with the mark?"

"Yutaro is convinced that he has magical powers, but nobody else believes him. For good reason, though. His ability to manipulate and read the thoughts of people around him is not strong enough to overwhelm, but it is a fine-tuned edge. He's practiced and honed already. I've been treading the balance of not saying I think he's crazy without revealing what I know. He's opened up to me enough to trust my advice, but not enough for me to convince him to join us. I have no read on how he would react upon being told by someone that he is not only sane but also welcome to a large community. He's a bit of a loner."

"Have you considered bringing someone in to hire him for his powers? It could be as simple as making him a freelance employee. We hire him to gather intel for us, with a couple tests to start, then we go from there. I can simply pose as his potential employer's hireling, and we can go from there." Madison stood up, gesturing toward the door. "Let's go see him and get this started."

Kenneth tilted his head as he considered her plan. It wasn't a terrible one, all things considered. They were in a hurry, and having an impatient but rich eccentric who believed in magic would speed up the process significantly toward putting him on their side of the line. It wasn't far off from Kenneth's own plan, which would have been slower and more careful. But he needed to rush things so he could free up his schedule to deal with Jake. He shrugged, walking out of the building with Madison and leading her to the nearest subway station. She had apparently already read the mark's file, given she hadn't suggested they teleport in. Yutaro had installed quite thorough security around his home.

Neither of them spoke as they made their way through the different train systems to reach their destination. Both of them knew their roles in the coming conversation. Kenneth did a final check of his appearance, making a couple of adjustments to make himself match how he typically looked when he met Yutaro to keep it as consistent as possible.

The intercom crackled to life before Kenneth even pushed the button. "Kenneth, who is that? Why are you here outside of our usual meeting times? Don't you know it's not safe?"

"Yutaro, calm down." Kenneth raised his hands defensively. "We weren't followed here. And this woman is Madison. She works for someone that has taken an interest in, well… your powers. I'll let her speak for herself."

Madison took a step forward as Kenneth moved out of the way. "Mr. Yutaro. We've been keeping an eye on you for some time now. Your… gift, as we like to call it, could prove useful to us. My employer would be willing to reward you handsomely for your services, assuming you accept. Kenneth here is safe, and you are too. But the magical world can be a dangerous place without friends in the right places."

"Ssshhh. Don't say that out loud like that." There was silence for a few moments before the door buzzed and locks clicked open. The pair made their way inside as they heard Yutaro speak loudly to be heard. "Come in and close the door behind you. We'll talk business."

They could hear the sliding of many locks echoing from the door as they approached it. It swung open, though Yutaro wasn't there to greet them. Kenneth resisted the urge to smile. It was amusing to think the man thought he was safe with mundane security despite his beliefs in magic. Once they were inside with the door properly shut and locked behind them, Yutaro walked out from around a corner. His eyes darted between them as he brandished his hand at them. Kenneth couldn't make out what Yutaro was holding before the smaller man pulled it back out of view and explained. "That was a dead man's switch. This entire conversation is being recorded. If I let go, the video will be released to the world. No funny business. Kenneth, I trust you, but you understand the precaution when you bring strangers into the mix."

"I am sure this rugged employee understands as well, Yutaro." Kenneth made a point of distancing himself from Madison as he spoke. He couldn't seem like he was comfortable around her. As he moved away, he forcibly relaxed some of the tension from his shoulders. The body language shift made Yutaro visibly relax as well.

Madison stoically waited for the exchange to end, her hands hanging limply at her sides, with the palms facing Yutaro. For most people, this would have been a sign of peace. Among pixies, it was a sign of distrust. Magic flowed easier from their palms. "If it would help… increase trust between us, my employer bade me to come bearing a respectable sum of money to hint at the potential for future payouts if you work for us. May I?"

Yutaro nodded wordlessly, his eyes twitching as he watched her every move. Madison reached up slowly, using two fingers to tease an envelope from her inner jacket pocket. Once it was free, she opened it and showed Yutaro the bills that filled it. Once she had held it out for Yutaro to see for a few seconds, she tossed the envelope onto the ground near his feet. "Consider that a sign of goodwill. Think about our offer. If you agree to it, mark your door with two lines of white chalk. I will be in touch. And Mr. Kenneth here can be a third party to make sure everything is legitimate."

Madison opened the door and walked out. Kenneth followed suit as Yutaro tapped the envelope with a toe before reaching down and snatching the money out of it. Once they were far enough away, Madison turned back to look at him. "Your assessment?"

"He'll be interested, but he'll still be wary. It may be best if I come with you for the first couple of visits. Once he's fully signed up, he won't need me around anymore. We can explain it by saying your employer decided to hire me and send me to work doing other things."

"Good. I will reach out to you when he's marked the door, so we can have our next meeting."

The two of them nodded and went their separate ways. Kenneth sighed to himself. He knew already that Yutaro was likely to mark his door as soon as the next day. Yutaro was too desperate to be recognized as magical to do anything else. Kenneth pushed the topic out of his mind and refocused as he went to see Silva. The restaurant had steadily grown since Silva accepted his place with the pixies. The layout itself had hardly changed, but the number of magical patrons that came and went had increased. Many paid with information instead of money.

Kenneth let himself smile as he walked through the door, whispering to the wait staff that he would like the chef's surprise. It was the code phrase Silva had given him to signal who he was. The waiter led Kenneth to one of the corner tables. Less than a minute later, Silva was seated across the table from him. "Kenneth, my friend. What brings you here after so long? Business or pleasure?"

"A bit of both." Kenneth let himself relax completely. His exhaustion turned him into a sunken mess in his chair. "I haven't slept in too long, and I need a proper meal. But I also came to say things went sideways at work. I will be settling some accounts then heading to the main office. I'll need you to keep tabs on things and reach out to me if anything happens. You should have told me about Maeva."

Silva's face tightened for a moment before he leaned in to whisper. "I only got that information two days ago and had just sent it up the chain of command. One of her underlings had a bit too much wine and became boastful. I figured you were scheduled to visit me soon enough that it wasn't going to be a problem for you."

"Yeah, well… it was a very problematic surprise. Still, I don't blame you for it. Bad luck happens to all of us. Would you make sure any more information about her movements gets sent to me as well? She and I have made contact with each other, and I need to make sure I'm prepared."

"Of course. For you, anything. And for your belly, a meal." Silva bustled off to cook, not even giving Kenneth an opportunity to order anything from the menu.

The pixie let out a sigh of relief. He wasn't sure he had the energy to make that decision, anyway. He didn't realize he had fallen asleep until the clack of a plate being set on the table roused him. He thanked the waiter, then dug into the meal. Silva had become an even more impressive chef over the time since he was brought into the magical fold. The combination of controlled magical enhancement and proper cooking was exquisite. Kenneth could feel himself become re-energized as the power slipped from the food and into his spirit. Silva had punched up the meal to make up for his lack of sleep. Kenneth made a mental note to express his appreciation to his friend properly some other time.

As he finished his meal and left, Kenneth stretched his shoulders and refocused. Back to work. A charmed life wasn't always an easy one.

Chapter 14

Sunlight was just starting to peek through the window, but Jake was already wide awake. His hands shook as he turned the knob off in his shower. Today was going to be the true first day of his magical exploration. His mind kept going back to what Kenneth said about training. Jake hoped that his nerves wouldn't get in the way of his learning. He needed to discover as much as he could.

A knock on the door interrupted Jake's thoughts just as he was finished clothing himself. "Come in."

"Good, you're awake. It's time for breakfast." Kenneth held the door open and gestured for Jake to go out first.

The two of them made their way to the dining hall and piled their plates with food. Kenneth led the way for Jake. "Try to practice glancing at people in the mist as we walk through the hall. They probably won't take offense to you glancing at them, and I can explain it if need be."

While shifting to the mist had become easier after the previous night's practice, Jake found it even harder to keep himself walking at the same time. His legs ended up stuttering and faltering every time his mind went into the mist, and he almost fell over repeatedly. The pressure of Kenneth's constant staring didn't help the human focus.

Once the two of them had worked through a large breakfast, Kenneth started to lead the way out of the hall. "Now that that's over with, I'm going to take you to the library."

"The library? Why there?" Jake shook his head. He didn't see how he could practice and master his magic by reading some books.

"Control over the mist is limited by what you know you can do. When you understand your limits, you can work to push at them and improve. When you don't even know that an idea or option exists, the door is closed." Kenneth lightly patted Jake on the shoulder as they arrived at a pair of large wooden doors. "In the library, you can learn about what others have done. And about the creatures around you, so you don't make a fool of yourself."

With that said, the pixie pushed the doors open and led the way inside. The doors closed behind them silently once the two men were past the threshold.

Kenneth led Jake through the stacks, gesturing to symbols at the ends of each row. "Each of these symbols represents a type of book. You can learn them on your own time. I'm just going to show you the area that we're mostly going to be working in. History."

Jake gazed curiously at the books as they passed by. The titles of some books were legible, while others were written in a language he didn't know. One section he guessed was bibliographies, as he saw books titled "The life and death of Mahogany" and "The tale of Archibald."

"Go take a seat at that table. I'm going to pull out the first books you're going to be reading." Kenneth stopped and gestured toward the reading tables nearby before walking down a row of books, his eyes scanning the titles with a speed that surprised Jake.

The human never really thought of Kenneth as much of a reader. There were so many things he did not know about the pixie.

Taking a seat, Jake let his thoughts wander as he waited. What kind of history book would he read? The history of how magic came to exist, perhaps? He tried to find some excitement, but he didn't understand how this would teach him to be safe. Did Kenneth really care about his safety?

After several minutes of searching the shelves, Kenneth came back to the table holding two books and a scroll. The books were bound in different materials; one in old, worn leather, the other in more modern resin. Kenneth placed the two books to the side before unfurling the scroll out across the table. "Here, take a look."

Jake stared down at the old scroll. The language written on it made no sense to him. There were words that looked almost like English if the letters were different shapes, then other places that seemed more like hieroglyphics. Jake squinted, as if that would somehow make things clearer. After a minute of struggling to make sense of the scroll, he gave up. "Okay, I've looked. Am I supposed to be able to read this?"

"Not like that, you won't." Kenneth moved to sit across from Jake. "Step one is to go into the mist. The older texts are written in a language that shifts to match the reader's language in the mist, but it's gibberish on the page normally."

Shifting into the mist, Jake took another glance at the scroll. The letters and symbols wobbled, and the ink seemed to come to life. The scroll's contents oozed together into a single black puddle, and Jake glanced up at Kenneth. His newly crowned mentor was silent. Once he looked back down, Jake gasped in surprise. The puddle had transformed at that moment into neat, long lines of English across the entirety of the scroll. Skimming quickly, Jake noticed it was about the first magical humans and how they came to exist.

Before reading any further, the human returned from the mist and smiled despite himself. "I can read it now."

"Good." Kenneth rolled the scroll back, tying it off and gesturing to the other two books. "The leather-bound one is also written in that language, but the other one is in English. Mist-writing is a lost art. Reading these books will teach you about yourself, the culture of the pixies, and more. Alongside your reading, you will be practicing shifting back and forth between the mist quickly until it is second nature to you. I am going to leave on other duties for several days. When I return, I expect these books to be finished."

"I guess I can do that. I won't have much else to do. Anything else I should know?"

"Yes. Look through the mist before opening any doors. If there is a visible mark on the door, do not open it. Some places are off-limits. Focus on coming to the library and practicing here. Feel free to read from other sections if you get bored or want a change of pace. The focus is improving your knowledge, so all reading here will be good."

Jake smiled and nodded. Seemed simple enough. Read some books, practice some magic. Don't get caught raiding any rooms. He felt surprised that Kenneth would leave him to his own devices so soon into their arrival. He would not squander the opportunity. "I'll try my best not to get in any trouble on my first days here."

"Then I will leave you to it. Remember to practice shifting." The Scotsman returned the smile, getting up from the table and turning to walk off.

Jake waved a hand, already thinking about the other books that might be in the library. Studying history still seemed pointless. Hopefully, he could learn how to do some real magic here as well. First, he needed to make sure he wouldn't get in trouble. Unfurling the scroll again, the human got to work.

Kenneth knew from his schedule that the next few days would be too busy to check in on Jake, but he was loath to leave the human alone, so he went to the administrative office and waited in the queue until he was called up. He leaned in, turning on his most charming smile. "Hey, good afternoon. I was wondering if there were any magical teachers free to handle a S-class mark that got brought in. I'm busy with other duties right now."

"I was just looking into this for a previous agent, but I'm afraid nobody's available on the rosters. You're going to have to deal with him on your own until it opens up." The secretarial staff sitting behind the desk barely glanced up, placing a file of paperwork on the counter. "If you wish to go on the waiting list, fill out those forms. Have a nice day."

Resisting the urge to curse, Kenneth simply walked away. A waiting list was pointless. He would be available to deal with Jake for half of the week. The issue was making sure Jake was settled into a routine over the course of the next few days. This time was crucial, but Kenneth simply did not have the option to abandon his other charges. He growled with frustration as he made his way back to his quarters.

Once there, Kenneth reviewed his schedule book. He had sent out invitations and received responses from one of his A-class marks and two of his C-class marks. He had been working on a weekly schedule with the A-class mark. She wasn't human, so Kenneth had an easier time being direct with her about things. He hoped that meant his meeting with her would be simple, even though he expected her to give him a hard time. The C-class mark was usually a monthly visit, but the pixie figured a second visit in the same month wouldn't be too much of an issue. He hoped the others would get back in touch while he dealt with his current responses.

The A-class mark, a minotaur named Lucinda, had simply replied with "Yeah, sure, meet me at the usual place."

Kenneth rubbed his eyes. He dreaded it even as he focused his thoughts and once again whisked himself back to Japan. As soon as he arrived inside the backroom of the warehouse, Kenneth felt a soft hand grip him by the collar and lift him in the air. He didn't bother struggling, instead waving over his shoulder. "Hey Lucinda. Do you always have to greet me like this?"

Lucinda turned Kenneth to face her, then set him back down. Her voice boomed so loudly that it echoed. "Of course I do. You pixies are so clever with your magic, I need to remind you that I'm made of tough stuff too."

"But we both know your toughness isn't just about that toned body of yours." He looked up at the buff woman with a small smile. Minotaurs had a reputation as some of the most stubborn magical creatures around. They were usually smart, but their culture valued direct approaches to things that made them seem stupid to the less informed. Kenneth felt the tingle of the magic Lucinda had used to check his defenses against his neck. If he hadn't been able to hold her off, he was sure she would have done more than just pick him up. "Can we get down to business?"

"To defeat the Huns?" Lucinda smiled at her joke but quickly straightened her posture as Kenneth frowned at her. "Yeah, yeah. Sure. What's the situation, boss?"

"A magical human's been compromised and has been taken into the kingdom to be worked into the organization. I have to be the one to oversee him, so I'm clearing out my schedule. That includes trying to convince you that it's worth joining us instead of other factions."

The minotaur reared up and puffed out her chest. "You're saying this puny human's more important than me? Those are fighting words, pixie boy."

"He's an S-class level human. Even Maeva took interest when she met him. I'm sure you understand." Kenneth wasn't phased by her posturing. He knew as well as she did that he would win a confrontation if it came down to it. Not because he was more powerful. Simply because he was a better fighter. Her frustration with that knowledge and desire to beat him was part of why he felt he had a chance to convince her to join his cause to begin with. Usually, minotaurs kept to their own business. It took a compelling reason to make one leave its chosen territory. "Look, Lucinda. I don't have time to mince words with you on this. You know it, I know it. You've been testing me and pushing boundaries this whole time. How about we settle this over a blood-oath wager?"

"A blood-oath?" Lucinda stared at Kenneth, visibly dumbfounded. He had hoped the suggestion would catch her off guard. Blood-oaths were bound by the power of the mist itself. Neither of them could break the terms of such an agreement without suffering a fate worse than death.

When several seconds had passed without another word from Lucinda, the pixie assumed he had called her bluff. "If you're not down for it, then I guess you could say you've lo-"

"What are the terms?" She cut him off. A fiery glint lit her eyes as she cracked her knuckles. "If you want to challenge me, I'll do it."

With a sigh, Kenneth took two steps back, focused his magic to form a small blade to cut open his palm, and flicked the blood into the air between them. It hovered as the mist itself waited for the terms of the oath. He then adopted a battle stance. "The terms are simple. We fight. Right here, right now. If I win, you will meet me here again in one week's time to bind yourself to the service of the pixies should we ever have need of you. If I lose, you will never hear from me again."

"Agreed." Before she had even finished speaking, Lucinda had launched herself forward, driving a fist down toward Kenneth's face. With her agreement, the small droplets of blood hovering in the air cut open her cheek as she passed, mixing her blood to bind the oath.

In the mist, Kenneth saw the twin-spikes of power extending from her knuckles and deftly side-stepped as they swung by, sliding his foot along the ground and leaving traces of his power in the dust that was starting to get kicked into the air. He hopped back as Lucinda swung her arm into a ferocious back-swing. He knew a single punch from Lucinda would be devastating as she channeled the mist to increase the force of her blows. He continued to seep energy outward into the dust particles that passed him, tracing the small lines of his energy as he formed a lattice in the tight quarters of the room.

"Stop running and fight me." Lucinda roared, grabbing the desk that occupied one of the walls and tossing it through the air at Kenneth. He ducked under as it slammed into the wall behind him, only to have Lucinda tackle him to the ground. She grinned as she rested her weight against his stomach. "I have you now."

"Correction. You almost had me." Kenneth snapped his fingers, letting the power he had poured into the dust flare to life. The small particles Lucinda had breathed in during their battle as well as the traces in the air all began vibrating violently. The pain caused his larger opponent to clench her stomach and fall to her side. He sat up, coughing a bit. "Yield or I'll let them tear through you."

"I yield." She spat up a small gobbet of blood as Kenneth reined in his energy, pulling it back to himself. They both sat there panting and staring at each other. "You pixies and your clever magic."

"We both know you could have won that if you had devoted some energy to shield yourself. You're too hot-headed." Standing up, Kenneth dusted himself off. He was glad it had ended quickly. He barely had any reserves after staying up so many days without sleep. At the thought of sleep, his knees buckled. He fell forward into Lucinda's outstretched arm.

"Whoa there, boss. I didn't hit you that hard with the tackle did I?"

"No, I'm just… I haven't slept." Kenneth wheezed in breaths. He had invested a lot into that one attack. In retrospect, he might not have even had the energy to follow up on his threat. The pixie was glad Lucinda had chosen not to test it. His eyes closed in exhaustion as he felt Lucinda pick him up and prop him over her shoulder.

"Well, I might as well start my service a week early. I'm taking you home with me to rest. Presumably, I was the last order of business for you today."

"Yes." Kenneth inwardly scolded himself for pushing so far past his limits. If Anissa were there, she would have given him months of flak for performing so poorly. He drifted to sleep, imagining her fingertips clacking on a desk as he made a report of his efforts.

Kenneth gasped awake, flipping himself out of the unfamiliar bed and instantly crouching. The tension in his muscles instantly relaxed when Lucinda's head popped out from around the corner. He wasn't in danger. Not immediately, at least.

"So you're up." Lucinda walked in with a bowl of soup, pushing it into Kenneth's hands. "Drink up. I assume you'll be headed out on business. And I'll go about doing what I can do to help you Pixies."

Kenneth drank the soup as he listened, barely tasting it as he worked himself to full wakefulness. "Yes, I have so much work left to do. I don't have any directives for you, but I trust you'll keep your word. As you are oath-bound to me now, I will return sometime to collect on that."

"Yeah, yeah. Go get 'em, boss." Lucinda clapped Kenneth on the back, then walked off.

Taking the opportunity to look around, the pixie noted how clean Lucinda's home was. He did not notice any personal objects. The sterility matched what he would have imagined a Minotaur's home would be if it were forced to travel often, yet Lucinda had been in Japan for quite some time. He decided to ask her about her history at a later date. For now, he had other business to attend to. Placing the bowl onto the nightstand, Kenneth concentrated for a moment, then appeared in his room within the castle. He needed to check on Jake before he wrapped up his final duty, just to make sure the human hadn't gotten into too much trouble.

It didn't even take thirty minutes before Jake grew tired of reading about history. The scroll talked about how humanity first came to break through into the mist and tap into magic, but he didn't see how that related to him. With a heavy sigh, he leaned back in his chair and looked around him. The empty silence felt at odds with the constant shuffle of feet and grumble of voices in the rest of the castle.

Rows and rows of books were neatly ordered in lines from the door to the other end of the library, with reading tables set at intervals. Despite the vast collection of knowledge, Jake didn't see anybody else as he got up to wander between the stacks.

As he walked, Jake practiced shifting back and forth between the mist. Each step came smoother as his transition improved. Pausing for a moment to catch his breath, Jake stared at the side of a bookcase, curious to see what it contained. There were no visible labels. The human stared for a moment longer before turning to look around. How had Kenneth known there were sections? He shifted into the mist, hoping to see a sign there, but the bookcase remained unchanged. There was no indication of its contents.

It was then that he looked up and saw, hovering above the bookcases, a series of strange shapes that shifted like the scroll to reveal lettering. Here, the words "Fiction" hovered in ghostly green and black lettering. A few rows down, the aisle was marked as "Educational" and Jake assumed it meant about magic.

To his satisfaction, he found there were some books that described magic and the usages of the mist as he perused the spines. Grabbing a few choice books, he decided how he would spend his time between sessions of boring history lessons—learning and practicing real magic. Things that could save his life one day, that Kenneth, for some reason, refused to teach him.

Sitting down, he got to work learning everything he could.

Jake took two days to finish the scroll and one of the books Kenneth had given him. He spent almost all of his waking hours in the library, poring over them and other things he could find. If he was in the library, the human felt he could avoid notice, and it gave him access to what he hoped would be the keys to understanding the magical world. The historical books seemed dull at first, but as he got through the initial, normal information, things became more interesting.

The scroll described how humanity's inventiveness and creativity eventually broke through the gap between humans and the mist. Ancient shamans and spirit guides were those able to cross the divide. Different names were given to these people across many cultures, and their abilities varied. Some communed with creatures in the mist, while others took their visions to be the sightings of demons. The description of visions and mentions of humans with supernatural foresight sent a familiar tingle along Jake:s spine. He couldn't explain it, but he felt a need to know more.

The smaller of the books described standard culture and customs of the various races. One of them was entirely devoted to Pixies and their way of life. He read about the queen and how there was never a crowned king. Instead, a new queen was appointed from the surviving nobility after the previous rulers' passing. By never sticking to a bloodline, the Pixies believed they could promote evolution within their culture. And from the modern appliances and conveniences in the castle. Jake had a feeling they were doing just fine.

More interesting than the royalty was a description of the Pixie spy system. Pixies regularly sought out magical humans. The spies typically roamed the same set of countries, using their ability to teleport to avoid having to deal with customs or money. The weaker humans were left to their own devices and monitored by lower ranked, locally placed Pixies and their allies. More powerful humans were typically handled one of three ways. Some were killed, as they were deemed too dangerous to let live. Others had magic hidden from them for the rest of their lives, and the spy's new job would be to prevent that person's exposure to the magical world. Failing this, they were brought to the Pixie kingdom. There, it would be easier to keep watch over them and convince them to see the Pixies as allies rather than as a threat.

Jake realized very quickly upon reading through the section that Kenneth had to be a Pixie spy. There was no other explanation for his behavior. It was jarring to think that the person he had trusted wouldn't have batted an eye at killing him. How much of their shared experiences were fake? The idea that Kenneth was still working to manipulate him only strengthened Jake's resolve to learn as much about the mist while Kenneth was gone as he possibly could. The less directed his path, the better. And the more equipped he would be to deal with potential betrayal.

Despite the knowledge he had gained over the past couple of days, Jake felt unsatisfied. He had learned almost nothing about himself or how to use the mist in more complex ways. Most of the books he read described techniques, yet he failed to mimic them in every attempt. The scroll sometimes described mystical feats performed by human sages, but there were no notes about how Jake could do these same wonders.

Jake groaned in frustration. Shifting into the mist, he left his body behind as he explored the shelves around him. He found it easier, after his practice, to explore the library while in the mist. He could move faster now that he wasn't relying on his body, and the floating symbols made his searches easier. Flitting from row to row, he searched. He wasn't entirely sure what he wanted to find. Wandering by instinct, he eventually arrived in a section devoted to subjects that the pixies had not yet fully researched. The bookcase was small and almost empty, but a book titled "The Types Of Mistical Humans" caught his eye. This was it. This is what he did not know he had been seeking.

Returning to his body, Jake rushed to where he had found the tome and collected it before returning to his reading table. With a glance through the table of contents, the human smiled to himself as he found a section titled "The Powerful Ones." Every story in the history books that included pixies bringing a human back to their kingdom involved someone powerful that they wanted to keep safe or control to keep themselves safe.

If what Kenneth had said before was true, then a key to Jake's ability to use and master his power was learning what he was. He spent the better part of the evening reading about every type of powerful mist-user known to the pixies. Whenever a skill or technique was described, Jake took a moment to attempt it. Most of them had no result. He simply could not do them. Others worked, but not as brilliantly as described. Whenever he had partial success, Jake noted the section for review.

None of the different types felt accurate until he chanced upon a section titled "Seers." Unlike most of the other types of humans, the description was lacking in detail. The author had merely written that Seers were capable of "seeing" and connecting to the very fabric of the mist. Their insights made them capable of piercing through illusions, at times able to see the future, and dangerous to let fall into the wrong hands. Seers were said to go on quests to unlock their power, but no pixie had ever observed the process to understand it. There were no techniques described. No great feats performed by previous humans of note. Instead, the author lamented the fact Seers were too rare and solitary to be researched.

Something within Jake's gut seemed to uncoil as he finished reading. Despite the lack of information, he knew this was what he was. He could feel it. Jake shifted into the mist, glanced about with a more critical eye, and noticed how the coiling tendrils of the mist seemed almost to reach out to him; beckoning. He could see it now. Or rather, he finally understood what he had always seen.

Chapter 15

On the morning of the third day, Jake cracked open the third book that Kenneth had assigned him. The title read "The Creatures and Entities of the Mist." Jake felt impatient as he read through boring descriptions about the eating habits of house gnomes. This wasn't nearly as exciting as the possibility of exploring the mist. If he wasn't afraid of Kenneth coming back, Jake would have just spent the entire time examining the mist and pushing himself to see more, to try and get some glimpse of the future or a hidden signal. Anything to confirm his belief that he was what he believed himself to be.

Jake turned the pages more quickly, flipping through to find anything that might be related to him. It wasn't until he reached the final section of the book that he stopped and read the first sentence aloud to himself. "The Dirges are an ancient, powerful race of creatures known to some as fonts of knowledge and others as living demons."

The mention of knowledge immediately piqued his interest. If these creatures were ancient and knowledgeable, perhaps one of them would know about Seers. Reading further, Jake learned that Dirges spent much of their time in dark places, feeding off of the thoughts and collected energies of other creatures in the mist. The older they were, the larger they grew. Their powers were fed by memories and emotions. Wherever there were large collections of magical creatures, there was a good chance that a Dirge lived underneath them and grew fat upon their accumulated energies.

All of the descriptions warned of the Dirges as being unpredictable and difficult to understand. Their motivations were unknown even after generations of researchers devoted their lives to the study of these living relics. Jake skimmed a few pages past numerous tales of those who had come across Dirges to find some mention of how he could find one. To his surprise, the author of the book had a personal anecdote of their own encounter with one. Unlike the calm, collected tone in the other stories, this page alone expressed the horror and fascination of the beast.

The author described how she had found one within the Underdark, a forbidden underground warren beneath the Pixie Kingdom. The hulking monstrosity had communicated through the mist with the author, yet even their brief conversation had been so straining that she had fainted before learning anything of note. The pressure of a Dirge's mind had nearly broken her. When she awoke, she found herself in her room again, yet she could still sense the Dirge's presence in the darkness below. Every few days, a piece of information or insight would bubble up from that connection, and she would learn some new secret about a creature she was studying or think of a new technique to cultivate herbs in her private garden.

In exchange, the emotions she felt dulled. Her day-to-day life took on hints of grey, and the excitement and passion she once felt for her work slowly drained from her. In the end, she wondered if her pursuit of knowledge had cost her more than she had gained.

Jake closed the book and stared at his hands. Someone had gone through the trouble of chronicling their own gradual decay from a short conversation with a Dirge. Yet his instincts were screaming at him to seek this creature out. Him. Someone with almost no experience with more normal creatures of the mist, let alone some inscrutable and powerful monster. His hands started to shake as his heart battled with his mind. Pushing against this strange sensation, Jake slammed his palms into the table and decided to delay the search. First, he would do research into the Underdark; how to find it, and what creatures he might encounter. Afterward, he would steel himself to survive his meeting with the Dirge. Then, he would go looking for it. Anything to stall what felt like an inevitability. When he closed his eyes, he could feel the mist wrap around him and whisper wordlessly. Against his better judgment, he could tell his path led down. Down into the dark.

The mist coiled and twisted as Jake focused his energy upon it. With his newfound vision, he was starting to learn, however slowly, how to bend the very fabric of the mist to his will. Grasping at a string of mist that lined the wall, he pulled gently at the tendrils until the line snapped, reforming the frayed ends afterward. He wasn't sure how this power would be of use yet, but he was intent on mastering it.

As he started his return to his body, Jake felt the mist ripple. Rounding the corner, there stood a massive, furry creature with pale-white eyes staring at him from the center of its body.

"So it is you! Seer. You are the one doing this."

Each word pounded against Jake's skull like a fist. He flinched, taking a step back from the monstrosity as it moved toward him. "I... I don't mean any harm. Kenneth brought me here."

The Guardian uncurled its body to tower over Jake, slashing a claw through the air above him. "I know, seer. That fool brought you here, and it threatens everything. You are already tearing at the security measures I placed within the kingdom."

"What security measures? I am just… just practicing. Kenneth told me to learn how to use the mist." Jake glanced about, wondering how he would escape if this creature attacked him. It seemed very angry. Kenneth had said this place was safe as long as Jake didn't go wandering about talking to people. What had he done wrong?

"You seers play with the mist without a thought to the weave. You just tore strands away from my delicate web of defenses." The furry creature curled its body inward, hovering its clawed fingers threateningly close to Jake's face. "I'm watching you. If you continue to sabotage our work here, I will not hesitate to kill you. Give me an excuse, human. I will savor it."

The Guardian turned, a ripple went through the mist, and it was gone. Jake stared at the place where it had vanished. His mist-form shook, and his thoughts raced. Urgently, he dashed back to his body.

Kenneth turned the corner of the library only to have Jake rush toward him and grab him by the shoulders. The urgency in Jake's voice was a stark contrast to his normal demeanor. Jake shook the one responsible for him being here, his voice echoing in the otherwise quiet library. "Why did you bring me somewhere so unsafe? You said I had nothing to worry about. But clearly, I do."

"Whoa, Jake." Kenneth pushed Jake's hands off and looked around. With a quick sweep, there were no visible threats to Jake's well-being. Not even in the mist. "What do you mean by unsafe? I promised you would be protected here, and I didn't lie. What's gotten into you?"

With his initial rush of emotions poured out, Jake gasped for air as he looked around for a sign of the creature before speaking.

"There was this… furry… thing. It threatened to kill me. Said it was watching me. I thought you said I was welcome here, Kenneth. That monster made it very clear I wasn't."

"The guardian was here? He spoke to you?" Kenneth copied Jake, looking around for some sign of the creature. Why had it approached Jake so carelessly? The Queen had put Jake into Kenneth's care. The disrespect and distrust chafed against Kenneth's pride. "What did he say? What did you do?"

Jake shook his head. "No, you don't get to interrogate me. You brought me here, but you would have just as easily killed me. I learned a lot while you were gone. Our friendship was a lie. All part of your job as a spy, right? Why didn't you just kill me and be done with it?"

"Jake, it's not so simple." Kenneth sighed. His shoulders slumped slightly as the weight of his exhaustion suddenly pressed against him again. Jake had put more pieces together than he had expected. "I had a choice to kill you or bring you here. I chose to fight to keep you alive because I saw you would be a good thing in the world. I got to know you. You are a good person. We need good people helping us."

"Oh, so it's just as simple as me being pure-hearted?" Jake scoffed. "Next, you'll say I'm the only one who can wake up the princess with a kiss."

"Okay, okay." Kenneth raised his hands in surrender. "You're right. It's because I thought your power was of use. Seers are known to change the flow of the world. Depending on who directs your power, it could force history down very different paths. I hoped, and still hope, you will choose to help us shape the world. Instead of acting against us."

Jake ground his teeth at the implied threat. He felt certain he didn't want any part of this, whatever it was. But he could tell he had no way forward except to at least pretend to help. If Kenneth believed in Jake, that could be a way to work toward his freedom. Trust. "Right. I won't forgive you, but I can still work with you. We both have the same goal. To help me master my powers. But… what about the creature from before? The guardian, you called it."

"The guardian keeps the pixie kingdom safe. He's a creature that specializes in defensive magics and the like. If he threatened you, he must have thought you were doing something to put the kingdom in danger. What did you do?"

"I…. There were tendrils of mist, and I changed how they were tied together."

Kenneth looked confused for the first time since Jake had met him. "You did what? How is that even… nevermind. If you mess with the defenses of the castle, the guardian will think you're trying to sabotage our security and feel threatened. Don't do it again."

The encounter with the creature had left Jake with a very different impression. That thing seemed like it had a grudge. Still, if Kenneth wasn't concerned, Jake couldn't show it. He nodded silently.

"Well… with that settled. I am going to teach you a technique of the mist. To help your training. Are you ready?" Kenneth determined the best way to move forward was to both test Jake's strength and distract the human from the unpleasant encounter with the guardian.

Jake stared at Kenneth in surprise. They were going to go from an argument to training? The shift seemed strange. Perhaps Kenneth hoped to distract him from his thoughts? Whatever the reason, Jake decided to play along. Learning more wouldn't hurt, anyway. "Okay, sure."

"The mist can be used for many things, but everything comes down to the same basic idea. It's all about the mind. Your will, the will of those around you, and the will of the mist itself. The tougher the task, the more willpower you need. If what you're trying to do involves another person or creature, then you have to push through their will and their resistances. For example, if I tried to convince you that you wanted to dance, I could do so like… this." Ken visibly focused himself, the mist forming not around him but around Jake.

The mist pressed inward toward Jake as he felt the desire to dance start to bubble from within him.

Not wanting to embarrass himself, Jake tried to resist. He reacted instinctively, mentally reaching out to the mist around him and tearing the coils, pushing them away. The feeling started to vanish.

Kenneth was shocked as Jake instinctively tore apart the mist and swiftly disarmed him. The ferocity of the counter caused him to instinctively reach out with greater strength, slamming the mist into Jake and overwhelming the human with the desire to dance. After a few moments, the pixie caught himself and relaxed his hold on Jake. His voice shook with the strain. "You… what you did there was impressive, Jake. You defended yourself well. With practice, you'll be strong enough to resist me at full power."

Jake nodded to Kenneth, frustrated that he couldn't defend himself but also happy to have realized that he could fight back. The idea that people could manipulate desires and thoughts was frightening but knowing that he would learn to keep himself safe from it gave Jake a feeling of empowerment. He could regain control, if he put his mind to it. And perhaps this could teach him how to do other things, in time.

Jake resolved to practice his technique on his own time as much as he could. That creature would not kill him if he had anything to say about it. "Can we do that again?"

Kenneth nodded, and the two of them spent the next few hours practicing until Jake was able to resist the Pixie's pressure for a full minute. "Let's call it a day here. You can practice controlling the mist on your own time, even without someone attacking you. Keep at it, and maybe you'll be able to stop me completely next time."

Jake was too wrapped up in his own thoughts to respond properly, but Kenneth was similarly distracted. It was clear that something needed to be done about Jake's development. The two of them left the library and went to their own rooms to rest and consider the recent events.

Jake woke up in the middle of the night with a start. Glancing around, he saw nothing. He strained his ears, giving himself a headache searching for something in the silence. The shadows cast by the moon loomed as he dressed himself. A moment's pause and the shadows turned into coiling mist. Empty, yet more alive for the transition.

He could tell that nothing was there, but it was too late to go back to sleep. His mind was fully awake, and the adrenaline was pumping through his system. The talons of the guardian flashed in his mind's eye. He had to do something more than wait for that thing to come for him. Jake shook his head as he recalled Kenneth's promise. Likely story.

Slinking out of his room, the human wandered the castle halls until he arrived at the library. His bare feet made no noise as he walked across the carpeted floor. Relying on the light filtering through the curtains, he moved between the stacks. Eventually, he found the section titled "History." With a soft sigh of relief, he pulled out the book about the Pixie Kingdom's history. He didn't know why he had felt concerned it would be missing.

Shifting into the mist, Jake was surprised by how crisp the lettering of the book was. Every word was clear despite the darkness around him. As he shifted through the book, he managed to find only one passage that mentioned the Underdark. It was a warren of underground tunnels, the entrances blocked from view by illusory magics. The researcher who had made their way down into the Underdark had managed to do so by summoning a rat-like creature called a Gibberer. These creatures were able to sniff out or even create alternative entrances and tunnels to bypass security measures. Gibberers were unable to control the mist properly, so they were easily attracted to mist-created food such as apples or peaches.

The other creatures in those depths were mostly unstudied and potentially very dangerous to the unprepared. Yet, there were also tales of great treasure and artifacts of power if one knew where to look.

Returning the book to the shelf, Jake shook his head. It had been less helpful than he had hoped. How was he supposed to know where to summon the Gibberer if the entrance was hidden to begin with?

While he was readying himself to return to his room, Jake heard the shuffling of feet and saw light shining from around the corner. In a panic, the human turned around, walking one shelf further away and hiding behind the stacks of books in a low crouch. He couldn't see the two figures through the shelf, but he heard their voices.

"Why does the boss need us to get a book this late?" A low, tired voice whined.

"You know how the guardian is. He makes strange requests about books all the time." There was a loud yawn.

"Still, a book on the pixie kingdom? Wouldn't he know everything by now?"

"That's none of our business. We're guards, not researchers. Let's go."

Jake listened tensely as their footsteps vanished, releasing the breath he didn't realize he'd been holding. The guardian had taken the book. How had he known to come read it now? Jake pondered the question as he hurried back to his room.

Slipping into his bed, the realization struck him. The story of seers being able to predict the future. What if this was the same thing? Had he detected something of the future in his sleep? The panic had been his instincts warning him. If that were true, then he had a way to find the Underdark's secret entrance. He had to learn how to pierce through illusions. Jake yawned as his mind slowly slipped into the darkness of sleep. It would be a consideration for tomorrow.

Kenneth tapped his foot impatiently on the carpeted floor of the Queen's waiting room. It had taken him several hours to get this audience, but the ten minutes he had been sitting on the couch felt longer.

Jake's power growing so quickly was a concern. He couldn't be left unchecked. With a heavy sigh, Kenneth thought over the events at the library. The human had shocked Kenneth by retaliating so effectively in the mist. Already, the seer was able to toy with the essence of magic. How much longer before he was too strong to be controlled?

The pixie spy immediately snapped out of his reverie when the doors were pushed open. Quickly walking in, he glared momentarily at the guardian standing off to the side before kneeling before the Queen. "My liege."

"Stand, Kenneth. You asked for this audience, what is the matter?"

"The seer that I brought is growing powerful. Faster than I expected. The guardian threatened him this afternoon. We can't be so direct, lest we scare him off."

The guardian hissed, jabbing one of its claws in the air at Kenneth. "If your pet human hadn't been subtly tearing apart the weave of our defenses, I would have left him alone. He is a danger to us all. You left him alone for days to wander the library and look what it has already wrought."

"It has wrought nothing." Kenneth clenched his fists. "But you are right. I was a fool to leave him alone. We must keep his education in check. Most books in the library are harmless, but there is… one. A book that details the Underdark. I believe we must keep him from journeying into those depths. I can not guess how strong he will be if he survives it."

The Queen looked quizzically at the two of them. "If that is all, then remove the book. This did not need my attention, Kenneth. You were told to handle this. Handle it."

"I can't be seen by Jake. If he knows I am limiting him, he will feel betrayed. I need to keep his trust. The guards under our guardian's command, however…."

The guardian's furry form trembled with what appeared to be excitement. "Yes, yes. I see. I shall order for the book to be confiscated. The human will be kept in check. I agree to this, if you will keep a closer eye on him. We can not afford for that monster to be let loose within the kingdom. He might very well unravel everything."

"Fine. I will make sure he is busy during the day, with no time to mess with things he shouldn't. If I take a more hands-on approach with his learning, perhaps I can stop him from exploring his limits beyond what we need. At least, until I can convince him to truly ally with us."

"Well, it is settled then. Guardian. Kenneth. Go about your duties." The snap of the Queen's fingers marked the end of the audience.

The guardian and Kenneth walked their separate ways, a thin truce formed between them.

The following morning, Kenneth waited patiently by Jake's bedside. He knew from their lengthy friendship roughly when the human usually woke up, so he had just enough time to mentally review what he was going to say before he said it. He had to be sure to not hint at the human that anything was wrong or unusual. He smiled as Jake's eyes fluttered open and focused on him. "Good, you're awake. Sorry about the intrusion, I just wanted to catch you as soon as possible. I know I've been leaving you to your own devices. Starting tomorrow, I'm going to be putting my other duties aside to focus on helping you learn more about our world. This way, you won't upset the guardian, and I'll keep you safe."

Jake rubbed the sleep from his eyes, using it as an excuse to cover his face as he worked through his rising panic. If Kenneth was going to be around all the time, that would be a problem. The human thought through his options in a rush, even as he forced a smile on his face. "Oh, good. I'm happy I'll have someone I can rely upon to guide me. I've felt so lost with all this knowledge that feels just out of reach."

"As a result of this, I have to spend today cleaning up the rest of my duties. Handing them off to other operatives and making sure everything is together. Can I trust you to behave yourself for one day?" Kenneth's tone was light, but even Jake knew the question was serious.

"Of course. I don't want to upset that... creature from before. I'll keep myself out of trouble."

Kenneth nodded and walked to the door, glancing back at Jake for a moment before leaving. He made his way briskly back to his own quarters and checked his appearance. After some minor adjustments, he focused and teleported himself just outside of Wilbur's office. If things went as planned, Yutaro would have marked his home by now.

Jake waited for a minute before hurriedly getting dressed and peeking out the door to see if anyone was around. If today was his only chance at finding the Underdark, he would have to start preparations for the journey right away. Who knew how long it would really take Kenneth to finish his affairs?

The human gathered food from the dining hall, focusing on non-perishables like bread and fruit. Stuffing them in a pack, Jake rushed to the library. He grabbed only the book that discussed Seers, hoping that it might help him in some way bargain with the Dirge. If that was how things would even work.

Lastly, Jake returned to his room to grab a stick of chalk and a flashlight. He did not intend to get lost in those maze-like tunnels if he could avoid it.

With his preparations completed, all that was left was to find the entrance to the Underdark. Jake started to explore the lower levels of the castle, using the quick-mist technique that Kenneth taught him to examine doors and archways for any signs that might indicate he was meant to stay out. As the day turned into afternoon, Jake came upon a wall covered by a drape. In the mist, lines of magic crossed the wall unlike any other location he had seen. Somehow, he could tell that these lines resembled trip-wires. If he cut them carelessly or walked through them, something would happen.

Jake instinctively wrapped his own energy around each line, gently teasing their connections and shifting their purpose. Instead of recognizing him as a threat, the tendrils understood him to be part of the system. They wouldn't break if he passed through them, unlike any normal creature. As he held out his hand to test his work, the wall behind the drape shifted, swinging inward and allowing access. Access to the Underdark.

Chapter 16

Finding the entrance to the Underdark turned out to be only the first half of the battle to find the Dirge. Despite marking each passage and tunnel that he explored, Jake continued to get turned around in circles. It was as if each new tunnel was just an alternate way back to the start.

The twisting tunnels and multiple dead ends were difficult to navigate and even harder to feel safe. Many times, he heard the sounds of growling or deep breathing that frightened him, and Jake hurried back the way he came for fear of being caught by some hungry dweller of the darkness.

More and more, Jake found himself searching for clues in the mist to no avail. Hours passed, and the human eventually stopped for a break. Jake took a moment to think about his options. His mind turned back to the mention of the Gibberer. Perhaps now was the time. Focusing his mind, Jake collected the mist. He carefully formed the most perfect apple that he could manage. He placed his creation in the center of the room and waited, curled up against the wall with the flashlight off.

Jake didn't notice the arrival of the creature at first. Only when it let out a loud squeak did he realize that his bait had worked. Looking up into the mist, Jake saw a mouse-like creature that was barely half his height, cowering backwards. "P… please! No eat me!"

Its evident fear helped Jake feel calm, the pounding of his heart in his chest slowly died down. He wasn't sure what he had expected, but he was happy the creature seemed docile.

Holding out his hands, Jake approached slowly. "Whoa, calm down. I won't eat you. I just want some help."

The whiskered nose protruding from its face twitched as its eyes darted around as if checking to see if there were any other potential predators. Jake could hear the small muffled squeaks and clicks of its tongue as it decided what to do, wringing its small paws against each other. "Me no want trouble"

Jake was sure this was a Gibberer. Jake knew he didn't have time to create anything and instead reached into his pack with one hand. Pulling out another apple like the one it had already devoured, Jake rolled it across the floor. He tried to keep his voice calm and even to avoid scaring the small creature. "Here, here. Eat that. I just want some information about these tunnels. I'm looking to go deeper. Do you know anything?"

The snout quickly went down toward the apple to inspect it, even as the beady eyes warily watched Jake's every move. The human kept very still, waiting as the little thing first picked up the apple, feeling its textures before taking a small bite. "S… so good!"

The Gibberer took another bite. And another. The entire apple was quickly consumed, core and stem included.

The nervous air around the Gibberer didn't vanish completely, but it seemed to relax more. Its body was no longer visibly tense. Its tail no longer swiped at the air.

Jake smiled encouragingly. "I'm looking for a way deeper. A safe way into the darkness. Can you help?"

The creature took a few moments, sniffing the air as it thought about its response. "More good?"

Jake stared at it blankly for a few moments before realizing that it was asking for more food. He begrudgingly took another apple from his pack, tossing it to the Gibberer.

The second apple vanished even faster than the first, and the little thing licked its lips with evident delight.

"So… will you help me f-" before Jake could finish, the mouse-man darted over to the wall that he had been resting against, pressing its small paws against the wall and pushing. The misty construction of the wall split open at the touch, seamlessly forming a new passageway. The path looked as if it had always been there.

The mouse-man turned to look back, squeaked, then darted off down the passage. Jake hurried after it, wondering at the little beast's power.

Several minutes passed with Jake simply following after his small, furry guide. The human made sure to mark each turn and corridor that split off with a symbol or two indicating where he needed to go. Jake could tell that we were getting deeper as the areas they passed through seemed to become rougher.

There were fewer signs of inhabitants, and fewer sounds overall. It was as if by being so deep that even the residents grew quieter. Suddenly, the Gibberer paused in a room, sniffing the air before turning to speak. "Is deep deep now. You happy, yes? Give good?"

Holding out one hand to placate the mouse as it stared expectantly, Jake concentrated on the mist. After having spent so much time in the mist, the apple formed almost instantly. Jake stared in surprise. It was getting easier every time. Perhaps there was some connection between spending time in the mist and his ability to control it?

Jake cast the thought aside as he handed the apple to his guide. Suddenly, Jake felt a tug on his mind. Turning his attention to it, the human didn't notice as the mouse-man squeaked and fled. It, too, had felt the tug.

He could sense something on the other end of that tug. He was being pulled. The feeling was faint, but it throbbed like a sore tooth. After a moment's concentration, he found that he could detect the general direction of the source. He started moving, carefully, toward it.

His steps led him to a corridor, one door barely visible at the end of it. The door was different from the wall around it. The frame and handle of the door seemed to pulse like a heartbeat, whereas the walls around were perfectly still.

The darkness seemed to grow deeper as he approached the door to where he hoped the Dirge maintained its solitude. Jake could feel a pressure, an instinct to run and never come back, growing stronger with each step forward. He shoved the irrational fear away. He had come this far, it would be pointless to turn back now.

The journey down that hallway felt like it stretched for hours as the shadows seemed to reach out for him. With a shaking hand, Jake pulled at the doorknob and opened it. Strangely, as the door swung open, the world seemed to grow brighter.

Jake's eyes, which had grown used to the dim, stung from the more normal lighting. It was as if, by crossing the threshold, the shroud of fear and dark was left behind. Slowly, his eyes adjusted to the light.

A hulking, shivering mass towered above him. Sickly green smoke flowed from twisted tubes in the flesh, vanishing upward into the invisible ceiling. Jake knew it had to be the Dirge, for its appearance was the same as the drawings in the books. Its words washed over him as the mass spoke through the mist.

"You… what pain have you come to deliver? What new misery will you invoke?" Jake gasped as its voice echoed through the mist, rocking his mind. He felt his mist-form fuzz under its scrutiny, as if the weight of the Dirge's mind alone was slowly eating away at him. The pain was overwhelming.

Jake couldn't focus long enough to communicate properly; images and snatches of thoughts bubbled up at random, barely forming before being split by a spear of agony. Jake could feel these fragments and emotions being read by the Dirge as its pressure seemed to decrease; the thundering becoming a heavy hand rather than a crushing fist.

"Ahhh… your pain is not for me. It is within you. But you seek my help. Help I am unable to give without a price." The words formed images in Jake's mind of previously paid prices. People crying as they sacrificed prized possessions, lost limbs, forgot memories of their loved ones. All of them experiencing new pain, new sadness, which fed the Dirge's magic. This understanding came to the human, unspoken, from the river of consciousness shared.

Jake saw himself sacrificing Ken to the Dirge. He felt the power surging through him as he gave his friend's life in exchange for the knowledge of who and what he was.

For a few moments, the sensation of total control was intoxicating in that imagined time. Then Jake came back to his senses, crying out in fear and shock. He was ashamed of himself and appalled by the offer being given. He ran.

Within minutes of Kenneth's arrival in front of Wilbur's office, Madison showed up. "Was waiting for you to show up back here. He's marked his home. Let's go."

The two made their way to Yutaro's home, and the locks on the doors clicked before they had even reached the intercom. Wordlessly, the two of them walked into the entryway of the paranoid human's home.

"Same as last time, any sudden moves, and this all gets broadcast to the world." Yutaro waved the small hand-held device around for emphasis.

Madison smiled slightly and nodded her head. "Yes, I understand. I assume from the marked door that you're interested in the offer. My employer would be most pleased to have you working with us."

"Yeah, about that. How do I know this isn't just a trap?" Yutaro's squirrelly expression flitted back and forth between both Kenneth and Madison. Kenneth noticed the tendrils of Yutaro's power as he reached out to read Kenneth's mind. The pixie carefully opened a controlled hole in his defenses, allowing the human to read just enough to make Kenneth seem open and honest. He watched as Madison did the same.

While Yutaro did his probing, Madison continued speaking as if nothing was happening. "Like all situations like these, it requires some trust between us. I, and my employer, are taking a risk by reaching out to both Kenneth and yourself. As an extension, we would appreciate you taking the opportunity to work toward a mutually beneficial arrangement. If you use your... abilities to assist us, we will pay you. Not just in money, but also in information. We could help you learn how to hone your skills. To grow even more powerful. Does that appeal to you?"

Yutaro's eyes flashed with greed at the mention of growing more powerful. The tension in his shoulders relaxed. "A tempting offer. I will accept working with you, if it means I can understand what my powers are and what it all means. But remember that I will be watching you. If anything happens to me, this whole shadow deal will be brought to light."

"As you wish. We are happy to have you onboard, Yutaro. I will be working with you directly from here on, as Kenneth is not within our circle. I hope you both understand this precaution."

The human nodded, and Kenneth bowed his head in understanding, walking out the door. Once he was out of range of Yutaro's surveillance, he let himself breathe a sigh of relief. It was done. The hand-off had gone even smoother than he had hoped. Madison had played well to mention power. Paranoia often was trumped by the desire to know and understand.

With his work done, Kenneth finally had his obligations completed so that he could focus on Jake. It had been longer than he had hoped. Shifting back to his room, Kenneth did not bother changing as he walked purposefully to the library. Not finding Jake there, he assumed the human was asleep and returned to his quarters for the night. He could start things off with Jake in the morning.

Jake ran through different passages, almost blind in his attempts to escape from the Dirge. It did not take long for him to become lost without his mousey guide. The human gasped and shook, leaning against a wall. Had the Dirge truly offered power and knowledge in exchange for Kenneth's life? Jake pushed the thought out of his mind. He needed to make his way back to the surface before anything else. Forcing himself to calm down, he remembered the chalk marks he had made earlier. Jake retraced his steps, eventually finding one of his chalked signs. The journey back felt twice as long as Jake constantly checked every wall for his signs, but he eventually made it.

Once he exited into the castle hallway, Jake started to notice a sensation in the back of his mind. It felt as if there was a constant rumble and pressure, like an engine providing power to some unseen machine. Poking around at his own mind, the human realized that it was the weight of the Dirge. Even after having come to the surface, the monster's presence was strong. The sheer strength of the creature became apparent. The reality that it had the strength to follow up on its end of the deal hit Jake. If Jake offered Kenneth to the Dirge, he would be able to learn what he needed to know to embrace his power as a Seer. He shook his head. The cost was too great. He would have to find another way forward.

Jake spent the next few days on auto-pilot. Because of this, the next few days with Jake were surprisingly easy for Kenneth. The human did as he was told and studied whatever he was instructed to study. He met Kenneth for his teachings, and he continued to search the library for more information about Seers. Despite the hours spent in the pursuit of knowledge, the human found nothing more about his powers, and he didn't grow at all. During Kenneth's lessons, Jake was, at times, too distracted to perform even simpler tasks.

The mistakes in his practice grew more and more common and problematic. When Kenneth tried questioning his charge, the human was evasive. After a particularly unproductive day with Jake, Kenneth grew tired of the secrecy. In the evening, Kenneth teleported into the middle of Jake's room as the human was changing.

"Jake… what did you do?" Jake turned to find Kenneth staring at him, his eyes wide with shock.

"What do you mean?"

Kenneth grabbed Jake's arm, dragging him to a mirror and forcing him to turn his back to it. "Look."

There was nothing in the mirror. Jake turned to face his former friend, confused. "What am I supposed to be seeing?"

"In the mist. Look in the mist, Jake." Kenneth's anxiety grew. The change in that too could only mean something bad was happening. While the pixie didn't know the cause, he knew enough to want to question Jake about his activities.

The anxiety in Kenneth's voice caught Jake off guard, and the human immediately shifted into the mist to check what was horrifying the usually stoic pixie.

After shifting into the mist, the mirror's reflection shocked him. The tattoo on Jake's back had twisted and changed. There was now a depiction of a sinister, clawed hand about to close around Jake's body. It wasn't visible to Jake when looking at himself normally, yet in the mirror, the truth was somehow revealed. Had Kenneth's talk about being marked for death become literal?

Jake stared, stunned, at the imagery. Some trick made it seem as if the thing were moving with every breath he took. The clutching talons appeared to flex and strain with each up and down motion. The human dragged his misty fingers across his own back, trying to see if he could disperse it. Nothing happened. His mind instantly went to the Dirge. Had it done this to him? The books hadn't mentioned anything like this.

As Jake stood silently and stared at his tattoo in the mist, Kenneth's concern was overshadowed by his suspicion. The human should have been begging him for answers by now. Still, outright distrust would only cause problems. Kenneth took on a confused tone, hoping to solicit some honesty. "Why haven't you freaked out yet?"

Jake knew he couldn't tell the truth. The tattoo wasn't nearly as strange as meeting the Dirge, and he felt this had to be connected somehow. In all the commotion with everything else that had been going on, the human had forgotten about the tattoo on his back. There had been no mention of it since he had arrived. Jake resolved to look into it on his next visit to the library. Returning to the moment, he tried to think of a proper response to Kenneth. Jake needed some way to deflect him and gain the space needed to find things out. "I, uh… I am. Or would be, if I knew what the hell this was. Just another thing I haven't learned about yet."

The words came out harsher than Jake had intended; his defensiveness making him lash out as the only alternative to keep Kenneth away.

Kenneth's face twisted for a moment with pain at the half-spoken accusation before his own anger came forward. The human so completely distrusted him after all he had done to keep him safe. "You think it's easy teaching you? You think I wanted this? You chose the painful path. You talked to Maeva. This is not on me. I could have made this a much less painful, more gradual process if not for your spontaneous foolishness."

Kenneth focused his will, quickly transporting himself through the mist. Arriving back in his own room, he grit his teeth as he considered what to do. Jake was clearly not going to be honest and forthright with him, whatever the human's reasons were. This left only two options. Kenneth could follow Jake around, or he could do research on his own into the change into Jake's tattoo. Walking back toward Jake's room, Kenneth used the mist to cover his presence and hide as he waited for Jake to exit. After an hour of waiting without the human emerging, Kenneth gave up. He instead made his way to the library.

Once there, Kenneth gathered several tomes relating to curses, illnesses, and creatures of the mist. At least one of them had to have an indication as to what might have caused Jake's current state. From there, he could perhaps get the full truth. The pixie spent much of the evening delving into the tomes, cross-referencing, and making notes as best he could. There was no point in investing so much energy to help Jake's magic improve if the human died in the process. Kenneth's sleep could wait, as could the training sessions with Jake. As long as he could figure out a cure to the problem. Kenneth spent several hours into the night poring through the volumes, eventually narrowing the possibilities down to a select few. With that done, he collected the useful books and returned the others. Making his way to his quarters, he began to search for clues in earnest.

Jake somewhat regretted having said something so cruel to Kenneth. He hadn't asked any questions about the tattoo, nor had he looked for information about it. It wasn't Kenneth's fault. Yet at the same time, Jake knew he couldn't trust the pixie spy with everything. At least, not until he came to a decision about how to move forward.

Once Kenneth had left, Jake let himself panic. Was this caused by the Dirge? It had to be. But how? He hadn't read enough in the book. He must have skipped something important. The only way Jake knew to make progress was to explore the library. At that moment, the human wished he knew of some way to get in contact with Maeva or Eve. Both of them seemed to know so much that they could surely have helped. But Jake had no clue how to reach out to Eve or anybody else through the mist. He had somehow attracted Eve's attention before, but he was afraid of simply shouting into the mist and summoning less-friendly individuals or alerting the guardian. The mere thought of the creature sent a shudder through Jake.

Feeling overwhelmed and alone, part of Jake wished to just undo everything. To go back to the simple times and easy life that Jake had had before. Was he really so unhappy with his previous life? He had good friends, a decent job, and a peaceful existence. There was so little stress and worry. Ever since joining the world of magic, it had been nothing but stress and worry. Jake had wanted a greater sense of purpose and control over his life, but even magic seemed useless. He still felt he had no control.

Jake shook his head. No point thinking about that now. He needed to deal with the decision rather than simply regretting it. The Dirge had done something to him. The human hadn't made any deals with it, yet for some reason it had marked him. Jake was sure of it. His fear of dragging Ken into it before he was ready caused him to hurt his only potential ally. Muttering darkly, Jake spent the evening planning his next move.

Chapter 17

The next day, Jake woke up early and managed to find time to go to the library to start up a new line of research.

His first order of business in the library was trying to find information about the tattoo on his back. It had fallen to the wayside because of everything else that had been going on, but it was clearly very important. Jake spent a long time in the mist, combing through the tomes to find anything he could about tattoos. Jake went through books about tribal tattoo markings, spiritual ascendance rituals, and so on without finding anything useful. All of them were inked or painted on. Perhaps the thing on his back wasn't a tattoo? But, if Jake didn't know the name for it, how could he find out what it was? Jake grew frustrated, returning books to the stacks and pulling out more without much hope of success. After some time, he gave up on the search and decided to focus on the other angle: the Dirge.

Thankfully, Jake had already found the books about Dirges. Spreading them out over the table and flipping through them, he hoped to find something he had missed. A clue about the changes in his tattoo, perhaps. Jake was sure there was some connection there. After all, his tattoo had been normal until after he visited the Dirge. Right? Jake wasn't too sure. He never took the time to look at it. Still, it only made sense. What other creature had Jake come across that was capable of doing such a thing? If it wasn't the Dirge, perhaps it was simply a representation of what Ken had told him. Jake was truly marked for death, and that was just the physical representation of a clock ticking down. Jake cast the thought aside. He wasn't going to give up hope.

To his frustration, Jake found nothing about tattoos or markings in the Dirge section. However, he did learn a lot of other details. Their typical deal-making involved the loss of something or someone of great value. Somehow they fed off pain, sadness, and negative emotion yet did not seek to cause it directly. For every single deal made, the person making the deal either requested something without naming a price and had it exacted by the Dirge or had a sacrifice that they offered. The concept confused Jake. If they needed pain, why wouldn't Dirges just hurt the beings around them? What kind of creatures took pleasure in the self-inflicted suffering of others?

The idea that Dirges were pain leeches was disturbing. This didn't explain the markings on his tattoo, though. Jake didn't feel any pain, but that didn't mean it was leaving him unharmed. What if there were aspects of the creature that simply weren't documented? Jake shook his head. There was no point wondering about that now. The Dirge had taken it upon itself to mark him and build some strange connection that Jake could sense through the mist. It was feeding off of him already: Jake was sure of it. It had no right. Jake ground his teeth, angry at the damage it had caused to his relationship with Kenneth. He had enough enemies and too few friends as it was. Jake thought about how to regain some control over the situation.

Could he perhaps stop it from feeding off his pain if he gave himself over to his anger? Perhaps he could use that to his advantage. If Jake could coerce the Dirge to help or give information by threatening to starve it, would it work? Jake read more details about them, hoping to find some suggestion of a weakness to see if his plan could work. The books described Dirges as if they were demonic barterers trading feats of magic of great power in exchange for terrible prices. Not a single story showed a Dirge willing to take anything less in value than the initial offer. Jake refused to harm Kenneth, and he couldn't just let the Dirge sink its claws into him either.

Despite all the mentions of pain, there was no record of a Dirge hurting the other party outside of the terms of a deal. Was it somehow leeching energy from the pain Jake was feeling in response to the offer? Was his emotional turmoil already feeding it? He needed answers. It seemed that he wasn't going to get much more combing through the library, so Jake resolved to go down to face the Dirge once again. If the information Jake had was correct, perhaps his plan would succeed. He returned the books, walking out of the library and making his way directly toward the entrance to the underground tunnels. Thanks to the markings Jake had made on the way down last time, the going was much easier.

Finding his way to the spot where he met the Gibberer, Jake fumbled in the mist to reveal the secret tunnel the creature had shown him until the wall simply slid out of sight. He continued down the passages, following his chalked arrows all the way down into the depths until he finally arrived at the hallway leading into the Dirge's lair. The entire way down, Jake recounted to himself every reason he had to be angry or frustrated. Ken's betrayals. The Guardian's threats. The markings on his back. The demand from the Dirge that he kill his friend. He paused in front of the door, taking a few deep breaths to ready himself for the confrontation.

Cracking the door open and slipping in, the human marched up to the Dirge. Gathering all the anger that he could, Jake yelled at it in the partial gloom. "How dare you try and harm me! What are you doing to me? What does it mean? We have made no deal, so I demand to know why you're exacting a price! I want answers, and you're going to give them! Nobody else in this forsaken place will."

He had become emboldened by the information that Dirges didn't harm directly. In combination with his fury, his fear of the hulking mass and its power was forgotten for a few moments. He pointed an accusatory finger at it, glaring up at the towering form as if somehow his force of will would make it do his bidding.

Its reaction was slow, but the rumbling that shook through its body was clearly laughter—mocking his anger and his demands. In turn, Jake wavered and became uncertain. Why would it be happy or mocking? Was the information he had found wrong? A part of Jake's mind thought about the fact that the being before him did have the power to kill him if it wished. Sweat started to bead on his forehead as he waited for it to speak.

"A deal, information for pain, has been offered. I shall take my price." And with that, Jake's finger, which had previously been pointing at the Dirge, was suddenly gone, leaving a smooth stump in its place.

He was shocked by the sudden loss, unable to understand how from one moment to the next, his finger vanished. He tried to move it, feeling the sensation of moving a finger while seeing that nothing was actually happening. Why had it taken his finger? What deal? He hadn't made an offer of anything! "You monster, you took my finger! I made no deal, I agreed to no terms!"

He had planned to try and pressure the Dirge into giving information, but this was not what Jake had expected. Had it mistaken his demands as an offer of exchange? Or perhaps it had done so on purpose? He didn't have time to continue to shout at it as the Dirge's flesh seemed to gain life. A gaseous substance shot itself down toward Jake and speared through his mind. He cried out, expecting to feel pain or even to die. Instead, his mind was flooded with information.

It was painless, except for how suddenly the knowledge filled him. How strange the perspectives were. He could barely grasp at some of the details before they slipped away, replaced with new ones. It was a black and white movie at six times speed. Glimpses of truths, blurred lines around lies. Jake tried desperately to grasp at as much of it as he could, to remember every unveiled truth. He had paid a terrible price for the knowledge being passed to him, yet he could not fully process the information that he was given.

What little he understood gave him far more perspective than the rest of his time in the Pixie Kingdom had. The tattoo on his back was not unique to him. Every magical creature was marked, these markings representing their magical nature and condition in the world of the mist. Others could interact with these markings if they knew how, offering aid or causing terrible harm. He learned that the library that he had been searching did, in fact, contain a book that could help him learn more about how to use the mist, if he could find it. The Dirge itself used the mist so differently that it could not transfer the knowledge to him directly. Moreover, Jake learned about the Dirges. There were other people who, like him, tried to coerce them to do one thing or another.

The result was always the same: an attempt to avoid a deal and get something for free was the same as trying to make a deal. So, the Dirge set the terms on its own. He was horrified to see in his mind depictions of previous people who had attempted to get even more from a Dirge than he had. Some of them lost whole limbs, lost their sight, or became paralyzed. Some of them received the gift that they requested, only to realize how terrible the reality of it was after the fact. Those that wished for ultimate power found themselves unable to control the energy they received, destroying themselves. Others that wished for harm to come to a political rival or enemies found themselves fallen from grace soon after. Many of those who sought a deeper understanding of the world ended up insane from the information they received. Their minds were simply not capable of containing all of the knowledge that was stuffed into them. They lost their grip with the world, becoming unraveled like a tapestry with its threads pulled apart. In his fear of becoming like them, the human thought about his own limits. Could he handle what it was giving him?

His head began throbbing as if the knowledge was truly causing his brain to swell against his skull. Whimpering and weakened, Jake curled into a ball as the Dirge continued to pump his mind full of other information. He wondered if this was how he was going to end up dying. Another person gone insane from interacting with a Dirge. At some point, he fainted. When Jake woke up sometime later, the light that had previously kept the room to normal levels had vanished, leaving it almost pitch black.

He could sense more than see the Dirge's presence, in the same place it had been before he collapsed. Getting up slowly, Jake left without speaking for fear of unwittingly making another deal with the monster. His hands shook with barely contained terror as he closed the door behind him, scurrying from the tunnels as quickly as he could. The human now realized just how dangerous everything was. Everything, including himself.

Once Jake finally made it back to his room, he took a moment to probe the new information sitting in his head. When he tried, he tapped into the knowledge as if he had always had it. Yet, the experience was unlike any of his other memories. Instead of having many other memories, experiences, and dreams that fought to gain his attention when he tried to remember something, the information that the Dirge had implanted into him popped up almost instantly. There were no distractions. It was as if he asked his mind for a file from a drawer, and it instantly supplied all of the documentation, with nothing else. While he found this experience unnerving, he reminded himself that he had already paid the price for what he knew. He needed to at least make use of it. Jake turned his attention to the biggest cause for concern; his tattoo.

Poking into the information bubble in his mind, Jake learned that his tattoo represented his existence and his experiences. That knowledge didn't help much. Turning his focus from "what is the tattoo" to "what made my markings change" allowed a whole new wellspring of information to come forth. The Dirge was not the reason for the change. It had not done anything to influence that part of him.

Jake's anguish was the source of the problem. Because he had been agonizing so much about the deal the Dirge had offered, his mind had developed a weakness. A way in for certain creatures to reach into him. The painful, internal struggle to make a decision had resonated on some wavelength in the mist. The parasite which had caused his tattoo to change appearances became attracted to him because of this.

It was called a Vyril. It was a being that existed only in the mist, which latched itself onto vulnerable minds and used the powers of the mist to manipulate the unsuspecting prey into a permanent state of indecision and feelings of hopelessness. In doing so, it kept its target in a state of emotional turmoil until it had finished feeding on the spiritual essence of its prey. When a Vyril finished eating, the host died, and the Vyril moved on in search of its next victim. All that would be left behind was a mindless shell, the physical body seemingly untouched.

Normally, Jake would never have seen the signs of its misty influence over his thoughts and emotions. Thanks to the Dirge, he was able to detect the tendrils of the Vyril's powers and build up his shields as Kenneth had taught him. Even with this resistance, the Vyril still fed off of his emotions and energies. But, it could no longer manipulate them. All that was left was to get rid of the beast completely.

Jake didn't find that information in his mind. Of course, the Dirge wouldn't share a vital piece of information. It gave him just enough to want more. He refused to go back and pay the price for its help. Losing a finger was bad enough, and he wasn't sure his mind could handle the strain of another flood of knowledge. The human shuddered to think of the experience: losing his mind and his ability to keep a grip on reality as some fell creature filled his mind until it popped. Better to try other alternatives if he could.

None of the bestiaries he had read in the library contained information about Vyrils. It was possible that he could find a different volume that could help, but Jake didn't know how much time he had left. There was no way to tell how long it would take before the leech in his mind would be done turning him into a braindead husk.

Knowing that he couldn't go back to the Dirge and that the library didn't contain the information he needed about the Vyril, Jake mentally winced but knew that he would have to ask Kenneth for help. It wasn't guaranteed, but it was possible that pixie would know something about the leech. Jake wondered if Kenneth would even help. Surely, he would, right? Kenneth hadn't brought him all this way just to let him die. At the very least, Jake was more useful alive than dead.

Jake hadn't talked with Kenneth since the argument between them. The human wasn't sure how to contact the pixie until another piece of information from the Dirge surfaced into his thoughts. It was possible to summon someone by focusing on them in the mist. It was like creating a beacon that tugged on the target's mind.

The human breathed out slowly, rubbing the stump of his missing finger as he shifted into the mist. It took almost no time at all for Kenneth to react to the summons. Popping into existence within moments, there was Kenneth in his human disguise.

Chapter 18

Kenneth had just finished compiling his list of possibilities when he felt the call from Jake. The pixie took a moment to collect himself before teleporting into the human's room.

He scowled at Jake, hoping to elicit an apology from the human. "Calling me here to blame me for more things?"

Jake shook his head, still rubbing his stump. "No, and I want to say I'm sorry. I was angry and panicking. What I said was wrong. Still, I don't have time to apologize for everything. There is a lot to say and not a lot of time to say it."

The human revealed to Kenneth the things he had learned. How he had searched for the truth behind what he was, and the resulting discovery of the Dirge. Jake talked about his adventures and the deal he had made with the Dirge, unwitting as it was. He left out the original proposition - the one where the Dirge asked for Kenneth's life. He finished with an explanation of the Vyril and how he would die if they didn't figure out some way to get it to detach from him.

When he finally finished talking, Jake looked at Kenneth. The pleading look in his eyes had no impact on Kenneth. Instead, the pixie focused on the information he had been given about the Vyril. That had been one of the possibilities that he had discovered in his research. He wished it had been something else. The solution for the Vyril problem was dangerous, and he hadn't spent much time formulating a proper plan for it.

"Don't worry. I'm sorry, too. Thank you for the honesty. There's a way to fix this. I won't let you die. You're important to me. To all of us." Slowly, Kenneth walked over and hugged Jake. He used the physical contact to make it easier for him to focus in the mist to determine the accuracy of Jake's diagnosis. While he was speaking, Kenneth pushed some of his senses through the mist toward Jake and felt for the presence of the Vyril. The creature's essence was subtle, but Kenneth noticed the difference in how it flowed. Confirming it, he finished buying time with his words and told Jake what needed to happen. "We're going to need to go out into the palace forest. We should go now."

With that said, Kenneth took a step back and offered his hand. Jake felt relieved, reaching out to start the journey to the forest. He didn't know what to expect, but some deeper instinct told him that everything would be okay. That confidence filled Jake as the mist closed around them.

Jake glanced about at the almost featureless forest. Bird song and the hum of insects filled the air. "Where are we?"

"It's dangerous here. Keep close." Kenneth was tense as he started walking. He struggled to keep alert to the dangers of the forest's natural denizens while at the same time forming a plan to assault the Arachnae.

Jake hurried after the pixie, grabbing his shoulder to stop him. "Ken, before we go any further, you need to tell me what we're doing here. You said we needed to come here. For what?"

With a small sigh, Kenneth turned. Time spent explaining was even more time when he couldn't focus on an actual solution.

"Okay. We're here to get a key ingredient to make the Vyril go away. I'll explain more once we get there. Trust me. It's hard to explain."

Frowning, Jake crossed his arms. "Try to explain, or I'm not going any further. I should know what we're getting into."

Kenneth ran a hand through his hair. Jake's stubborn streak was frustrating. Why couldn't the human just trust him for once? Their lives were at risk the longer they stayed in the forest.

"Look, Kenneth. You keeping secrets from me is what caused us to be in this mess to begin with. I've told you the truth about things. It's about time you be straight with me, too." The two of them glared at each other. Kenneth eventually shook his head and sighed.

"Alright, fine. We have to go into the forest and find a creature that lives in it. An Arachnae, to be precise. We need the Arachnae's webbing to create a drink that will trap the Vyril and allow us to pry it off of you."

Jake stared at Ken. "We have to… take a spider's web from it? A magical spider's web?"

"Pretty much. First, I want to show you where it is, then we're going to have to talk about the plan. I can keep us from being noticed by most of the less powerful creatures because Pixies have immunity. The bigger ones… don't care as much." Kenneth turned and continued to travel through the forest. He quickened the pace to try and make up for the wasted time.

Not wanting to be left alone, Jake followed him. The human didn't like how things were going, but he couldn't go back without Kenneth's help. Jake had no choice but to trust him, however begrudgingly.

Eventually, Kenneth stopped at the edge of a clearing. On the other side was a massive spiderweb hung across the limbs of an even larger tree. The creature nestled inside could hardly be called a spider, since it moved with surprising fluidity and grace. Jake had imagined a grotesque, spider-like monstrosity with dripping fangs and a spider's typical start-and-stop, jerky movements. Instead, the Arachnae was beautiful. The creature's water-like motions were mesmerizing. Jake felt a strange peace come over him as it flowed across its web. The peanut butter-like scent of jimsonweed filled the air. There was nothing wrong or dangerous here. The human had been afraid to see the beast, but Kenneth had made it sound so much worse than it was. Why would he be worried about such a lovely thing? As usual, Kenneth wasn't being entirely truthful.

Jake started to walk from their hiding spot toward the opening of the clearing itself, hoping to embrace the invitingly open arms of the Arachnae. Kenneth grabbed him and held him back. Jake didn't even look at the pixie. "Kenneth, don't worry. Can't you see? It's just a gentle creature. It wants us to come to it."

Kenneth spoke through the mist in response. "Stop. It's an illusion. Close your eyes and focus. Break free."

The human continued to think the pixie was being ridiculous, but he complied anyway. As soon as Jake's eyes were closed and he focused in the mist, he could detect the glamour. He shook with horror, his eyes still closed as he remembered what he had actually seen. Involuntarily, he stepped backwards into Kenneth in his desire to gain some distance from the beast that had almost fooled him into walking to his death.

There on the web was a creature much like a giant spider. Its eight limbs sprawled over the length of the silky trap, vibrating to some secret rhythm which sent out waves of enchanting energy into the mist to influence those that saw the motions. Its multi-jointed limbs were covered in sharp-looking, hooked hairs, and the fangs were long enough to pierce through a human's arm. With careful inspection, Jake could detect the small warning fibers placed around the edges of the clearing and along its floor to alert the trapper of approaching prey. If he had moved just two more steps forward, it might have eaten them both.

Focusing his thoughts in the mist, Jake spoke to the pixie who had just both endangered and saved his life. "Next time, warn me before we walk up to a creature with enchanting powers. I could've gotten us both killed."

"I figured you'd be more careful. Still, I needed to show you. We have to make a plan to harvest its silk." Jake had no idea how they were going to do that, but Kenneth answered half of the question for him. "We're going to have to kill it."

Jake knew he had heard Kenneth correctly, but it still seemed like madness. "What?"

"I know you aren't happy with this solution, but… we have to kill it. It'll eat us if we try to take its silk. The Arachnae aren't the type to make friends. And without its silk, we can't save you from the Vyril. At least, any way that I know works."

A giant, magical spider. They had to kill something that came out of nightmares. Jake shuddered at the thought of dealing with the creature. Even with his newfound powers, he wasn't confident he had what it would take to deal with such a beast.

Jake stared at Ken incredulously. "Do you have some kind of special plan, or are you just crazy? It'll kill us! And I'm supposed to drink its silk? That's beyond nasty and makes no sense. How is that going to help?"

Kenneth grabbed Jake's arm and led the human slowly away from the clearing. His voice was barely more than a whisper. "Come on, I can't get us out of here using my powers until we're further away. We'll talk when we're not so close to it. It can sense motion in the mist and trap us if we try to teleport near its lair."

The journey back seemed to take much longer. The sun was just starting to set. Jake's fear and anxiety increased with each step that seemed to bring them no closer to their destination. Nothing about this situation made sense. They were supposed to be figuring out a way to kill the Arachnae and steal its silk. Yet there was no planning being done, as far as he could tell. Kenneth suddenly stopped and pulled Jake into the crook of a tree.

Once they were far enough from the clearing that Kenneth could act in the mist without attracting undue attention, Kenneth stopped and pulled Jake into the crook of a tree. Kenneth kept half of his attention on their surroundings as he considered their options. Jake clearly still had very little understanding of his powers, and Kenneth did not have the strength to kill an Arachnae without some risk. And he could not risk an injury when he needed to get them both back safely afterwards. "Okay, we're going to sit here while I think. This should be far enough that we're mostly safe."

Jake didn't understand why they had to hide out. Did Kenneth not have a plan? The seconds turned to minutes as Kenneth seemingly stared into space and presumably made plans. The longer this took, the more worried and frustrated Jake became.

Jake tried to find some information that could help them from the pool of knowledge he had gained from the Dirge. Despite his efforts, nothing surfaced. He wasn't sure if that was a sign that nothing could help, or that he simply didn't have the knowledge. Either way, it left him feeling more impatient and desperate to get this over with than before. Jake's thoughts moved on to the next potential danger. What if the Arachnae came and found them in the dark? Perhaps there were other, deadlier creatures waiting for their opportunity. Jake felt more certain with each passing moment that they were going to be attacked.

He couldn't just stand by and wait for Kenneth to figure out where they were going. He was scared, and his trust in the pixie was thin enough already. Jake grabbed Kenneth by the arm. "We can't just sit here. Surely we've travelled far enough from the Arachnae to talk. How are you going to just bring me out here and not explain anything? I could've died from that glamour because you came into things just assuming you could keep me safe. You can't. I've almost died several times now. You've gotta give me something. If nothing else, let's just use the mist to search for safety or set a trap or something. You taught me how to search my surroundings, at least."

Kenneth shook his head. He didn't feel Jake knew enough to help him plan, and he didn't want to risk the human's impulsiveness getting in the way of a good strategy. "I already said that we should be safe here. You just don't trust me. And the plan is to trick the Arachnae into leaving its nest or eating something poisonous so that we can harvest the mist of its silk. The Vyril is a mist creature, so we need mist silk to capture it and pry it from you. We can't go walking into the mist, or my attempts to keep us hidden won't work anymore. Giant spider creatures aren't the only things out here. In the mist, a lot of things get a tad bigger even if their brains don't get much smarter. Let's not kick the hornet's nest. Now shush and let me think about the details, will you?"

Jake shook his head. Kenneth's entire plan was to sit around imagining ways to distract a giant spider? Or to poison it? Jake couldn't think of a better plan, but the ideas both seemed equally ridiculous. Spiders could sense vibration, and if they had to go into the mist and collect the silk there, it would detect them no matter what. It was obvious that Kenneth didn't have a real plan. If he knew what they needed to do, they would have done it by now.

How was he keeping them safe, anyway? They were simply sitting in the roots of a tree. Jake refused to get caught out in the woods unprepared without at least some knowledge of what was around them. He could feel a tug. A desire to go out and be proactive. Jake announced his decision. "I'm not going to wait around for you to figure out everything. I can do some things, and I'm going to do them."

With that said, Jake shifted into the mist and left his body in Kenneth's care.

The pixie called out to Jake a few times, hoping to convince him to come back. When the human kept going, Kenneth swore under his breath. Jake hadn't given him many options going into this. And now the human had just run off to figure things out on his own. The pixie wasn't even sure what to do in this situation. Staying out in the forest for too long was a hazard, but he couldn't leave with Jake not in his body. Trying to teleport would likely kill both of them. Jake's empty vessel of a body would try to pull Kenneth in, and he was certain things would go haywire.

So, on the one hand, he was stuck. On the other, this gave him time to think things through. While he had no choice but to wait for Jake, he could plan how to move forward. He set about hiding their presence in the mist. Focusing his mind, Kenneth sent out very small feelers into the mist to check for anything that might notice his behavior. When nothing caught his attention, he shifted his focus to gathering nearby mist in small pieces. He molded them, working carefully to shape the mist to match the tree that stood above them in the physical world. He layered the coiling energy and twisted it until it appeared to be a natural growth from the tree itself. It wouldn't fool an intelligent creature, but it would do for most of the wandering insects and hunters in the area.

With that done, Kenneth could finally relax and think. There hadn't been any opportunity to completely process everything Jake had shared with the threat of the Vyril looming so close. Kenneth thought back over what he had been told: a deal in exchange for a finger, individual study in the library, and not much else. How had the Vyril come to him? There wasn't a real connection. Jake said he suspected the Dirge, but that explanation was nonsense. If the Dirge wanted Jake dead, the human would be. It was only possible for the Vyril to grow powerful enough to threaten Jake's life if he was emotionally vulnerable. Some internal struggle or pain had to be wearing away at his mind and creating a weakness in the natural mental walls that living creatures, especially magical ones, built up over time. Otherwise, the Vyril could never absorb enough energy to be fatal. There was something Jake was keeping secret. There had to be. But what?

Kenneth sighed. There was no way to know for sure. An additional problem was Jake's power. It had been growing far too unrestricted over the past few days. At this point, Kenneth wasn't sure if he could deal with Jake if it came to a direct confrontation. The pixie still knew tricks to surprise and manipulate Jake, but the human's strength was staggering. Was it even possible to keep Jake under control? Had Kenneth been mistaken in thinking he could harness a Seer's might? Perhaps the Guardian had been partially right.

Mulling over other thoughts, Kenneth arrived at the other key question: how did a Vyril find its way into the castle undetected? The Guardian's security should have kept such leeches from ever entering. Only two explanations sprang to mind: Jake had opened a gap in the security measures, or the Guardian had let the Vyril into the castle of its own free will. The first seemed unlikely. What reason would Jake have for threatening the kingdom in this way? It made little sense. Kenneth's experience at reading people told him that Jake wasn't the type to endanger his hosts in such a fashion.

The Guardian, however, was not so trustworthy. He could imagine the creature using an agent like the Vyril to keep its hands clean when Jake died. Kenneth's first instinct was to plan a conversation with the Guardian once he returned. But, if it really did do this, Kenneth couldn't trust that it wouldn't try to kill him as well. He wouldn't stand a chance in a fight with the Guardian. That wasn't a real option, no matter his feelings. Gritting his teeth, Kenneth thought about reporting to the Queen everything that had happened. It would be a mess to explain, and she might not be happy to hear of Jake's rapidly increasing power. Still, it was better than the alternative. Surely, the Guardian wouldn't dare to oppose the Queen directly. There were too many problems to think about. He didn't even have a plan for acquiring the silk threads of the Arachnae. And he couldn't even think about that until Jake had returned. If he returned.

Chapter 19

Kenneth had the decency to catch Jake's body as it fell over.

Jake wasted no time, immediately heading off in search of a way out. He let his mind wander, radiating outward in slow circles and trying to be alert. He ignored the whispers of Kenneth's voice in the mist as the pixie tried to call him back. They had each made their choices.

Jake hoped that being in the mist might allow him to see some secret breadcrumbs home or at least a safe location. After several minutes of searching, he thought of an idea. What if he could call out to Maeva or Evelynn out here? Surely one of them could hear without the guardian detecting it, if he were careful? Kenneth had mentioned there being dangers in the mist, but the human decided that his best hope of having someone help was calling for it. Kenneth had just repeatedly left Jake out of the loop while dragging him through different, yet perilous circumstances. Even if the pixie meant well, good intentions weren't enough.

Focusing his mind, Jake tried to project his thoughts outward, up and toward the mist's outer limits. The knowledge flowed from the Dirge's gift, showing him how to craft and loop the mist into a pair of beacons. All he had to do was imagine his targets, every detail of their appearances, how they felt, and their influences on him.

First, one to draw Maeva's attention. The dangerous one; the woman who had started him down this path.

Then, another to attract Evelynn. The spirit; the entity that saved him, for a price he had yet paid.

It was a mystery how long it would take them to come, if they even heard the call. Hopefully, one of them could arrive before something disastrous happened. After he'd sent out the distress beacon, Jake continued to look for a place that seemed somewhat safe to rest in.

Eventually, he noticed a faint buzzing sound in the atmosphere. It had been slowly growing louder the longer he spent in the mist, starting from about when he had made the call for help. Jake hadn't paid it much mind at first, being so focused on what he could see rather than what he could hear. But it was a nagging pressure on his mind at this point, and he became afraid of being caught by something he didn't understand. If it was growing louder, that meant it was also growing closer. Jake shuddered.

Desperately searching through his memory, Jake tried to make his way back to his body. He could feel the tug of his body calling back his mind. He hurried in the hopes he could make it before the source of the sound caught up to him. Yet, despite going what he was sure to be the right way, the human only found himself twisting and turning through the forest with the buzzing growing all the louder with each passing moment. It was as if the forest was keeping him trapped.

Jake attempted to make things easier by memorizing the features of the trees around him in hopes that he could recognize the way back. As he came to the same tree with a knot in its bark, he confirmed his suspicion. If he couldn't outrun the creature, he would have to come up with a new plan. He thought of his options.

A deeper instinct told him that he couldn't fight the creature that was coming. He had to survive.

A strange calm took hold as he honed his thoughts on that one idea. Survival. Instincts he didn't know he had took over, and his mind reached out to the mist around him. He gripped the essence of magic, and he started to slowly mold it into a sphere around himself. As he worked, the buzzing stopped. The silence rang in his ears.

The sensation was strange, as he felt he watched himself work the mist into a defensive ball. He understood what he was doing, as clearly as he didn't understand mere moments before. The sensation of power filled him as he completed the barrier, turning at the sound of the trees parting. The sphere was see-through, and he half-wished it wasn't when the insect-like beast emerged from the trees.

Jake stared in a mixture of horror and fascination as the insect twice his size crawled forward on its several pairs of sharp, spear-like legs. The creature looked like a giant praying mantis mixed with a hornet. Its shape seemed to melt and reform, features of its carapace and head switching between the two. Almost as if the two sides battled for control. Poison dripped from its vicious-looking stinger. The claws were sharp yet deformed; strangely angular and disjointed. From its mandibles, saliva dribbled yet never fell. The wings, the source of the buzzing sound, were in a constant state of flux. First, one tearing through the other, then the reverse. The horrific nature of the beast made Jake think it was one of the forest guardians that Kenneth had mentioned earlier. Surely, no natural creature could form like this.

Jake shook his head to free it from those thoughts. It didn't matter how this creature came to exist. He had to focus and stay alive. Despite its aggression, the tearing in its shape made the beast almost seem as if it were more designed for self-injury than for hunting. Jake quickly found out this was not the case when it made a loud, keening sound and lashed out with its claws. The human could feel the crushing strength of those claws as they attempted to clamp on the sphere, finding no purchase against its smoothness. The barrier held, but he sensed the ravenous, insectoid hunger on the other side. Its hunger frightened and disturbed him. Its buggy eyes stared into his. The glassy, deadened sensation that came from them was unnerving and almost made Jake lose his grip on the mist that surrounded him.

He would have thrown up if he were in his body. Its mind pushed against his, and he could sense its desires. They were very straightforward: to dismember and eat him, then Kenneth, then anything and everything else. Jake grimaced at the thought of being food, feeling his stamina take a hit as the creature blindly struck at his shield. He couldn't hold it up forever.

Jake knew he had to figure out a way to escape. Kenneth probably wouldn't be of much use. There had to be something else. As the beast pressed its grasping mandibles against the spherical defenses he had put up. He could feel it. The clock was ticking. The time to act was now.

Each moment stretched into an infinity of buzzing wings and flailing, shape-shifting limbs as the forest defender tried to find a way to break through Jake's barrier and devour him. He held back a shiver, trying to keep his mind focused on the task of survival, even as half of his mental energy was spent maintaining his defenses.

Jake's fear of the creature before him made each second of clashing mandibles turn into a miniature movie of what would happen if his defenses were to fail. He considered the possibility of forming a weapon to defend himself with. He looked at its body in search of a weakness. Its abdomen seemed hardly connected with its thorax. Aside from the two scythe-like arms, the legs ended in vicious-looking barbs that could easily penetrate flesh. Its entire body was covered in small spikes, all facing one direction, like scaled armor. The joints all looked like potential weak points if he could hit them hard enough.

What weapon could he make that would work? It seemed too risky. Who knew what special properties the beast's body had? If he even managed to cut it apart, would it grow new heads or bodies like a hydra? Would it spray him with poison? He had no clue what would happen, and the human doubted his strength to survive a direct confrontation. Giving up on that line of thinking, Jake shook his head. He couldn't die like this, and he wouldn't risk death for the sake of bravery. He had to live, no matter what. A slow, dull ache started to form in the back of his mind. Holding the barrier was taking its toll.

Thankfully, the mantis creature seemed to be growing tired as well. It had stopped keening at him every few moments, and its swinging scythes were still. Instead, the beast just stared. It was unnerving, but Jake couldn't help but stare back into the lifeless eyes of the creature before him. His frightened face stared back at him from the multi-faceted lenses.

Taking another approach, Jake tried to push his mind into the monster's. Perhaps he could influence it that way. The monstrosity flinched before snarling at him. Flashes of imagery passed from its mind to his; sparks of hunger and need and fear and death. The beast was starving and was only so patient because it knew it could eat him eventually. It needed to be sated with something, anything.

It was at that moment that Jake had an idea. If it were so hungry, perhaps it wouldn't care about the target of its hunger? He knew from his hatred of spiders what their predators were. Praying mantises and hornets both had the aggressive tendencies to hunt and consume spiders. What if he could use this to solve both of his problems? If he could lead the creature to the Arachnae's clearing, could he get the creatures to attack each other? It was a long shot, but once he thought of the idea, he couldn't let it go. It was his best chance at escaping alive. But, in order to do that, he needed to be able to move. Perhaps there was some way to move his defensive shield with him? He wouldn't know until he tried.

Focusing his mind, Jake imagined the shield around him moving, gliding with him through the air. To his pleasant surprise, it worked. The shield floated along with him as he made slow, steady progress through the forest. The creature clacked its mandibles together and followed after him, not wanting to let him go that easily. Tentatively, he tried sending out feelings of hunger to the creature. The monstrosity pressed closer, entirely consumed in its desire to eat him. Jake smiled despite the danger of the situation. He had used the manipulation technique he had seen Kenneth do in their practice on his first try. It had been so easy. Jake continued to manipulate its hunger in the hopes of kicking it into a mindless frenzy. That way, it would attack the Arachnae when they arrived.

After figuring out that he could stimulate the creature's hunger, the rest was much simpler to perform, if nerve-wracking. He guided the creature back, using himself as a carrot, to where he thought the clearing with the Arachnae had been. The beast in front of him eagerly followed, at times lifting up its body to jab its powerful stinger into his defenses. He couldn't help but flinch seeing a sharp, jet-black needle the size of his hand come flying at him.

The displays reminded him of what would happen if things failed. The creature would tear him apart. He had already committed himself to this path, but his hands shook as the horrific results of failure sunk into his mind. The way to the clearing was long, and each rabid strike from the hybrid creature felt more jarring. Jake wasn't sure how much longer he could hold the barrier. He could feel the manic hunger of the creature behind him. He had successfully pushed it over the edge, and its attacks had become wild. Its swinging limbs cut through the surrounding trees and rang against his shield with a visibly resounding impact.

Jake couldn't keep this going forever, and he still wasn't sure how far we were from the clearing. Could he even make it in time? What if he made a mistake and the shield dropped because of it? He shook his head, trying to shake off the feeling of self-doubt along with it. Surely, the Vyril was trying to manipulate him again. He couldn't be weak. Not now. He could do it. He had to, or else he'd die. His reserves were almost gone by the time he arrived with his delivery.

The forest guardian didn't pay much attention to the Arachnae at first, so focused on Jake that it stepped into the clearing completely before it noticed the shifting movements of the spider-like entity. The moment of recognition caused it to visibly tense, ready to pounce but waiting for some signal. Jake couldn't tell if his attacker was completely distracted or if it had stopped moving to bait him into making a mistake. Nervously, he tried to slide to the side of the two creatures.

It was at that same moment that the Arachnae, which had been attempting to cast its glamour, realized that it hadn't mesmerized its prey. With that realization, it reared up on its hind legs and hissed loudly. The sound was so horrific that Jake vowed to avoid forests for the rest of his life if he could. Fortunately, it seemed that both monsters were so focused on each other that he became an afterthought. They had more important things to deal with.

The hornet-mantis keened as it flew forward, wicked claws scything through the air as it struck out. The Arachnae showed surprising agility for a creature of its size, popping off of its web and landing behind its assailant. The slicing motion of the other beast's claws tore through the webbing that the Arachnae had been resting upon. Tendrils of silk flew into the air as the Arachnae reeled, turning around to face its enemy. With silky webbing flying in the air around him, Jake was reminded of the whole reason that he was out here to begin with. If not for Kenneth, he would have never come.

Jake flinched, wondering where the pixie was for a moment. The human closed his eyes and breathed deeply to try and calm himself. Focusing on the sphere, he slowly pulled it apart. Once free, he grabbed some of the silk, feeling it strangely smooth against his skin. Prize in hand, Jake hurriedly started to make his way back to his body. He left the two monstrosities behind without a second glance.

Jake could hear the terrible sounds of the creatures' deadly combat behind him. He shuddered and tried to avoid thinking about what could have happened if they had taken a particular interest in human flesh. It was surprisingly easy to find his body, with Kenneth cradling it, now that the forest guardian was out of the picture. Jake was exhausted, mentally calling out to Ken in a whisper.

Kenneth's anxiety grew as he waited for Jake. The pixie considered what to do if Jake were to die in the forest. He could tell from the breathing body that Jake was still alive, but that didn't indicate the human was safe. Kenneth's contemplations were interrupted by the sound of Jake calling to him in the mist. Shifting his focus, he saw the human approaching. He gasped and almost stood before remembering that he was cradling Jake's body. "You're alive. I thought for sure you were a goner. How…?"

Jake shook his head. "I'm alive. And you were right, it was dangerous. I shouldn't have done it. But I made it back. It would've been easier if you kept fewer secrets."

Kenneth sighed, using one hand to rub his face as he took a moment to collect his thoughts. Jake was probably going to push even harder for answers now that he had gone through this ordeal. He decided to turn the tables instead. "Yeah, yeah. We should both be honest with each other, right? So how about you be honest with me. Just how much of the mist have you studied and learned about in the library and other places? What did you do to attract the Vyril? You should have figured that one out by now, but you're refusing to tell me. Why?"

Jake hadn't expected to have to defend himself against Ken's suspicions. He wasn't ready to reveal the full truth. Frantically, he tried to think of a way to change the topic. He held up his hand to show several strands of the Arachne's web. "Speaking of the Vyril, I got the silk. What am I supposed to do with it? Is this enough to create that… thing we needed?"

Kenneth stared in surprise at the strands. The fact Jake had managed it indicated much about the human's creativity and power. His growth since he had been brought into the mist had been stunningly fast. Kenneth wondered if he even had what it took to restrain Jake if they were to come to blows. Perhaps if he got the drop on the human, it was possible. Returning his focus to the moment at hand, the pixie decided to follow Jake's lead in the conversation. "You… you did it. You're crazy, but you did it. You're going to have to tell me how you managed that, too. Hand them over, I can keep them stored properly for our journey back."

The human complied, more than happy to get the strange things away from him and shivering at the thought that they'd be key to his freedom from the Vyril's clutches. While Kenneth wrapped the strands in a pouch made of mist, Jake slipped back into his body.

Once he was safely within himself again, Jake tried to stand. His legs buckled, and Kenneth had to catch him. "I'm drained. Are we safe to head back now?"

"We should be fine, yes." Kenneth shifted so that they were facing each other. "I'll take us back."

Nodding, Jake reached out and took Kenneth's hands. He shuddered to think of what monstrosities might come out at night.

Kenneth quickly transported them back inside Jake's room.

Once they arrived, Kenneth kept his grip on Jake. The human stared at his companion. "You okay, Kenneth? We're here. You can let go now."

"No. We need to talk." Kenneth's gaze was stern. He had dropped it long enough to get Jake back into the castle, but he still had a duty to find out what had transpired in his absence. Jake's wild, uncontrolled developments were a threat to Kenneth's ability to keep control of the situation. "You haven't told me everything, Jake. The Vyril wouldn't be attracted to you for no reason. And the Dirge had nothing to do with it being summoned. What's the truth? I want to hear all of it."

Jake shifted, uncomfortable at having to reveal what he'd been hiding about the Dirge and its offer. What could he say? How much could he really share that wouldn't break the tentative peace they had found? With a sigh, Jake looked Kenneth in the eye and resolved to be honest. If he couldn't tell the truth, how could he expect any help at all? He couldn't keep being a hypocrite; expecting Kenneth to reveal everything while keeping everything so close to his chest. "Okay, Kenneth. You're right. I haven't been completely honest with you. You weren't around, and I wanted to learn more about being a Seer. I had finished your books and explored the library in search of more. Eventually, I found out about the Dirge and the Underdark. So, I went down and found the Dirge. It offered me a deep, true understanding of what I am… in exchange for your life. I was supposed to sacrifice you to the Dirge."

Kenneth managed to keep his anger from showing on his face. It was directed at his own foolishness in how relaxed he had been around the human. The temptation of power had been enough to leave Jake distraught and open to assault from the Vyril. Jake had actually considered the option, and Kenneth had been overconfident in his assessment of the human's connection. Jake hastily tried to defend himself. "Of course, I didn't do it. I couldn't do it. Even if it wasn't completely real, our friendship meant something to me."

The last comment got a small smile from Kenneth. Perhaps he hadn't been overconfident after all. He kept his tone soft and caring as he spoke. "Oh, Jake… if only you had just talked to me. It's my duty to teach you about being a Seer. About the mist. If you had a little more trust and patience, I would have worked you toward it slowly. It's too dangerous to learn everything at once."

Jake growled in frustration. Even now, Kenneth was deciding what was too dangerous for him. "It's not your place to let me out or keep me in. I'm not your son, Kenneth. I have a right to know what's going on. It's my life you're talking about. My identity."

"Okay, you're right. We're both right and wrong here. We need to tell each other everything. But, this isn't the time to do it. There are things that need to be handled first." Kenneth shifted his focus. If Jake were insistent on taking control and having little trust, then Kenneth needed to buy some time to make sure he could keep ahead of the human's antics. The only way to do that would be to incapacitate his charge for the time being.

"Fine, but what?" As he spoke, Jake felt a push in the mist. Someone was trying to influence his mind. Reflexively, he pushed up the barrier that Kenneth had taught him. For a moment, it held back the wave. With that second of time, the human realized that Kenneth was the one trying to control him. "What are you doing?"

"My duty." Kenneth's face was neutral as his power surged forward, overwhelming Jake in his moment of surprise and distraction. Kenneth sent Jake into as deep a sleep as he could manage.

The human's world went dark as sleep overtook him.

Once he had confirmed that Jake was truly knocked out, Kenneth immediately set about creating the formula needed to detach the Vyril from Jake. He shifted the strands of webbing, crushing and mixing them with the mist before forcing it into Jake's essence. The strands would catch the foreign element, the Vyril, and force it forward. All that the pixie could do now was hope Jake was strong enough to fight back. He stood. In the meantime, he would report to the Queen. The situation had become too dangerous to proceed without reporting.

Kenneth stretched, looking down at Jake. He almost felt guilty for keeping so many secrets, even though he still felt it was the right thing to do. Jake wasn't ready yet. He was still too brash and impulsive to learn everything and take his place as an active member of their magical users.

Leaving Jake behind, Kenneth focused on his main task. He quickly arranged for a meeting with the Queen. There were supposed to be wards in her chambers that would prevent the Guardian from spying on them. As long as the creature wasn't there, it wouldn't be able to try and convince her of anything. Kenneth couldn't risk it knowing anything. Jake's life could be at stake, as well as his own standing in the pixie kingdom. The Guardian had been stupid and foolhardy to send the Vyril after Jake. More importantly, it was two-faced. The Guardian had promised to the Queen that he'd do nothing. He had pretended to be okay with the measures they had taken together. Clearly, it was a ruse. Kenneth just wasn't sure about the reason behind it.

Chapter 20

Kenneth waited once again to be beckoned into the Queen's presence. The sound of the clock ticking made him flinch. He could feel the air move over his skin, and every shift of the guard at the door made him turn his head expectantly. He wrung his hands together. How long was he going to have to wait? If this took too long, he wouldn't be there when Jake woke up. Kenneth wasn't sure what would happen if that were the case.

Finally, the guard reached out and opened the doors, gesturing Kenneth into the Queen's audience room. Kenneth took a deep breath, pressing his shaking hands firmly against his thighs as he walked inside. He kept his face as smooth as he could, kneeling before her. "My Queen."

"Rise, Kenneth. The message said you had urgent news for me. Speak."

He stood, taking a deep breath. "I have reason to believe that the Guardian attempted to kill Jake, despite your orders to not get involved. And in doing so, he put our relationship with Jake in jeopardy. The human has grown extremely powerful as of late. Far beyond my expectations. This act of violence towards him will poison the well if it hasn't already. I've done some of the work to fix things by helping to save his life, but the situation is precarious. It seems that with every new encounter, he becomes more deeply seated in his own magic than the last. In raw strength, he's greater than I am. I believe that his value as an ally, if he continues to improve, will be unprecedented. But so will the threat if we alienate him."

Kenneth stopped, pausing to see her response. The only sound was of the Queen's fingertips tapping against the arm of her throne. He shifted uncomfortably as he waited for a response. Every passing second felt like an eternity. Kenneth's mind wandered to think about Jake. He should be fighting for his life with the Vyril right now. With his strength, he should win. But what would it do to him? Kenneth could only hope that Jake didn't hold it against them. Only the Guardian was responsible, after all.

"You have said a lot here, Kenneth. Things I would like to confirm myself. If this human is as powerful as you say, perhaps I should see him. An ally of such strength would be better than an enemy. But first… explain to me how he grew so strong so suddenly. You were assigned to control his learning to keep him in check, were you not? How did you fail so spectacularly?"

He winced at the question. He had been avoiding thinking about that the whole time. Jake's sudden growth should have been his to maintain and direct. And he had failed. Clenching a fist, he looked back up at the Queen. "I took time to perform wrap-ups on my current assignments, to make sure that other agents could take over. During that time, Jake somehow found information about the Underdark. He explored it in search of the Dirge. And he succeeded in finding it. It granted him knowledge about himself and about the magical world. For the price of one of his fingers. I believe this was the tipping point that caused his power to grow so explosively. He kept all of this a secret from me until I found the marking of the Vyril upon him. At which point, we went into the forest to harvest Arachnae silk. He trekked off alone and managed to get some without my help. At which point, we returned here, he told me the truth, and I put him to sleep. I then administered the silk to enable him to fight the Vyril. Which he is doing now."

"Very well. You are not forgiven for your errors, but you seem to have handled the aftermath respectably. Your next task is to return to the human. When he wakes, bring him to me." The Queen waved a hand. "Dismissed."

Kenneth turned, resisting the urge to run out the door. Things had gone better than he had expected. Perhaps she had heard some news of things while he had been busy. Or there were other changes. Regardless, he had orders. Once he walked out of the audience antechamber, Kenneth started sprinting toward Jake's room. If he didn't arrive before Jake woke up, there was a chance the human might do something rash. The pixie ran a hand through his hair. This had turned into a complete mess.

At first, Jake's sleep was empty. There was only darkness until, slowly, the area around him began to fill itself in. He was in the Underdark of the castle. The Dirge loomed before him. Its foreign presence pressed on his mind. In front of him lay Kenneth tied to an altar. The mist along the floor seemed to shift and move in the corners of Jake's eye, but it was still when he stared at it. What was happening?

"Come, Seer. Present me with your sacrifice. Free yourself. Empower yourself." The Dirge's voice rang in Jake's mind, though it seemed different from before. More distant; like an echo.

As the monstrosity spoke, a ritual dagger appeared in his hand. He almost yelped as it slid in his grasp. The blade passed through the place where his old finger had been. A reminder of the Dirge's strict resolution of an agreement. Jake wiped sweat from his brow with his free hand, staring down at the weapon. None of this made sense. First, Kenneth had knocked him out. Now they were together in the mist? He winced as the Dirge's voice rang again through his skull.

"Do not tarry! I have the knowledge you seek. Simply plunge your knife into the pixie. Offer his blood to me."

Jake watched in horror as his shaking hand held up the knife. He grasped it with his other hand to fight it. As soon as he started to resist, the strange pull stopped. Was this a dream? Was this a representation of his inner emotions? It couldn't be. He had decided he wouldn't sacrifice Kenneth to the Dirge. Even with the offer so free to take before him, the human felt no temptation. The Dirge's price was too great. Jake leaned down to examine Kenneth and tossed the knife aside. The blade vanished before it hit the ground.

The pixie was breathing. A good sign. Once he had confirmed that, Jake realized that Kenneth's wings were the wrong color. Their usual blue, gold, and red had been replaced by brown, black, and grey. Dark, dead colors. Jake stood, shouting up at the Dirge. "If you're killing him, stop. I am not taking this deal. I reject your offer. Now leave him alone."

The creature laughed. The rumbling shook the air. "Puny human. I am a Dirge. What I want, I may take. You have no power to stop me."

Jake paused for a moment. This wasn't right, either. Dirges didn't simply take things. It was always a trade done willingly. It was one of the strange quirks for beings of their power. As he thought of an explanation for this strange behavior, Jake noticed silver lines along the monster's body. They hadn't been there moments ago. He was sure of it. Instinctively, he reached out with his mind to touch them. The pressure of his thoughts tore through every strand, and the Dirge simply vanished. The sudden emptiness loomed larger than the creature had.

With the Dirge gone, Jake turned to look at Kenneth. The altar was still there, but the captured pixie was not. The faint sound of buzzing wings came out of the darkness around him, but Jake couldn't see any hint of his friend. Dreams usually didn't make sense, but this dream was more unusual than most. Without any signs of what was around him, Jake was unsure of what to do. He felt at ease now that he at least wasn't being forced by the Dirge to kill Kenneth. The moment of relaxation was short-lived as he was plunged back into darkness. The buzzing sound grew louder for a moment then stopped.

Jake knew this was supposed to scare him. Normally, it would have. A deeper instinct told him this wasn't a real threat. The mantis creature couldn't truly be here, or he would already have been attacked. Slowly, the mist started to coil around him. As he stared at the mist, he could see the same silver lines that formed the Dirge. With a quick push, they were severed again. This time, Jake followed the trail with his senses. The tendrils of energy flared brightly against his mind's eye in the supernatural darkness. Now that he was focused on them, he could see how these lines criss-crossed across everything. The darkness seemed to be caged within the lines.

Tentatively, he concentrated his thoughts into a needle and poked a hole in one of the threads. The darkness let out a hissing sound, like air escaping a balloon, as it started to leak out. Jake's suspicions were confirmed. This was an illusion. Knowing this, he quickly pushed out with his mind, focusing on the silver tendrils that held the illusion in place. He heard a high-pitched whine of pain as his power surged. The illusion fell apart under the weight of his strength. There, floating in the air in front of him, was the creature he could only guess to be the Vyril.

The Vyril resembled a human-sized mosquito fat with blood. The insectoid carapace was bloated, the chitin stretched so that its contents were visible. Jake felt drawn to the streaks of blue held in the creature's stomach. His throat grew dry as he realized that the blue streaks were his essence. Parts of him sucked out by the foul creature.

"You are more powerful than I waszz expecting. No matter. I have abszorbed enough of your energy to finish this." Its voice was thin and reedy. "The rest of you will susztain me for a while yet."

Jake growled, focusing his mind and readying his defenses. He could feel the weight of his lost energy now that he was aware of it. It was like a missing limb. The ghost of sensation. If he wanted his full strength back, he would have to kill this thing. If only Kenneth had given him more information about the strange creature before knocking him unconscious. That bastard. Jake refocused. He could deal with Kenneth later. First, he had a bug to swat.

It floated in the air, glowing from the energy it had stolen. The rumble of its laughter shook through his mind, and Jake readied himself to fight.

Jake reached out for his power to focus on creating a weapon to defend himself, but it slipped out of his fumbling grasp and failed to form into anything. The Vyril's satisfaction emanated from it as it simply hovered there. He didn't understand what was happening. He had managed to manipulate the mist without problems for a while now. He wasn't distracted. Focusing his mind again, Jake reached out and attempted to collect the mist. Once again, the mist started to form then simply slipped out of his control.

A glint in the air drew Jake's attention. He watched as the power he had extended to grab the mist was sucked into the Vyril's proboscis. The creature was somehow absorbing his power as he tried to use it. Jake shook his head. He could feel the new emptiness inside him, but he couldn't afford to be distracted. He backed away slowly from the Vyril, unsure of what to do. If he couldn't extend his power into the mist, how was he supposed to fight?

The Vyril flew forward, aiming its sword-length needle directly at him. Jake dove to the side, narrowly avoiding the lunge and instinctively trying to control the mist once more. This time, he saw the Vyril's body flare as he attempted to wield his power. It was lit by a series of tubes that extended from Jake to its mouth. It must have been waiting for Jake to drop his defenses to control the mist to reach in and devour his power.

A thought bubbled from the Dirge's pool of knowledge: the Vyril had no powers he could not emulate. This bounced in his mind for a moment before he realized what it meant. If he could not handle the mist, perhaps Jake could tap into his power within the Vyril? He could see, now, that he was not cut off from his energy simply because the Vyril had absorbed it. The Vyril had to digest all of the essence that it took in. Its body acted as a storage chamber while it digested. But what if he could reach in and use it directly?

Dodging another lunge from the Vyril, Jake turned and shouted. "I will slay you, monster. Right here, right now."

The floating menace waggled its appendages in mirth as it laughed at his proclamation. "What can you do with no power? I will eat away all that you are! Give up now, there issz no hope."

Jake could feel it attempting to press its will against his. It was trying to make him feel hopeless. To give up. Despite all the power it had taken away, the effort felt weak to Jake. Now that he was aware of its influence, it was almost laughably easy to resist. The human made a show of collecting his energy, harnessing as much of it as possible. The Vyril didn't wait, charging forward and plunging its proboscis directly into his chest. Greedily, the mosquito-like creature siphoned his essence.

It began drinking, lowering its guard, and Jake focused his energies within his body. He shaped his energy like a vice and gripped the Vyril's mouth around where it had struck him. He sealed himself around it. As the Vyril sucked hungrily at his outpouring of energy, Jake reached out with his mind into the stomach of the beast. He could feel his connection to himself grow stronger the more the Vyril absorbed. Eventually, it reached the tipping point. Jake seized control of the power in its belly and heaved. It was only then that the Vyril realized what was happening. That it had been tricked. Jake could hear its gibbering fear and panic as he held it in place. "N… no! Releassze me! P-P-Pleassze!"

"Die." Jake kept his mind focused, collecting more of his energy within its stomach and increasing the outward pressure. He could see as well as feel the creature's body start to strain. It wasn't long until its chitinous form burst apart. Unlike the small splatter of a real mosquito, the Vyril's body slowly dissolved into mist as it died. A whisper in Jake's mind told him to cast his mind like a net. He reached out with his power around the life force of the Vyril, pulling it within himself. He had recovered his own energy and felt a new strength. He felt renewed and invigorated. Somehow, the fight with the Vyril had refilled and even overflowed his previous reserves of energy. He must have absorbed its remaining essence like it had planned to do to him. Jake shuddered. What had pushed him to do that? Had he just absorbed a soul? Did Vyrils even have souls? The horror of the realization shook him. He had just performed an atrocity. Was this the Dirge's doing? No, the feeling had come from something else. A different voice. If this was what it took to become stronger, Jake wasn't sure if he was ready for it.

Turning, Jake looked around. This strange blankness was part of his mind. He stopped himself from giving in to the urge to explore. Now wasn't the time. He still had to deal with Kenneth. Among other things. Focusing, Jake tried to draw himself out of his sleep. He gasped in pain as the light of the room hit his eyes. Blinking repeatedly, he slipped out of the bed where Kenneth had presumably placed him. Where was that damned Pixie? Jake frowned to himself, turning as he felt a ripple in the mist. A strange tear was forming in the air in the center of the room.

What was happening now?

Chapter 21

The fragrance of rhododendrons filled the air. Jake could feel the power wafting from the portal in waves even without reaching into the mist. Whatever was coming was powerful, and he had a feeling he knew what was coming. Claws gripped the edges of the cut in reality, slowly pulling it open. Jake shuddered in both fear and anticipation as the Guardian of the Pixie realm climbed its way into the room. It pulled its body forward, plopping into the room in a small bundle before stretching to its full height. Despite the pure white of the creature's eyes, Jake could feel the hatred and animosity emanating from it.

The beast growled, its words projecting through the mist strongly enough to be heard despite Jake's focus on the physical world. "I knew you were a danger. Your power grows by the day. The Pixies must not have you. You must not be left to unweave the lies we have set in motion."

Its words surprised him. Jake knew it to be a guardian of this realm, but did this creature actually serve a different master? He shook his head, pushing those thoughts out of his mind as he focused on the present. He couldn't let himself get too distracted.

"The Vyril did not perform its job in killing you. I have no choice but to handle this myself." Not wasting any more time, the furman tensed its muscled body and lunged at him with surprising agility for something so large. Jake hastily jumped out of the way of the attack.

He readied himself for it to strike only to have his feet lurch out from beneath him, as if the ground itself had shifted. Jake fell backwards, rolling to the side and narrowly dodging another swipe from the beast. He rose to his feet again, shifting his gaze into the mist. As Jake stared at the furman, its form began shifting. No longer was there a furry creature. Instead, before him was a gangly-looking spider with a human man's torso rising from the abdomen. While the creature's body shared basic human features, eight bright eyes gleamed in place of the normal two, and fangs visibly protruded from its lips. Each of the spider's legs ended in sharp, cutting points like glossy, black knives.

Jake remembered seeing one of these creatures in the bestiaries within the library. They were called driders, and the entry mentioned that they were extremely dangerous and powerful creatures capable of all manner of spells. He gazed in horror as the beast's multiple legs clacked against the stone tiles of the floor. For a moment, Jake could see strings of misty power extending from it in every direction. The energies of the guardian's mind tied directly into the walls.

Power snapped and crackled like lightning along these lines of influence as the drider hissed, somehow recognizing that he could see its true form. "That fool Kenneth should never have saved your life. Your powers could ruin my master's designs. I will strike you down here, Seer!"

Jake watched as the beast began siphoning power from somewhere. The lines of energy glowed bright enough to make him squint.

He resolved to not wait for it to attack him, this time. Instead, Jake focused on the mist and formed a spear. Willing it to strike, the spear shot forward like an arrow directly at the joint between the human and spider halves of the beast. He watched as the spear sank directly into, and then through, the drider's body. The Guardian laughed, its voice shrill. "Your magic is powerless against me, Seer! Give up, make this easier. I will give you a quick death."

He stared at the powerful monstrosity before him and knew that he stood no chance in physical combat. If it could ignore a spear, direct assault was out of the question. He had to find some way to make his powers meaningful. From the corner of his eye, Jake noticed that the portal was still glimmering in the center of the room. He did not know how it worked, but lines of energy connected at points from its edges to the joints of the drider. After a moment of thinking, he realized that the glimmer was much like the illusion the Vyril had placed around him in his mind. Perhaps it was the same technique? He would just have to get near it to find out.

Meanwhile, his enemy finished channeling its powers. It spread its arms outward and strands of webbing spewed toward Jake. Instinctively, he raised a barrier from the mist, diving for the portal. Extending his mind into the mist, he wrapped his will around the tendrils of energy. With a sharp tug, he managed to disconnect several of them at once. The drider realized what he was doing and tried to lunge for him, but its body jerked in reaction to the severed ties. It collapsed on the ground, crippled.

Jake turned toward the portal. He hesitated, apprehensive at the thought of diving into the unknown. But it seemed clear to him that this body was a puppet. Taking a moment, he tore the rest of the strings apart. The drider illusion vanished. Turning back to face the portal, Jake could see the twinkling of the drider's eyes in the darkness beyond.

"This is far from over, Seer. You tricked me for a moment, but I have you now." A blast of energy shot forth from the portal directly at him. This surge was matched with the floor beneath him seeming to yawn into a gaping maw, snapping him up within it. Jake knew that it hadn't truly eaten him. Knowing this did not help as he stared into the darkness. Focusing his mind, the human attempted to find the lines of power that made up the previous illusions he had encountered, yet he saw none.

The skittering of a spider's legs echoed from the dark.

Jake stared into the darkness blindly for a few moments, twisting to face every new sound. The small noises of the drider's movement stopped. He took a deep breath, thinking he had a moment to refocus. As he did so, one of the drider's legs swung out from the darkness. Its razor-sharp edges cut Jake's cheek as he barely managed to avoid being decapitated.

He held his hand up to his bleeding face, wincing at the pain. If he couldn't see, how was he supposed to fight back? Closing his eyes, he looked through the mist. The darkness seemed no different. The drider swung out again, and Jake saw the shadows shift before its leg came close. This time, he jumped clear of it without getting struck.

"So you managed to see already. I do not have time to continue toying with you. Kenneth may be bringing people here soon." As it spoke, the darkness started to move away. All of the shadows that had blocked Jake's sight coalesced into a small ball. A ball that the drider held in between both of its hands. It held up the ball and dipped its fangs into it. The blackness started to roil with sickly green energy as its poisons mixed with the magical sphere.

Jake shuddered at the thought of being struck by such dark power, hastily shifting into the mist to gather his own strength.

As he did so, he reached into the new reserves he had gained from consuming the Vyril. The mist roiled and shifted, gathering around him. With his power harnessed, Jake saw more clearly what the Guardian was doing. It had gathered the dark energy of evil creatures that had been caught in the security measures he had put around the kingdom and was going to release it all as a single attack. Jake could trace the lines of power from the walls of the castle, extending out into a vast net that surrounded the nearby forest as well. He felt the defenses weaken as more power was drained from them. If this kept up, the drider would leave the pixie kingdom almost defenseless.

The Vyril's energy that Jake had absorbed tugged against his mind. Almost as if it, too, was being beckoned into the sphere. As it did so, the human could feel the parasite's knowledge seep into him. With enough finesse, Jake could use the drider's focus against it. Much like how the Vyril had absorbed his power. He wasn't sure if this would work, but he had to try nonetheless. He reached out with his mind, pressing against the drider's consciousness. He could feel the barriers around its thoughts, but that didn't matter. He wrapped himself around those defenses like foil around a piece of chocolate. In doing so, he found the conduit between the drider and the kingdom's defenses. This was not as well protected as the drider's mind and proved simple for Jake to penetrate.

Using his Vyril-induced insight, he channeled his energies to form a needle and injected himself into the stream. The drider continued its power-gathering until it noticed that Jake was siphoning from it as well. Swiftly, it broke the connection. It chittered in a language Jake didn't understand, but he could feel its shock and fear. Having shared some of its power, the drider's mind was almost simple to understand. He could see clearly that it realized it was outmatched. This realization emboldened him as he stepped forward, reaching out his hand to the sphere the drider had formed.

"No. You can not have it." The creature hissed as it resisted, trying to keep control over the accumulated energy. Jake smiled as he felt the power flowing through him. He was winning. Slowly, inexorably, he pushed the destructive ball forward until it collided with the drider's human chest. The effects were devastating. The drider's skin boiled and hissed, sagging into the ball and vanishing. The sphere grew larger the more its form disintegrated. Jake watched in a combination of fascination and horror as the spell worked its way to completion. After a minute of consumption, all that was left was the bloated sphere. No trace of the drider remained.

Jake stared at the thing as it floated in the air. He had done it. A smile pulled at the corners of his mouth. He had survived and killed the beast. The high of victory was short lived as the sphere continued to sit there, unmoving. He had expected it to vanish once it had consumed the drider. What was he supposed to do with it now? He was too afraid to touch it, and he had no idea how to get rid of it. He didn't even really know what it was.

Hesitantly, he reached out with his mind. The sphere's surface went from a smooth, black-green ball to a roiling mass. As he stared with his mind's eye, Jake saw the drider inside the sphere. It wasn't dead. Somehow, the ball had contained it. Like a genie in a bottle. The instinct that called him to absorb the Vyril's energy came surging forth again, stronger than before. A voice too soft to recognize urged him to reach out and take it and consume the drider's power. Jake reached his hand out and touched the sphere. With a quick burst of light, the entire thing began to shrink as it was sucked into his skin. The entire sphere, with its captive, spread through Jake's body and filled him with a euphoria he had never experienced before.

The power from the drider surged through Jake. He shook from the mixture of adrenaline and the sensation of energy flowing through him. He watched the coils of raw power leave the drider's body and flow into his own. As it did so, the drider's form started to flatten like a deflating balloon. Once Jake had finished absorbing his adversary, all that was left was a thin, deflated husk of the drider's body lying on the ground. Jake stood, staring at the corpse. Having just faced two fights without rest, he expected to feel tired. Instead, he felt fuller of life than ever before. Still, he barely felt any relief as he glanced around the room. He thought he would be safe in the kingdom, yet he had only been going from one dangerous situation to the next. It wasn't safe here. But how was he to get out?

Evelynn let out a sigh of relief. For a few moments, she had been worried Jake was going to die. That would have been a major setback to her plans. While the human marveled at his newly acquired strength, Evelynn took the opportunity to slip through the kingdom's wards using her bond with Jake and hop into the other side of the portal. She needed a plausible explanation for why it took her so long to arrive in case Jake ever questioned her about it. "Perfect timing. Jake! Over here."

Jake's thoughts were interrupted by the sound of a voice coming from the portal. Turning, he recognized Evelynn. She was floating on the other side of the rift in the center of his room. He took a step forward, staring in confusion and surprise. "Evelynn? What... what are you doing here?"

"I'm here to help you get out of this mess before the pixies get you all tied down again. Hurry up, come through the portal. There's no time to lose." Evelynn gestured impatiently at him to come through. This was her chance, while the pixies couldn't stop him. While they couldn't stop her. She tried her best to keep her anxiety out of her voice.

Jake hesitated, turning to glance back at the door to his room. Was he really going to let himself be whisked away by another person? No. Not without an explanation. Squaring his shoulders, Jake turned back to Evelynn and shook his head. "Unless you give me an explanation, I'm not budging. I trusted Kenneth, and look where that got me. How am I supposed to trust you? You all have agendas."

"Ugh, fine." Jake's resistance came as a surprise. He was a fair bit more grown than the lost lamb she had helped the first time they met. Evelynn grit her teeth and waved a hand at the portal. She didn't have much time. She could see the heat of a pixie's energy coming toward them. "Look, you just absorbed the drider's power. That means you have inside you the knowledge, and the ability, to control this gateway. You can leave now. But you won't be able to once they start trying to seal it back up. You've got at most a minute before someone comes running through that door to keep you in their gilded cage. Do you want to be free to discover who and what you are or not?"

Jake narrowed his eyes. Reaching out to the portal, he felt it react to his mind. Instantly, the drider's knowledge started to bubble to the surface: how to operate it, the limits of its travel, and the fact it was a one-way trip. She hadn't lied. But he knew she wasn't telling him everything, either. She had avoided telling him what she got out of all this. Still, the pixies clearly weren't on his side. Jake clenched his fist in frustration. He didn't like feeling as if he was just being led by the nose, but what choice did he have?

Jumping through the portal, the human reached out with his mind and filled it with energy. He turned to Evelynn. "Where should I go to get away from them? To find myself?"

"Someplace you know well and feel at home in." The ghost shrugged at him.

Jake frowned at such vague direction. After a moment's thought, a location lit up in his mind. He nodded to himself. It was the only place that made sense. As he remembered his destination, the portal came to life, vibrating with the energies flowing through it. Evelynn floated down to place her hands on Jake's shoulders, smiling to herself. Moments passed. Then, the pair was suddenly sucked through the misty pathways to their destination.

Chapter 22

Kenneth threw open the door to Jake's room, panting and sweating as he rushed inside. The pixie arrived just in time to watch as a gateway in the center of the room flared bright with energy and closed with an inward rush of air and a soft pop. On the ground lay the deflated corpse of a drider. It didn't take much time for Kenneth to put two and two together. The guardian, a drider, had attacked Jake. And lost. After which, Jake opened a portal and left the kingdom despite the numerous wards against teleportation magic. "Damn it. Damn it all to the pits."

The pixie slammed his fist into the wall next to him. The pain helped clear his head as he turned back to the corpse. He had no choice but to report back to the queen. More experienced pixies, possibly even the elders, would be brought in to examine the situation, and a verdict would be made. Kenneth knew already that he wasn't going to go unpunished for the events that transpired. While bringing in Jake revealed and dealt with a threat to the kingdom, it also potentially created an even greater one in the process. Who knew what Jake intended to do? The human's powers were only growing with each passing day.

Kenneth shook his head. He couldn't do anything for Jake. Kenneth could only hope that his former charge was safe and had no ill intentions toward the kingdom. The pixie chuckled mirthlessly at the situation. He stared at the spot where the portal had been. "What a mess I've made of things. I'm sorry. Stay safe."

The pixie knew his words fell on deaf ears but saying them felt right. He hoped to see the human again under positive circumstances. Until then, he had a job to do. Turning his back on the drider corpse, he left the room to make his report. Kenneth shivered as he walked. Dark days were coming, and there he was. Wholly unprepared.

* 9 7 8 1 9 5 3 9 7 1 1 6 6 *